West

# THE
# KILLING TRAIL

Center Point
Large Print

Also by Johnny D. Boggs and available from Center Point Large Print:

*And There I'll Be a Soldier*
*Top Soldier*
*Return to Red River*
*The Kansas City Cowboys*
*Wreaths of Glory*
*The Raven's Honor*
*Poison Spring*
*Taos Lightning*
*Greasy Grass*
*MacKinnon*

**This Large Print Book carries the
Seal of Approval of N.A.V.H.**

# THE
# KILLING
# TRAIL

## A KILLSTRAIGHT STORY

# Johnny D. Boggs

CENTER POINT LARGE PRINT
THORNDIKE, MAINE

This Center Point Large Print edition
is published in the year 2019 by arrangement with
Golden West Literary Agency.

First US edition: Five Star

The text of this Large Print edition is unabridged.
In other aspects, this book may vary
from the original edition.
Printed in the United States of America
on permanent paper.
Set in 16-point Times New Roman type.

ISBN: 978-1-64358-137-8 (hardcover)
ISBN: 978-1-64358-141-5 (paperback)

Library of Congress Cataloging-in-Publication Data

Names: Boggs, Johnny D., author.
Title: The killing trail : a Killstraight story / Johnny D. Boggs.
Description: Center Point Large Print edition. | Thorndike, Maine :
    Center Point Large Print, 2019.
Identifiers: LCCN 2018057153| ISBN 9781643581378 (hardcover :
    alk. paper) | ISBN 9781643581415 (paperback : alk. paper)
Subjects: LCSH: Apache Indians—Fiction. |
    Murder—Investigation—Fiction. | Western stories. |
    Outlaws—Fiction. | Teenage girls—Fiction. |
    Indian captivities—Fiction. | Large type books.
Classification: LCC PS3552.O4375 K545 2019 | DDC 813/.54—dc23
LC record available at https://lccn.loc.gov/2018057153

For Hazel and Tiffany

# THE
# KILLING TRAIL

# CHAPTER ONE

Sand and grit peppered his face, and he clamped the hat on his head with both hands. The dust became so thick, he could scarcely see the railroad tracks, but managed to glimpse a newspaper sailing in front of the depot. He thought: *Well, in an hour, someone down in Mexico will be reading today's* Socorro Chieftain. *Unless that paper has blown all the way from Santa Fe.*

Head bent, Daniel Killstraight made his way to the ticket window at the Rincon station. The hard gust of wind died, and the agent looked above his bifocals, but didn't give Daniel more than a glance before going back to stamping his papers. Daniel said nothing. He just waited. At least now he didn't have to keep pulling down the brim of his hat. Instead, he reached inside his coat pocket and brought out an envelope.

Once the agent wearing the funny cap stamped the last of his papers, he wiped the ink off his fingertips on his blue jacket, pushed the bifocals farther up the bridge of his nose, and asked: "Help you?"

"Next train?"

"Northbound or southbound?" The agent didn't wait for an answer, kept right on talking. "North to Socorro and Albuquerque and Lamy . . . train don't go into Santa Fe, but there's a spur to take you there . . . to Vegas to Springer to Raton and out of this god-forsaken hell hole. Pulls in tomorrow evening at Seven-Nineteen, if she's on time, which she won't be. South to Deming to pick up the Southern Pacific. Or south to Las Cruces . . . an omnibus'll take you from the depot to Mesilla . . . and to El Paso, Texas. Which, if you were to ask me, ain't no better than this sump. But anywhere's better than here."

He stopped, Daniel assumed, merely to catch his breath. A station agent at a place like Rincon likely didn't have too many opportunities to talk to someone other than himself.

Before the man could continue, Daniel said: "Sump?"

"Swamp," the man snapped. "Bog."

Daniel looked north, then south. All he could see was desert, a harsh, ugly land that wouldn't know what to do with rain if it ever fell.

"A cesspool, son." The agent sighed. "A latrine."

"North," Daniel said. "Dodge City."

Envious, the man sucked in a breath, let it out, shaking his head. "By grab, I hear that was a wild town in its day. Full of debauchery forty-four hours a day. Forty-four. Get it?" Grinning, he made a pistol out of his right hand, and pulled the

10

imaginary trigger. "And still a mite wicked, even if them days of trail drives is gone."

Daniel hadn't seen anything of Dodge City other than the depot, but the railroad man had pulled out a catalog, and thumbed through some papers. "Let's see your spondulicks, son."

Daniel said: "Spondulicks?"

"Your money, boy. Cold, hard cash. Nobody rides these rails free."

Daniel opened the envelope, pulled out one paper, then another, and slid both to the agent.

Again, the old agent adjusted his spectacles, unfolded the paper, held it out at arm length, then moved his head back and forth until he found an appropriate range. He read. Aloud.

15 March 1889
This introduces the bearer of this letter as Sergeant Daniel Killstraight of the Tribal Police and requests that he be treated with proper respect as due any white peace officer.

He is a personal friend of the Northern Texas Stock Growers Association and members Dan Waggoner, Burk Burnett, and Captain Lee Hall; Quanah Parker, chief of the Comanche Nation; Captain Richard Pratt of the Carlisle Indian Industrial School; Isaac Parker, district judge for the Western District of

11

Arkansas; and William Henry Harrison Miller, recently appointed United States Attorney General.

Respectfully,<br>The Rev. Joshua Biggers, Agent,<br>Kiowa-Comanche-Apache Reservation<br>Fort Sill, Indian Territory

Folding the letter and sliding it back toward Daniel, the agent said: "It ain't no letter of credit, boy. It . . ."

Then the agent saw the second paper, a railroad pass, good for any seat on any Atchison, Topeka, and Santa Fe train. He picked it up, studied it, turned it around to look at the blank back, even examined the sides and edges, and finally ran his fingers across the letters, before sighing and returning that to Daniel, as well.

"Reckon I stands corrected. Some folks do ride these rails free." He peered over the bifocals, examining Daniel, probably trying to figure out how a Comanche tribal police officer could rate a free pass on the AT&SF. "You must be some top-dog soldier," he said after his examination.

Daniel merely returned the items into the envelope, and the envelope inside his jacket.

"Or maybe . . ."—the agent grinned—"you're just a dog soldier."

"I am not Cheyenne," Daniel said.

"Chasing some rapscallion?"

*Running away myself,* Daniel thought. *Or trying to.*

"Well, you don't need no ticket, sonny." The agent was out of jokes, and got down to business. "Just show the conductor that there railroad pass, and you can go anywhere you'd like, from one end of the tracks to the other. Wouldn't want to sell that pass there, would you?"

Daniel ignored his question, and said: "The northbound train leaves tomorrow night?"

The agent sighed. "Seven-Nineteen. Or thereabouts."

Another gust of wind brought Daniel's hand back to the crown of his black hat. He stepped back, and looked down the tracks. The depot, a two-story frame with a long single-story supply shed attached, was the biggest building in town. If you called it a town. All Daniel saw were a handful of picket cottages on the west side of the depot, and one adobe saloon.

The agent had removed his bifocals and busied himself wiping the lenses with a dirty handkerchief, as he informed Daniel: "Ain't no hotel. No place to sleep. On a bed, that is."

"What do people do when they wait for the train?" Daniel asked.

"They drink."

Daniel nodded. What else would a person do in a sump like this? If he had enough spondulicks.

"Alice . . . over to the saloon . . . don't serve

13

Injuns no liquor, but she does offer pickles and sandwiches free if you're drinking. If you ain't, she only charges a nickel. And she don't charge for the water, though she ought to. It's harder on your belly than the whiskey she pours."

"Thanks."

" 'Course," the agent called out as Daniel walked toward the grip he'd left at the edge of the platform. "You being a personal friend of the U.S. attorney general and that hanging judge from Arkansas, she might make an exception and serve you a foamy draught beer, more suds than beer, and warm, but that's what you find in this wasteland."

Daniel didn't drink liquor or beer, for he had seen too much of what the white man's whiskey did to his people. Did to their own people, too. He thought of the miners back in Pennsylvania, the soldiers at Fort Sill.

His throat felt raw, but he wasn't sure he wanted to walk down the dusty path to that adobe saloon and ask for water. The only sound in Rincon came from the saloon, and he could see two horses and three mules tethered in front of the ramshackle building. He sat down on the edge of the platform, felt the wind again, and took off his hat to let the wind blow through his hair.

It was shorter than it had been. He had thought about letting it grow back. Braids again. But

14

. . . no . . . not yet. It was a *taibo* haircut, not Comanche, though long enough in the back just to touch his collar, and cover maybe a quarter inch over his ears. His right hand fell to his left forearm, and he massaged it through the canvas jacket and the flannel shirt. He could feel the old gashes throbbing, even though they had healed long ago, leaving just the scars on his forearms, and his thighs, and his calves. Everything had healed, more or less, except his heart. And his head.

He thought of Rain Shower, dead, murdered by one of her own people, and let the cold wind dry the tears before they could even fall.

The agent's words echoed in his brain. *Just show the conductor that there railroad pass, and you can go anywhere you'd like, from one end of the tracks to the other.*

What good would that do? As the crow flies, Rincon had to be roughly seven hundred miles from Cache Creek. The train ride from Dodge City had been slightly farther, and it had been a jarring two hundred and eighty-five mile wagon ride by military conveyance from Fort Sill to Dodge City. All of that traveling, and his heart still felt heavy.

And coming to the Mescalero Apache reservation had done him no good.

Again he looked down the path. The hand-painted sign above the open door to the adobe saloon was crooked, and the paint job seemed far from professional, but he could read it.

Alice's Grog Shop
We Don't Claim to Be Much,
But We Are HERE!

"I'm here, too," he said aloud, and slid off the platform. The valise came with him as his moccasins carried him down the dusty road. He stopped to watch a tarantula move across the road and find some shade beneath a palm-size stone.

Maybe all of The People who would trade for or buy contraband whiskey from the Creeks or the Pale Eyes—or steal it—knew what they were doing. Getting drunk made you forget. Or so he was told. Daniel Killstraight would like to forget. He had been trying to for months now.

As he kept walking, the noise from inside the dark building became louder. Laughter. Friendly curses. The clinks of glasses, and the sound of spurs. He reached Alice's Grog Shop, put a hand on the rump of the nearest horse, a strawberry roan, and slid between it and a slumbering mule, then ducked beneath the hitching rail, and stepped under what passed for an awning— ocotillo slats that blocked some of the sun. He breathed in deeply, already smelling the cigarette smoke, exhaled, and stepped inside.

Three Mexicans sat at a table by the front

16

window. Two cowboys stood at the makeshift bar, between them was a chubby woman, her red hair disheveled, a cigarette between her lips, and wearing a flimsy dress missing several buttons. On the other side of the bar stood two railroad workers with arms like railroad ties.

Every conversation, every drink, every drag on every cigarette ceased when Daniel Killstraight stepped inside the saloon.

He nodded at the Mexicans, and one even returned the gesture. Leaving his grip on the nearest table, he walked toward the bar, found a spot between the cowboys and the railroad workers, and withdrew his envelope and a beaded leather pouch. The pouch dropped on the warped plank that passed as a bar, and the jingle of coins caused the red-headed bartender to move toward Daniel.

She flicked away the cigarette. "You ain't Apache." Her voice had been tarnished by cigarette smoke and whiskey. She could have been thirty, or she could have been eighty. Her eyes were bloodshot.

He could have told her that his mother had been Mescalero, which was why he had come here from Indian Territory. He could have told her that he was Nermernuh. One of The People. A Comanche. He could have showed her the letter of introduction, but he wasn't sure anyone in this bucket of blood could read, except himself.

Instead of opening the envelope, he reached back inside his pocket, and pulled out the shield badge. He slapped it beside the pouch, which he then tugged open, and withdrew a dollar coin.

"Water." He knew he wouldn't—couldn't—drink whiskey. "And the man at the depot said you serve sandwiches?"

She stared at the pouch, then put both elbows on the plank between them, and leaned toward him, squeezing her breasts together and giving him something else to consider.

"Is that all, sugar?"

"Hey, Alice!" one of the cowboys called out. "I ain't sure if he's skunk, coyot', Apache, or some half-breed greaser, but he sure ain't no man. He ain't nothin' but a boy."

"The men's down here!" his partner called out. "And we need some more . . ."—he flashed an unfriendly grin at Daniel—"some more *firewater*."

Shaking her head, the barmaid straightened, picked up the coin, which she bit. Satisfied, she pulled a jug from the backbar, placed it in front of Daniel, along with a shot glass, and walked back to the cowboys. "Fixin's for the sandwiches is next to them boys, but I'd avoid the bacon unless your stomach's made of cast iron." Her jaw jutted toward the railroad men.

"Leave him be, Roy," she told one of the men. "He's a payin' customer. Unlike some sidewinders

who drink and eat here. Help yourself, Marshal."
She emphasized the last word. Maybe to make
all of the patrons think twice before starting a
fight.

Daniel picked up the badge. It said *Indian
Police,* not marshal, and if that weren't enough,
two crossed arrows and a bow had been engraved
between the two words.

The envelope, the pouch, and the badge
returned to his jacket, and, leaving the jug and
glass, he moved down the bar. The railroaders
watched as he carved stale bread with a knife,
and fixed two sandwiches made up of butter,
green chiles, and what looked like red-tinted
pork. Or beef. It wasn't bacon, which he avoided,
heeding Alice's advice. With the two sandwiches
on a tin plate, he returned to fetch his jug and
his shot glass, and, balancing everything, moved
back to the table by the door.

Conversations had resumed. The two cowboys
drank and smoked and laughed with Alice. The
railroaders huddled on their end of the bar, and
whispered. The Mexicans simply turned and
stared as Daniel bit into the sandwich.

His mouth erupted in flames, and he slammed
down the water from his shot glass, then lifted
the jug.

The Mexicans laughed, and the railroaders
stopped their whispers to turn and chuckle. The
cowboys cackled harder, and Alice called out:

"You want a beer, sugar, to cool yourself off?"

Daniel's head shook. He couldn't tell which was hotter, the red meat or the green chiles. Both burned like the hinges of hell.

One of the Mexicans rose, moved to the bar, and returned with a plate of tortillas, which he placed in front of Daniel.

"*Señor,*" the man said softly. He pointed at the sandwich. "*Carne adovada. Muy caliente.*" He fingered a tortilla, tearing it in strips, leaving a pile on the plate. "Better," he said in English. "Water no good. Eat. Help cool."

Daniel's nose ran. Tears welled in his eyes. His head bobbed so hard, his hat toppled onto the floor, but he reached for a strip of tortilla, cramming it into his mouth.

"Shoulda stuck with bacon," one of the cowboys commented, laughing.

After wiping his nose, then his hands on his trousers, Daniel picked up the sandwich again. He was one of The People. His name was His Arrows Fly Straight Into The Hearts Of His Enemies. He would not be defeated by *carne adovada.*

He bit again into the sandwich, making sure he took a healthy portion of stale bread with the red-spiced meat. His tongue burned, but he did not drink water this time, merely took another piece of tortilla.

The Mexican who had assisted him had returned

to his table. Daniel glanced at him, and nodded his thanks. The cowboys snorted, went back to talking to Alice. The railroaders dismissed him. The fun was over.

Daniel finished eating, surprised that his tongue had not been reduced to ash. He drank water, which indeed was hard, finished the tortillas, and returned his empty plate, glass, and jug to the bar.

"Well," Alice said as she left the cowboys to dump the dishes in a tin basin behind the bar, "at least this lawdog's got manners. Thank you, Marshal."

Daniel picked his hat up off the floor where it had fallen, and put it back on his head. He touched the brim, muttered as much of a thank you as his tongue could manage, and prepared to head back to the depot.

It was then he heard the horses and shouts. As he picked up his valise, two dusty, young, sweaty cowhands stormed inside.

"Hey, Vince!" one of the newcomers shouted. "Charley and me's goin' to Deming. You and Frank oughta come along."

"Why in hell would anyone want to go to Deming?" the cowboy nearest Alice said. His pard sniggered.

Daniel was stepping through the door, figuring he could sleep at the depot, when one of the newcomers responded: "To see the hangin'."

"What hanging?" asked the cowboy at the bar who had been addressed as Vince.

"Hell, man!" the other newcomer shouted. "They's gonna string up an Apache."

# CHAPTER TWO

Daniel's free hand gripped the frame of the doorway, but then he let go and turned, watching as the two newly arrived cowboys leaned against the bar to shoot down the whiskey Alice had already poured for them.

"What Apache?" Vince said, his voice laced with something stronger than skepticism.

"Not just any Apache," one of the newcomers said. "Chiricahua."

"Crap." Vince turned away, sipped his drink, grinned at his partner who had been addressed as Frank. "These kids don't know a bull snake from a rattler, or a Cherry Cow from some digger Injun."

"Chiricahua," Frank agreed, shaking his head, mocking the two younger cowhands. "Boys, all them Cherry Cows got shipped out of Arizona. They're in Florida now. Or is it Alabama?"

"Same damned place," Vince said.

"No, Jimmy's right, fellas," the newcomer argued. "It's a Cherry Cow, sure as hell. And we figured you'd wanna come along, Vince, seein' as how this buck killed Melody . . ."

Jimmy jabbed his partner's side with his elbow, spilled his whiskey. He hissed: "Shut up, Charley."

Charley must have realized his *faux pas*, because he practically dropped his shot glass on the bar, his face paling, his Adam's apple bobbing.

Whirling, Vince came at the two young cowhands, reminding Daniel of an old buffalo bull ready to fight some young bull ready to challenge him for the herd.

"The hell did you say?" Vince yelled.

Neither Jimmy nor Charley spoke.

Jimmy stood tall, sandy hair underneath a bowler hat. He wore a tan collarless shirt, blue bandanna, dusty vest of duck canvas, striped britches, no chaps, tall black boots, and thin brass spurs. He probably was younger than Daniel. Charley appeared a few years older, but was shorter, solid, built more like one of those railroad workers than most cowboys Daniel had seen. He sported a fine walrus mustache, and a nice shirt of silk. At least, it had been a nice shirt, until Vince stormed at the cowhand, grabbed the shirt front, and jerked the startled Charley forward. Mother of pearl buttons ripped from the shirt, and rolled across the floor.

"What did you say about Melody?" Vince roared.

"Vince!" Alice yelled, and picked up a bung starter. "I'll have no fisticuffs in my place. It cost me twelve dollars and three days to get it back in shape the last time you boys had a row."

Ignoring Alice, the cowhand pulled Charley closer. "What about Melody? And some damned Apache buck?"

Daniel stepped aside to let the Mexicans exit. He moved back to the table he had been sitting at, and placed his grip atop it.

This was not his affair. He didn't know a girl from Deming named Melody. He didn't know Charley, Jimmy, Frank, or Vince or anyone else in this bucket of blood. He had no jurisdiction in the Territory of New Mexico. To top it all off, he had never cared much for any Apache he had ever met.

"She's dead, Vince." It was Jimmy who answered. Frank had come up behind the enraged cowhand, and put a hand on the tall man's shoulder. Alice had raised the bung starter, but now she lowered it.

"I'm right sorry to have to tell you, Vince, but she got . . . killed . . . the other night."

Vince released Charley, who leaned, practically fell, against the bar. Alice was busy pouring him a drink, and not one from the jugs of rotgut. Rather from a fancy bottle with bold script on the label.

A week's worth of dark stubble, sprinkled with gray, covered Vince's face, except for a white half-moon-shaped scar on his left cheek. He stood a good six inches taller than any of the other cowhands, was thin but solid. He wore a black hat, black pants, black boots, fancy leather suspenders, green calico shirt, red polka dot bandanna. He wasn't the oldest of the four. That had to be Frank, whose clothes looked as ancient as the dirt and grime that caked them. And his hair was a steel gray, although his mustache revealed some brown.

All four cowhands carried revolvers—Vince's, Charley's, and Jimmy's in holsters on shell belts, Frank's stuck into a mule-ear pocket of his trousers.

"An Injun kill her?" one of the railroaders asked.

"Chiricahua," Charley said, his voice cracking. "Or so we got told."

"Who?" Vince took the snifter Alice had handed him, and drank.

The railroaders moved over near the cowboys. Daniel found himself walking toward them, also.

"Who told you?" Vince polished off the drink, and set the snifter on the bar, next to the bottle.

The writing on the label was French. Daniel could tell that much. Brandy, he figured, something rarely poured in a place like this.

"Luke McAfee," Jimmy answered.

"Of the Ladder J?"

"Yeah."

"He's a good man," Frank told Vince. "Ain't prone to lying. Or exaggerations."

26

"Luke was in Deming when they found her body," Jimmy said.

"By the railroad tracks." Charley had steadied his nerves with a shot of whiskey, not the brandy that Alice had poured in his shot glass. He dropped to the floor and began picking up the buttons.

"This Melody girl?" one of the railroaders asked. "She a white woman?"

"Melody Rivera," Frank said.

"Half-Mex then." The railroader nodded, as if that settled everything.

"You don't think they'll hang an Indian for killing a sixteen-year-old girl?" Vince said, his voice breaking with anger.

"I'm not saying a damned thing," the railroader said. "But in a trial, a Mexican . . ."

"Half-Mexican," Frank blurted. "But most of her's whiter than any of us."

Daniel found a chair, and sank into it, bewildered at the cowhand's comprehension of mathematics.

"There ain't gonna be no trial," Jimmy said. "That's why me and Charley rode here to fetch you, Vince."

Charley added: "And everybody knows that that calaboose down in Deming ain't strong enough to hold a fart."

"You know the town law won't put up a fight to protect no damned redskin," Jimmy said. "And we heard the deputy sheriff rode out right after the killin'."

Charley chimed in: "Besides, Luke McAfee was saying that Matt Callahan had his boys all ready to invite that Apache woman-killer to a necktie party."

"That town law sure won't stand up to Mister Callahan," Jimmy said.

"Lynchin' an Apache buck!" Frank whistled.

"That would be something to see," one of the other railroaders said, and his fellow worker's head bobbed with enthusiasm.

"Let's ride," Vince said. He gulped down another drink, and stormed outside.

"Train's faster, fellers!" a railroader called out, but none of the cowhands listened as they stormed out after Vince.

Hoof beats sounded, and dust drifted through the open doorway, settling on the dust-caked floor and furniture. The railroaders finished their drinks, tossed some coins on the bar, and walked outside. Neither paid any attention to Daniel. Even Alice didn't consider him as she walked down the bar to collect the money.

Daniel opened his grip, reached inside.

"You still here?" Alice had finally noticed him.

After retrieving a blank Old Glory writing tablet, a Columbus lead sharpener, and a Faber's No. 2 pencil, Daniel approached the bar, the tablet stuck underneath his left arm.

28

Alice found a fairly clean glass, and filled it with water. She poured a whiskey for herself.

"Do you know who they were talking about?" he asked.

She considered him, her eyes suspicious. "Is it any concern of yours?"

He set the notebook, pencil, and sharpener on the bar, and picked up the glass of water. He drank, not answering her, not looking at her. Over the years, he had learned that it was best not to make eye contact with Pale Eyes when asking them questions. They seemed threatened by Comanches, an idea that often caused him to grin. In the old days, they had good reason to feel threatened by The People.

"The girl? You know her?"

Alice killed the whiskey. "Melody Rivera. Just some young strumpet all the boys around Deming's struttin' over." She leaned toward him, eyes no longer suspicious but gleaming. "Bet you wouldn't believe it, but twenty . . . er, ten years ago, boys acted like they was the cocks of the walk when they come to pay me a visit."

"I believe it." Smiling, Daniel set the glass down, picked up his pencil, turned to the first page in the tablet.

He wrote: *Melody Rivera.*

"I never met her," Alice said. "Only been to Deming three, four times. You ain't Apache, are you?"

His head shook as he wrote another name: *Luke McAfee*.

"What about this Vince?" he asked.

"You wrote Luke McAfee," she said, and refilled her glass.

"Luke I know about," he said. "He rides for the Ladder J." Which was all he knew about Luke McAfee, although he appeared to be a cowhand in good standing among his peers.

"Vince works for the Four-Five-Connected. It's across the river."

"Know his last name?" he asked.

"Just know him as Vince. We ain't that sociable here."

He wrote down Matt Callahan's name, and turned the notebook so that Alice could see it. He sipped more water, hoping his stomach was made of cast iron. He would know soon enough.

"The Four Gates Ranch. Biggest in the southern part of the territory. At least on the west side of the Río Grande. Probably larger outfits in Lincoln County and off to the east, though."

After turning the tablet back toward him, Daniel wrote that down beside Callahan's name. Then he wrote: *Vince, Charlie*.

"It's with an e-y," Alice corrected him, "not i-e. I know on account Charley always tells folks that's how to spell his name. Showin' off, he is. Figgers hisself to be an educated man."

Daniel corrected the spelling, and scribbled the

30

names of the two other cowhands—*Jimmy and Frank.*

"They all work for the Four-Five-Connected?" he asked.

"Just Frank and Vince. The others ride for the Hanging Slash-W. Or did, last I heard. Some of them boys jump around from brand to brand as fast as fleas."

He wrote: *Melody R., half-Mexican teen-ager. Body found by RR tracks. Killed by ????*

He stopped writing, tapped the lead on the page, pursed his lips.

"An Apache," Alice told him.

This time he looked up at her. "A Chiricahua?"

"You heard the boys," she said.

"I also heard that, after Geronimo surrendered," Daniel said, "the American government rounded up all of the Chiricahuas, and shipped them to a prison in Florida." By now, however, some of those Apaches would have been sent from Florida to the Carlisle Industrial School in Pennsylvania, where Pale Eyes would teach them how to look like a white man, how to read and write like a white man, how to pray like a white man, how to act like a white man, how to be a white man. . . . The same as they had taught him—how to forget everything he had known about being one of The People.

"Maybe it was a Mescalero," Alice said.

"Maybe." That made more sense. He had just

31

come from the Mescalero reservation east of Rincon.

*Chiricahua,* he wrote, and stared at the word, wondering.

"There are stories," Alice said, sipping her whiskey, "that not all of Geronimo's boys surrendered to Gen'ral Miles. They say a lot of them's been livin' in the Sierra Madres south of the border. So it could be . . . could very well be that one of them bucks . . . er, one of them Apaches . . . come up to Deming, and he found that little strumpet, and he . . ." She downed the rest of the liquor in a smooth gulp.

His head bobbed slightly. "Yes," he said, "it could be."

A gust of wind blew more dust through the open doorway, moaning through the cracks in the walls.

He stared at the words he had written, and asked himself why he had even bothered. Mescalero or Chiricahua? A girl dead? It was not his concern. He should forget about the dead half-Mexican girl, and some rumored Apache in some Deming jail.

His hand dipped into his pocket, and he felt the tin shield badge, fingers tracing the etching and edges, and he remembered something a Pale Eyes, a friend, a deputy U.S. marshal named Harvey P. Noble, had told him.

*That badge you're wearin' means that you are*

*a duly appointed peace officer with jurisdiction on your reservation only, and that means you can't arrest white men, only Indians. My badge says that I'm a federal lawman for the Western District of Arkansas, which includes the Indian Nations. But that ain't what these badges mean at all. You pin on a badge, you fight for justice. White, black, red, don't matter. You may have to risk your life for the meanest sum-bitch you ever met, who ain't worth savin'. Like as not, we'll both get killed by some drunk nobody ever heard of. It ain't much of a life, Daniel, but you pin that badge on, you got to believe in it. You got to believe in justice. Now I'm done preachin'. You got the makin's for a smoke?*

His hand came out of the pocket. He would let Noble's words guide him. He would go to Deming, for justice. He was a peace officer, and he had a railroad pass that could get him to Deming.

Even if he didn't care much for Apaches.

Even if he knew that he wasn't going to Deming for justice.

"How far is it to Deming?" he asked.

Alice shrugged. "Sixty miles, I reckon."

Two days, he figured, for Vince and his friends to ride. Maybe three. But Vince would push his horse. Two days.

"When is the train due?" he asked. "The west-bound?"

As if answering for itself, a faint train whistle sounded in the distance.

"Be here directly," Alice said.

"Why didn't Vince and his friends wait for the train?" he asked, more to himself than to the barmaid, but she answered anyway.

"Trains cost money. And ain't many cowboys I know who'd pass up on a good long ride. Even if they's ridin' to the end of the earth, which is what Deming is."

He picked up the pencil, stuck it over his right ear, grabbed the sharpener and tablet, and nodded his thanks at Alice.

"You goin' to stop a lynchin'?" she asked.

"I'm going to help an Indian," he said.

Sighing, she leaned against the bar again, and almost reached for him. "Deming's full of railroaders and cowhands, and, from what I hear tell, Matt Callahan ain't a guy to stand up against, sugar. You stand in their way, and they'll string you up, too. Or just shoot you dead." She contemplated him, as he stared at her, just briefly. Sighing, she said: "You got the head of a mule." Finally she gave him one final argument: "But you said you ain't Apache."

"My mother was," he said.

# CHAPTER THREE

"He is brave," his father had said after Daniel, then a young boy known as Oá, or Horn, had counted first coup while on a hunting party that had turned into a raiding party. He was Kwahadi, the last band of The People who had not been driven to the Pale Eyes reservation. On this hunting trip, The People had caught four *Tejanos* slaughtering buffalo for only the skins, so they had killed those men. Only eight years old, Daniel had reached one of the wounded men, touched him with the tip of his bow. As the men celebrated and told stories about that small but memorable fight, his father had given Daniel his own name, His Arrows Fly Straight Into The Hearts Of His Enemies, and taken a new name— Marsh Hawk—for himself.

*He is brave.*

Daniel remembered something else about that evening around the campfire. Another warrior had said softly, contemptuously: "Considering his mother . . ."

Daniel remembered his father well. He could still picture his face, feel the *puha*—the power— his father held. Closing his eyes, he felt that he could reach out and touch his father's buffalo-hide shield decorated with hawk feathers and the drawings of talons the color of vermilion. He smelled the hat of otter fur and buffalo horns. He saw the lance dripping with feathers of crows. Marsh Hawk had been a powerful warrior of The People. Even Quanah, the Kwahadi leader who the Pale Eyes had later designated chief of the Comanche Nation—despite the fact that The People had never been ruled by one man—had respected Marsh Hawk.

Those days were gone forever. The *Tejanos*, the Long Knives had proved too powerful for even Nermernuh.

Although Daniel had spent the first of his boyhood years living with the Kwahadi, eventually they had surrendered. With his men, women, children, dogs, and horses starving, Quanah had led The People into the soldier fort called Sill, once in the middle of the land ruled by Nermernuh.

Some of the braves had been allowed to stay at the reservation, to follow the white man's road. Others, the most recalcitrant, had been sent east to St. Augustine, Florida.

His father had been one of those removed. "Too war-like," the Pale Eyes had said. "Apt to cause trouble." So Marsh Hawk had been sent to Fort Marion by train, but Marsh Hawk had been a fighter to the end. He had tried to escape, only to be shot by Long Knives along the railroad tracks in Florida. Marsh Hawk had staggered into the woods, and then . . . ?

If one believed the Pale Eyes, Marsh Hawk had died from a bullet through a lung, or both lungs, and had been buried where he had fallen. Isa Nanaka, an old holy man who had been on that same train, however, had told the story a different way.

Marsh Hawk had fooled the Long Knives, for Isa Nanaka had seen a hawk fly from a tree in those woods. Isa Nanaka had heard the hawk's cry, and watched it circling over the trees, laughing at the Pale Eyes below. Marsh Hawk had turned himself into a hawk, for the hawk was his *puha*, and the hawk would always be there to guide Daniel.

That is the story Daniel tried to believe. Every time he saw a marsh hawk, he saw his father.

His mother, though? He had tried to picture her, but the face never came clearly to him. She was Mescalero, taken captive by his father on a raid. No, that wasn't right. Once, she had been Mescalero, but she became one of The People, although many boys, and quite a few men, had ridiculed Daniel as not being whole, being only half Nermernuh. Some had whispered similar snide comments about Quanah, whose mother had been a *Tejano*. Only they hadn't spoken up quite as vocally when insulting Quanah.

After four years on the reservation, the Pale

Eyes had taken Daniel away, loading him into a wagon, sending him to Pennsylvania, to the Carlisle Industrial School, where he had been forced to give up his Comanche name, where he had become Daniel Killstraight, where he, along with one hundred and thirty-six Lakotas, Cheyennes, Kiowas, and Pawnees, had been taught the ways of the Pale Eyes.

When they abducted Daniel—albeit with Isa Nanaka's permission—his mother had tried to return to her first people, the Mescaleros. It's likely she believed she would never see her son again, and she knew her husband was already dead, buried in some unmarked grave—buried the Pale Eyes way, not the way of The People— in some terrible land called Flo-ri-da. But she had not made it to New Mexico Territory, had not even made it across the Red River into Texas. She had drowned trying to cross the river.

Eventually Daniel had returned to the reservation near Fort Sill. After seven long years living among the Pale Eyes, learning the white man's ways at Carlisle, on the Franklin County farms where they sent him to work, and finally in those dark, dreary, wet coal mines. He had seen Philadelphia, Pittsburgh, all the power of the Pale Eyes. He had come home—if he could call the agency home—a stranger, unsure in which world he belonged.

Few Comanches called him His Arrows Fly

Straight Into The Hearts Of His Enemies any more. Many had forgotten the old ways. Children were still sent to Carlisle, or one of the closer schools, like Chilocco—which The People call Prairie Light—in Kansas. Not many remembered his mother, and it was not good to say the names of those who had gone to The Land Beyond The Sun. He was Daniel Killstraight, part Comanche, part Mescalero, turned Pale Eyes.

So he had taken a job as a Metal Shirt, a tribal policeman, earning $8 a month to be mocked at, shot at. He spent most of his time chasing after whiskey-runners, or arresting Comanches who had fallen prey to the lure of Creek whiskey, Choctaw beer, Pale Eyes rotgut, any kind of liquor. He had been promoted to sergeant. He had solved a few murders, too.

Solved? No, that wasn't the right word. He had bungled around until finally stumbling across a killer, or killers. *Tejano* cattlemen like Dan Waggoner and Lee Hall, Judge Isaac Parker, and a few of his deputy marshals, maybe even the Cherokee policeman named Hugh Gunter, plus one or two newspaper reporters might have considered him a detective, even a hero, but Daniel knew better.

If he had been any kind of hero, any kind of detective, any kind of a man, Rain Shower would still be alive.

But she had been murdered—not by a Pale

Eyes, but by one of The People, one of her own—because Daniel hadn't been smart enough. Rain Shower had figured out who was responsible for having almost killed Quanah Parker long before Daniel had, and it had cost her.

Cost him.

Coming to New Mexico Territory had been Agent Joshua Biggers's idea. No, that wasn't exactly right. Quanah had thought of it—of that, Daniel felt certain—and Quanah had suggested to Biggers that he persuade Daniel to make the trip southwest.

"Daniel," Biggers had said, leaning against the desk in the cabin that served as his office at the agency. "You've been through a lot these past few months. Rain Sh— . . . well . . . you've lost a . . ." The agent's hand moved to the Bible, picked it up. The Bible, Daniel realized, held Joshua Biggers's *puha*. "I think it would be a good idea for you to get away for a while."

Not back to Carlisle. A knot had formed in Daniel's gut.

"We'll keep you on your salary."

As if $8 a month might be worth saving.

"I've talked to Quanah, and Captain Hall, and they're pretty confident they can get the railroad to provide you with a pass. Take you anywhere you want by rails."

"Where would I go?" Daniel asked.

"You're probably too young to remember this,"

Biggers said, "or you may have already been at Carlisle, but years ago Quanah Parker himself got a pass from the agent. All it said was that he was a good Indian, and was looking for his mother, a white woman. . . ."

Cynthia Ann Parker. Daniel remembered her name. By now, everyone in Indian Territory and Texas, even beyond, knew the story of Cynthia Ann Parker and her son, the "chief" of the Comanche Nation.

Cynthia Ann Parker was her *taibo* name. Among The People, she had been Nadua. *Tejanos* had struck a Comanche village when Quanah himself was just a boy. They had captured Nadua, returned her and her daughter, Prairie Flower, to the *Tejanos*. Eventually both had died. Of broken hearts.

"From what Quanah told me," Biggers said, shifting the Bible to his other hand, "he had quite a few adventures on that journey. He had many stories to tell. The trip helped strengthen the bond between the Texans and the Comanches, helped forge the peace we now know."

Daniel had nodded. He had said to himself: *I think it is the Big Pasture on our reservation, all that grass the Tejano cattlemen need for their beef, I think that is what has forged our peace.*

Aloud, he had said: "You wish for me to go to Texas?"

He had been to Texas as a tribal policeman.

To Dallas. To Fort Worth. To Wichita Falls. He would rather not go back to Texas. Once, The People had ruled that land, too.

"I have been told that your mother was a Mescalero Apache," Biggers had said.

Daniel had stepped back, needing to brace his back against the wall, needing something stronger than his legs to keep him upright.

"My mother is in The Land Beyond The Sun," he had said.

"Cynthia Ann Parker was dead, too, by the time Quanah made his journey. But he found her relatives."

Daniel had not been able to speak.

"I've already written the agent at the Mescalero reservation. If Captain Hall can acquire that railroad pass, we can get you to the railroad in Dodge City, Kansas, where you can catch a westbound train. Go all the way to New Mexico Territory, then by stagecoach to Tularosa, and from there to the reservation. I understand it is beautiful country."

So was Pennsylvania, Daniel had thought. So hilly. So green. So thick with forests. But it had not been home. In fact, it had taken him probably two years just to get used to the enclosed sur- roundings. Those forests had made Daniel feel like he was trapped in a tunnel, or a cave. You couldn't see where you were going. You couldn't see anything but trees. He had gotten used to it, though. Seven years away from the Staked Plains, away from Cache Creek and the Wichita Mountains.

*You adapt,* Hugh Gunter had once told him. *We Cherokees are damned good at adapting. You adapt, Daniel. Else you die.*

He had adapted. Otherwise, he never could have survived those coal mines.

"I don't know your mother's name," Biggers had said.

"We do not speak the names of those no more," Daniel said. But he remembered her name, if not her face. Tsomo Korohko. Bead Necklace. She had been wearing one when his father had captured her. But Daniel could not remember the necklace, either.

"Well, you would have given her a Comanche name, anyway. Do you remember her Mescalero name?" Biggers had asked.

Daniel had said no.

"Well, you're the detective." Biggers had laughed. Daniel had remained stoic. "You can solve that one, I warrant." Straightening, Biggers had set the Bible down. "Do you want to go?"

Daniel had nodded. "It would be good, perhaps, to meet and visit with my mother's people."

Which hadn't been quite the truth. That's something else Daniel had learned while living with the Pale Eyes. How to lie. Or at least how to tell the Pale Eyes what they wanted to hear.

Quanah Parker had found his mother's grave, had found his *Tejano* relatives, but Quanah always had *puha*. But Daniel had found nothing on his journey so far. No one remembered a Mescalero woman having been taken captive by Comanches, or at least they would not admit to it. Oh, the Mescaleros had been friendly to Daniel—so had the agent—and the mountains were beautiful, taller and more rugged than the Wichitas, nowhere near as green, as lush, as tree-studded as those in Pennsylvania.

On his journey, Daniel had soon realized that his heart was not into finding anyone who had known his mother. They would have known her as a Mescalero, not as one of The People. What good was it to forge a peace between The People and the Mescaleros when they were no longer enemies, just "wards of the government," as the Pale Eyes said? Prisoners.

Thus, he had bid his farewells, thanked the Mescaleros who had befriended him, the agent, and managed to find a ride on the back of a freight wagon from Blazer's Mill to Rincon.

So now here he stood, showing the conductor on the westbound his railroad pass. A white-haired man with neatly groomed mustache and beard, the conductor looked at the pass, and pulled it away from Daniel, hiding it behind his back.

"How do I know you're this Daniel Kill-straight?" His accent sounded Irish.

Daniel found the letter of introduction, and while the conductor read that, holding the letter in his left hand, the pass still in his right, still behind his back, Daniel fished out his Indian Police badge, pinning it to his lapel. The conductor stopped reading, glanced at the badge, then back at the letter. Both hands dropped to his sides, still holding pass and letter.

"Kiowa-Comanche-Apache Reservation," the conductor said. "Which one be you?"

"Comanche," Daniel replied.

"So you must know Geronimo."

A silly test. Or an ignorant conductor. "No," Daniel said. "But Quanah Parker, chief of the Comanche Nation, calls me a friend."

The papers were returned. The conductor smiled briefly, but Daniel saw no warmth in the grin. "You speak good English for a Comanche, so I guess I'll have to give you the proper respect due any white lawdog. Where you bound?"

"Deming."

That seemed to relax the conductor. He wouldn't have this Indian aboard his train very long. "Well, we're full up. You don't mind riding in the caboose, do you?"

It was better than the boxcar full of horses, which Daniel had been forced to ride in from Dodge City to Trinidad.

45

# CHAPTER FOUR

Actually, now that he had time to think on it, Daniel had not minded riding in the boxcar with the horses. Back on the reservation, he shared his home with horses. The People loved horses, loved their smell, their power. They knew everything one could know about horses. To Pale Eyes, a Comanche might not look like much. Short. Squat. Fat. Dirty. But when a Comanche was on horseback, Pale Eyes, and even other Indians, marveled at how they rode, how they could become one with the animal, or maybe it was the other way around. The horse became one with the Comanche.

When the brakeman farted, Daniel wished he were in that boxcar with the horses. To him, horse apples had a pleasing aroma. He waved his hand in front of his nose, while the brakeman laughed.

"You think that stinks, wait till I eat some of them things." He pointed to the pot of beans simmering on the stove. "Want some?"

Daniel's head shook.

He liked the brakeman, a heavy-set *taibo* with a drooping brown mustache, hands the size of anvils, arms like tree stumps. His grip had practically crushed Daniel's hand when they

46

shook, and the man had introduced himself, Ladislaus Radegunde.

"How about some coffee then?"

The brakeman was moving to the potbelly stove, and Daniel was thankful when he reached for a coffee mug, and not a bowl for beans. He hovered, staring, waiting.

"Sure." Daniel started to stand, but the brakeman waved him off.

"I'll fetch it." The big man picked up another mug. "Hope you like it black. Ain't got no sugar. Ain't got no milk or cream or even John Barleycorn." He was already filling the mugs before Daniel could say anything. "Some folks would say that we ain't even got coffee. But it does the job."

He brought the cups over to the table in the corner by the door that led to the rest of the train: 4-4-0 locomotive, tinder, express car, baggage car, three passenger coaches, a Pullman sleeper, a smoking car, two boxcars, and the caboose, where he and the brakemen were riding. Radegunde sank onto a stool, sliding a cup toward Daniel, about a quarter of the steaming black liquid spilling onto the table top, which didn't seem to bother the brakeman. He was too busy drinking his own brew.

Daniel took a tentative sip, and made himself smile. It was like drinking tar. Without cream and sugar.

47

"So you're headin' to Demin'?" the brakeman said.

Daniel made himself take another sip of the wretched coffee, just to be polite. "Yes, sir."

"Don't *sir* me, boy. You don't even have to sir my old man. On account he was a son-of-a-bitch."

Daniel couldn't think of anything to say, so he took another sip, and set the cup on the table. He felt himself leaning, realized the train must be rounding a bend.

"Why would anyone want to get off in Demin'?" the brakeman asked.

Daniel decided to answer truthfully. "There's been a killing."

Radegunde drained his coffee, as if he were drinking water, began twirling the empty cup on an oak branch he called a finger. "Was a killin' in Trinidad. Probably was a killin' in Tucson. Lots of killin's. Lots of towns. I can think of better places to go to because some idiot got killed than Demin'."

"It was a girl." Daniel didn't want to tell the man that she had been killed by an Apache. Or was thought to have been murdered by one.

"It's still Demin'." The brakeman grinned, slapped the table, and pushed himself up, striding back to the stove for more coffee.

Suddenly curiosity struck Daniel. "You know Deming?"

"I live there." The brakeman chuckled. "End of the line for us. I'll have a few days to find a way to occupy my time till my eastbound leaves." He was coming back toward the table, walking on his "sea legs," as he called them, to the rhythm of the train. Daniel had already pulled out his note tablet and a pencil by the time the big man was settling onto his stool.

"Can you tell me about the city?"

The brakeman sniggered, drank some coffee, sniggered again. "City? You been readin' too many of 'em railroad guides."

Daniel shrugged. "How many people live there?"

The leviathan pursed his lips for a moment. "Last I heard, somebody tol' me it was right around sixteen hundred." He grinned. "But that was before the killin'."

To Daniel, sixteen hundred sounded enough like a city. Maybe not Philadelphia or Pittsburgh, but far too many *taibos* for Daniel to feel comfortable.

"Used to be a stop on John Butterfield's line of stagecoaches." The big man had turned talkative. "My pa worked for one. Then he went to work for the railroads. Brakeman, like me. Only he was workin' before air brakes come along. Got caught between two cars while couplin' 'em. Nasty way to die. So that's how come I'm here. Anyhow, 'bout Demin' . . . they moved the

49

original settlement to what's now Demin' on account of better water." He spat, missing the cuspidor. "But that's a matter of opinion. Tastes terrible."

*Like your coffee?* Daniel mused.

"Wasn't many people livin' there till the Atchison, Topeka, and Santa Fe reached there back toward the end of Eighty-One. That connected that desert burg with the Southern Pacific. So folks started callin' her New Chicago . . . figurin' she'd replace the old one. Didn't happen." Another sip of coffee. "So they renamed her Demin'. Some top dog of the S.P.'s wife's family's name. Or somethin' like it." He drank more coffee, then pointed a massive finger at Daniel's tablet.

"You writin' a book or somethin'?"

"No, sir."

"Told you don't *sir* me. You a newspaper reporter?"

That made Daniel laugh. "No. Nothing like that."

"Then what interests you about some killin'?"

Daniel hesitated, but decided to be honest. "They say an Indian killed the girl."

"Friend of yours?"

"The girl? No . . ."

"Not the girl, kid. Do I look blind to you? The Injun?"

"No. I don't think so. Couldn't be. I couldn't

50

know him." A wild thought popped in his head: *Could I?*

"An Apache?"

"That's what they say."

Radegunde rocked back on his stool. "Mescalero, I reckon," he said to himself. "That's odd." Daniel wasn't about to tell him about the cowboys claiming the killer was a Chiricahua. Lowering the stool legs back onto the floor, the brakeman leaned forward, putting his elbows on the table and drinking coffee again. "Yeah, I guess events might make my brief sojourn in my ol' stampin' grounds a mite interestin'."

Quickly Daniel tried to steer the conversation in another direction. "The county sheriff, I understand, left town after the murder."

"Wouldn't know about that. Sheriff spends most of his time, I'd reckon, in Silver City. That's the seat for Grant County."

Daniel glanced at his notes. He had written *sheriff,* but now that he thought about it, he realized he had made a mistake.

"The deputy sheriff, I mean. Do you know him?"

"Moran." The brakeman's rugged face showed no emotion. "Nah. See him in the saloons from time to time, but we ain't pards or nothin'. Minds his own business."

"And the town marshal is . . . ?"

"Called the police chief. That's how fancy

51

Demin' figured itself to be. Young fellow. McLyler. Or as we call him . . . McLiar. He's all right. For a snot-nosed kid. Likely ain't no older than you. About the only thing he polices, though, is stray dogs and dead rats."

He had no idea how to spell McLyler, so he wrote down: *McLiar. Police chief. Young.*

"So . . ." Daniel studied the man opposite him. "Where does a fellow like me sleep in a town like Deming?" he finally asked.

The brakeman had drained his coffee again, resumed twirling the cup on his big finger. "Best hotel's the American. Right next door to the depot. But I don't reckon they'd have a room for you . . . no offense . . . just like that bastard we call a conductor stuck you in here with me and not with the fools who pay to ride this train. You know, I moved from car to car, checkin' the brakes and such, makin' sure nothin' looked too hot. Plenty of empty seats up yonder."

Still twirling the cup, the brakeman waited for a reaction. Daniel gave him something he thought might be unexpected.

"I like riding with you."

It worked. The man laughed, spitting saliva across the table. He set the cup in front of him, and leaned back on the stool again, rocking in time with the movement of the train.

"You likely could get a cell," Radegunde

said after a while. "Just see Police Chief Mark McLiar. I guess he has cottoned to puttin' Injuns in his cells."

*Actually,* Daniel thought, *that might not be a bad idea.*

Then the brakeman began tossing the cup from one giant hand to the other. "Two smithies are in town. Hickox. He's the biggest. Probably the best. Even runs advertisements in the *Headlight*. But there's another, east side of town, G.K. Perue's. Perue often puts up folks in a stall for four bits." He grinned. "It's a clean stall." He farted again.

This time Daniel had to laugh. "What would you know about clean?"

Which got the brakeman cackling so hard, he pounded the table, spilling Daniel's coffee cup over and onto the floor, somehow missing Daniel's Old Glory tablet as well as his pants. Radegunde finally got himself under control, before reducing the table to kindling, and picked Daniel's cup up off the floor and took both of them to the wreck pan by the stove.

He opened the rear door, and Daniel immediately felt the rushing wind, saw the blackness of the New Mexican desert night. The brakeman disappeared outside for a moment, but soon was back inside. He shut the door.

"More coffee?" he asked.

"No, thank you." Daniel glanced at his notes,

then called out: "What can you tell me about Matt Callahan?"

That stopped the brakeman like a pole-axe. "Matt Callahan. What on earth would have a young Comanche buck interested in a big rancher like Matt Callahan?"

"I just heard his name mentioned in Rincon."

"Well, here's all you need to know about Matt Callahan. He's got a son, probably close to thirty years old, but the boy's a simpleton." He tapped his temple. "Nothin' in his noggin'. Dumb as a brick. You savvy?"

Daniel nodded.

"But that boy . . . Jules is his name . . . has got the strength of ten men. One Fourth of July, the two of us got into a wrestlin' match. Just for fun. To see who's the strongest man in New Chicago . . . er . . . I mean, Demin'. I didn't last five minutes before young Jules had me beggin' for my mama. Whupped me good. And fair. That's how strong Jules Callahan is."

Daniel sat still, holding his pencil, waiting.

"But," the brakeman said, then paused, "I'd rather tackle Jules Callahan than his pa. That's all you need to know about Matt Callahan." He moved back to the stove, retrieved his cup, refilled it with coffee, then shook the pot. " 'Bout empty, but that's all right. We'll be in Demin' soon." Slurping the coffee, he leaned against the wall. "No, here's somethin' else you might ought to know about Matt Callahan. They say that when some lawman or vigilantes would catch up with some tough *hombres* over in Arizona Territory, they'd send 'em to Demin'. Just give 'em a one-way ticket to Demin'. And keep in mind that our fair city wasn't founded, not official-like anyway, till Eighty-One. But that's how tough a town this place was. Back before we got civilized, and all. You follow me?"

Daniel didn't, but his head bobbed anyway.

"Well, 'em boys, 'em tough ol' birds who got run out of Arizona Territory . . . they's all workin' for Matt Callahan these days. If he ain't buried 'em."

So now all Daniel knew about Matt Callahan was that he had a powerfully strong son with a boy's mind, hired rough men to work his cattle, and was feared by one giant of a brakeman for the Atchison, Topeka, and Santa Fe.

He looked again at the notes he had written, and once more wondered what kind of fool's errand he had sent himself on. He was riding the westbound AT&SF to a city he had never seen, in a territory he did not know, to help out an Apache Indian he had never met, who was being jailed for the murder of a young girl that a bunch of drunken cowboys in Rincon had fancied.

What he was really doing, of course, was just postponing the inevitable—returning to the reservation, to Cache Creek, to agent Joshua Biggers, to the Wichita Mountains, and to his friend Ben

55

Buffalo Bone and the *taibo* house that his family had turned into a barn for horses. That's where Daniel slept. That's why Daniel did not mind riding in a boxcar with horses. Yet that was another reason Daniel didn't want to return home. Ben Buffalo Bone was Rain Shower's brother.

"Wait a minute!" Radegunde shouted. "Now I got it."

Daniel looked up at the grinning brakeman.

"Now,"—the big man jabbed a finger toward Daniel—"I got you pegged." He laughed. "You're goin' to Demin' 'cause you aim to prove that the Injun who killed that girl is innocent. Ain't that right?"

Daniel couldn't answer.

The brakeman shook his head. "Well, Mister Detective, you tell me this. What you gonna do when you figure out that the Injun's guilty as hell? You thought about that?"

Daniel studied the lead tip of his pencil.

"Apaches have been known to kill white women. Even worse," the brakeman informed him.

Daniel could only stare at the Old Glory tablet.

"Who was this girl that got kilt?"

That gave him something to do. He flipped back a page and read the name. "Melody Rivera," Daniel answered with hesitation, not wanting to say the name of the dead girl.

The coffee cup dropped to the floor, and the

brakeman came at him, all the laughter gone, his face masked by a blinding anger, his massive hands reaching out. He could crush Daniel easily.

"You damned liar!" the brakeman roared. "You lyin' red-skinned son-of-a-bitch!"

# CHAPTER FIVE

At first, Daniel thought, the screaming whistle saved his life.

It seemed to stop the burly man, bring him out of some murderous trance. He straightened, the huge arms dropping to his side as he blinked. Then the brakeman laughed.

"Boy, I fooled you. Ha! That was a good one. You thought you was done for."

Daniel, now standing, could only stare.

"Had you goin'." Radegunde snorted, spit, missed the cuspidor, and cackled again. "I gots to . . . check the brakes," he said. "I'll . . . we'll . . ." His head shook, and he moved to the corner, grabbed his club, and walked past Daniel, opening the door, then turning. "Melody Rivera, you say?"

Daniel nodded slightly.

"You sure?"

"It's just what I heard," Daniel said, almost as an apology, while thinking that cowboys weren't known for getting their facts straight, especially not cowboys in saloons.

"Melody Rivera." The brakeman tested the name. His grin reappeared, and he laughed again. "Kid, I ain't never heard of her."

The door closed behind him, and Daniel sank back down onto the stool.

That brakeman was just like the Cherokee policeman, Hugh Gunter. He thought he was so damned funny.

When the door reopened, Daniel rose slightly, only to see the conductor step inside, followed by the big brakeman and another railroad employee. Radegunde nodded slightly at Daniel, before dropping his club in a bucket in the corner. The conductor removed his glasses, and told Daniel: "We'll be in Deming in ten minutes."

"Thank you," Daniel said.

"Might as well gather your grip." He stuck his glasses in a pocket, and removed his watch, opening the case to check the time. "You can get off that way." He nodded toward the rear door.

Daniel shoved his Old Glory tablet into his grip, fastened it, stuck the pencil above his ear.

"You drunk all the coffee, damn you!" the third railroader swore at the brakeman.

"Your stomach can wait ten minutes. Then you can have a cup at the Harvey House." The brakeman looked at Daniel. "My advice is for you to pay four bits and stay at G.K. Perue's. Tell ol' G.K. that me, Ladislaus Radegunde, sent you."

The two other railroad men snorted. Daniel

wondered if this were another of the big brakeman's jokes.

"See you around town, kid." The brakeman was heading out the door. "Come on," he said to the two men. "We gots work to do."

"Remember," the conductor said a few moments later, and he gestured to the rear door. "That door." Then he was gone, too.

Daniel retrieved his writing tablet and wrote— *Ladislaus Radegunde*—sounding out the name. *What is that? Russian? German?* Daniel had known a number of men from those countries while working the mines in Pennsylvania, yet the brakeman had no accent. He studied the name, then wrote after it: *Asshole*.

He was waiting by the door when the train lurched to a stop, sending him leaning one way, then the other. Daniel didn't know how many times he had traveled by rails, but he never could get used to the feeling. He wondered how the brakeman and conductor managed to make a career out of this. After opening the door, he stepped onto the rear platform, leaped down, and made his way through the shadows amid the commotion of the train's arrival. He heard shouts, a baby crying, the hissing of steam as he climbed up onto the depot's platform, and moved through the throng of people waiting for the passengers, who had begun alighting from the coaches.

It was dark—Daniel didn't know the time—but, near the railroad tracks, Deming felt as alive as the coal mines when crews were changing shifts. Black men called out to passengers. Others carried bags from one car to the depot, to an omnibus, or just followed the passengers into the night. An organ-grinder did his best to entertain some children. Mules brayed at the hitching rails. From somewhere in town came the sound of an out-of-tune piano.

The American Hotel stood across from the depot, just as the brakeman had said, and already passengers were making their way for the hotel's open doors. Next door, he saw a restaurant, figured it to be the Harvey House as the drifting aroma of food reminded him that he had not eaten since Alice's groggery in Rincon.

Food would have to wait. Besides, he doubted the Harvey House would serve an Indian, anyway. A black man stopped near him to wipe his face with a dingy handkerchief.

"Do you know where the marshal's . . . the police department is?" Daniel asked.

"Silver Street," the man said. "Near the customs house." He pointed, then stuffed the rag into his pocket and hurried to a woman needing help with her trunks.

Daniel glanced back at the train, looking for the brakeman, but saw only strangers. One man in a bowler hat and sack suit checked his watch, so Daniel walked over to him and asked: "Pardon me, sir. Do you have the time?"

The man slid the watch into his vest pocket, turned, and said: "What do I look like? A damned clock?" The man picked up his grip, and scurried away.

*In the old days,* Daniel thought, *I would have cut your throat, gutted your body after I filled it with arrows, cut off your manhood and stuck it in your mouth, then taken your scalp. And I would not have cared what time it was.*

He looked at the sky, but clouds obscured the stars and moon.

A woman came to his rescue.

"Young man," she said. "I apologize. Not everyone in Deming is so rude." She was checking a watch on a necklace. "It is eleven-thirty. Why, we arrived right on time."

"Thank you, ma'am," he told her, tipped his black hat, and walked away before she realized she was talking to an Indian.

He made his way to Silver Street, moved down the dust-coated boardwalk. The first building he passed was a saloon, only it wasn't really a building. Daniel studied it as he walked past, smelling cigar smoke from the open doorway, seeing the glowing light from lanterns hanging in the corners, hearing the laughter and the clinking of glass. It was, he realized, an old railroad car that had been transformed into a saloon. He chair, leaned back against the wall, and closed his eyes.

The energy and traffic of Deming picked up. Daniel yawned, and let the front legs of the chair tip back down. Footsteps sounded—no spurs—and Daniel opened his eyes to find a tall, thin man in a gray suit and straw hat walking toward him, eyes filled with suspicion. Sunlight glittered off a badge pinned to his coat pocket.

Daniel stood, leaving his grip by the wall, and walked toward the jail door.

The man unbuttoned his coat, and Daniel saw the strap to a shoulder holster. Slowly Daniel pulled back his own jacket, revealing that he was unarmed.

That seemed to relax the man in the fancy suit, and he sped up his gait, stopping before the boardwalk, sizing Daniel up with hazel eyes.

"Can I do something for you?" Indeed, he was a young as the brakeman had said. Daniel didn't think the man even needed to shave, and he certainly wasn't Indian. His nose was straight, hair blond, fingers slender. The revolver in the shoulder harness probably was the only thing keeping the twig of a man from blowing away in the southern New Mexico wind.

"Chief McLyler, I presume."

The badge read *Deming Police*. And below that: *Chief.*

would pass similar buildings as he moved along, plus *jacales*, huts, adobes, before he came into the main, more permanent, business district. He passed Hickox's livery and blacksmith shop, which led him to believe that the AT&SF brakeman hadn't exaggerated when he said Hickox was the best. The building was made of decorative brick and parapets, unlike the shabby frame structures with which he was familiar in Fort Smith and Texas.

He walked on, past a hay store, another saloon, a barbershop (another one of those railroad cars), a mercantile—all closed at this hour, except the saloon—more brick buildings, stone structures, even a handful of frame stores with façades, a fancy structure with Greek columns and a double gabled roof covered with shingles.

Finally he saw a small frame building with DEMING POLICE written in broad black letters over the door. No lights shone through the windows, but next door stood a small structure. A man stood outside near a large wooden door with a small barred window, smoking a cigarette. The sign above the door read: *Cárcel* Jail.

Deming certainly wasn't the New Chicago, Daniel agreed. Most of the street lamps burned coal oil, instead of gas, but here, at the jail, the lamp on the wall flickered from a candle. As he approached the jail, the man—Mexican, Daniel realized—pitched the cigarette into the dust, and tensed.

"What do you want?" he said.

"I'm looking for Police Chief McLyler." He had to stop himself from saying McLiar.

"He is not here. Come back *mañana*."

"Deputy Sheriff Moran?"

"No." He spouted something off in rapid Spanish.

"It is important. Very important."

"*Mañana*," the jailer repeated. Stubborn man.

Sighing, Daniel tried to think of another approach. "Where would I find the police chief?"

"*¿Quién sabe?*"

"Deputy Moran?"

The Mexican shrugged again.

"How is the prisoner?"

The jailer did not answer. Instead he turned, opened the door, and disappeared inside. Daniel heard the lock catch, and a bar being lowered. But what was it he had heard someone say: *The Deming jail couldn't hold a fart?*

Probably not quite midnight yet. He was hungry. He had no place to stay, unless he wanted to find that livery stable owned by G.K. Perue. No. Those cowboys from Rincon wouldn't make it here. Not tonight. But perhaps others might want to lynch the Apache prisoner.

Spotting a chair sitting underneath the *portal* in front of the jail, Daniel walked with his grip, feeling stubborn. He set the valise by an ▮ frame building, its paint stripped away by wind blown sand and the desert sun, and sank into the chair. It creaked under Daniel's weight. He probably weighed twice as much as the raw-boned Mexican jailer. He pulled his hat down.

He wasn't sure what he would do, what he could do, if some lynch mob came to hang the Apache inside, but he would be here. Besides, he was out of the wind. For now.

Sleep came in fits, and he often felt as if he were still riding that train. Eventually, dawn broke, and he lifted his head slightly, pushing back his big black hat, staring at the unopened door, then toward the streets. A few people moved slowly along the boardwalks—where boardwalks actually existed, that is—and a silver-haired Mexican led a burro past the jail, disappearing around the corner. He could smell eggs and bacon frying. Daniel still hadn't eaten.

He stretched, rose, stamped his feet, and sat back down, wondering if the jailer would ever get around to opening the door. When he did, Daniel would still be there, waiting. Mexicans and Pale Eyes didn't know just how patient a Comanche could be, although most of those that were old enough knew how relentless they could be.

Pulling down the brim of his hat, Daniel found what passed for a comfortable position in the old

"That's right. Mark McLyler." He didn't extend his hand.

Daniel reached inside his pocket, pulled out the envelope, withdrew the papers, and presented these to the lawman.

"I am Daniel Killstraight," he said.

"Killstraight?" McLyler stared at the papers, then, apparently struck dumb, returned them to Daniel. "I don't understand," he said.

"I'd like to see your Apache prisoner?"

"Apache?"

"The one you're holding for the death of . . . the girl . . . a few nights back."

The young police chief stepped back, his eyes intent now, his thumbs hooked in his waistband. "How the hell did you hear about that killing all the way over in Indian Territory? By jacks, Melody's body wasn't found till the morning of the Fifth."

"I was in Rincon." Daniel had decided to be helpful. "And there are some cowboys heading this way who'd like to hang the man you have behind bars."

"You mean . . . ?"

Daniel's head bobbed. "Yes, sir."

"You a lawyer?" McLyler immediately dismissed the thought. "No, you're just a tribal copper. But . . . ?"

"All I want to do is talk to your prisoner," Daniel said, and added: "I'm after justice, same as you." Sounding like Harvey P. Noble now. Daniel considered trying to explain: *If the Apache's guilty, I'm fine with that.*

McLyler just stared. Finally he smiled, and moved past Daniel, banging on the door. "Miguel! Open up. It's Chief McLyler. Hurry up, *hombre.*"

The door and heavy walls muffled much of the sound, but the door opened, and the wiry old Mexican stepped into the morning light. He looked as if he had slept as well as Daniel.

"Man wants to see the prisoner," Mark McLyler said. "Take him back there."

Then the chief was through the door, heading toward the stove in the corner, where a coffee pot waited.

Daniel followed the jailer inside.

The interior wasn't much better than the outside, just dustier, stuffier. The jailer opened another door, held it open, motioned for Daniel to follow down a dark corridor that smelled of sweat and mold and urine.

"Last cell!" McLyler called out while pouring coffee. "Only prisoner we have!"

Daniel stepped through the door, feeling his way through the darkness, until Miguel stopped him and handed him a candle he had just lit. That helped, and Daniel continued down the hall, feeling a wetness on the bottoms of his moccasins. No longer did he feel certain of anything. There was movement on his left and farther down the hall, and he saw the outline of the Apache prisoner, sitting up in his bunk. The man snorted, spit.

"How 'bout some coffee?" he bellowed. "Before I swing."

Daniel moved on, the candle casting meager light into the last cell. The prisoner was rising, moving, then gripping the iron bars with his hands.

"Who the hell are you?" the man asked.

By then, Daniel was already sure of one thing. This prisoner—this killer of Melody Rivera— was no Apache, but a white man.

# CHAPTER SIX

Certainly the prisoner looked Apache enough. Deerskin trousers, stained and dirtied with age, and tan moccasins that rose to just below his knees, the tops bound around his calves with rawhide. The blue cotton shirt, with dingy, once-white piping around the buttons and collar, could have come from a sutler at any reservation, as could have the red cotton bandanna, but the scarf's silver concho likely came from some Navajo. He also carried a ration ticket pouch, heavily beaded, hanging from a rawhide strap over his left shoulder, and his hair was dark, hanging well past his shoulders, unkempt, unruly. No hat, either, just another scarf, this one red with floral designs, used as a headband.

The thick, dark beard, however, gave him away. So did the blue eyes. And his voice.

"Well?" the prisoner demanded. "Coffee?"

"No," Daniel said.

The white man snorted. "No rope, neither, I warrant?"

To that, Daniel just stared blankly.

The man snapped: "Then what good are you?"

"I'd like to help you." Daniel wanted to add: *If I can. If you will let me*. That, however, seemed more *taibo*, not something one of The People

70

would say, even now after all these long years living as the Pale Eyes wanted them to live.

The man spit between the iron bars, missing Daniel, the glob landing somewhere where the candle's flame did not illuminate. "Nobody can help me," the Pale Eyes said.

Daniel waited.

"Besides, I don't want help." The prisoner stared at his own dirty moccasins, then looked up, meeting Daniel's eyes briefly. No defiance, just weary resignation, which led Daniel to remember something Ladislaus Radegunde, that big AT&SF brakeman, had told him: *What you gonna do when you figure out that the Injun's guilty as hell?*

This had been some fool's errand. A silly crusade. Daniel had come all the way to Deming to save an Apache from a lynching. Thinking himself a real detective, not a lonely, heart-broken Comanche in his mid-twenties with nothing but bad memories waiting for him if and when he returned home to Indian Territory. Now, Daniel realized, he had no reason to stay in Deming.

He almost turned to leave, but again found himself looking into the man's eyes. A dead man's eyes. Daniel knew those eyes, for, since Rain Shower had been murdered, he had seen such sadness in his own reflection in mirrors.

Briefly the man appeared curious, but that,

71

too, died in his eyes. Still, he cocked his head, studying Daniel, then said: "What are you?"

*A good question,* Daniel thought. *Comanche father, Mescalero mother, mostly educated by Pale Eyes back in Pennsylvania.* He said: "I am Comanche."

Again the man spit. He possessed an amazing amount of saliva. "Figured. You sure ain't Apache."

"Nor are you." Thinking, but not saying: *At least, not by blood.*

Silence. The man's eyes burned with intensity, his grip on the iron bars tightening, then relaxing. He even smiled, but the grin held no warmth, no humor.

"Bet you ain't got any smokes on you, neither," the prisoner said.

"Cigarettes? No."

"Like I said . . ." The man had turned away, moved to the corner, where he unfastened his pants and urinated in a foul-smelling bucket. "What good are you?"

Dismissal. Yet something held Daniel there. He waited for the man to finish relieving himself, hitch up his buckskin trousers, and turn around. The prisoner saw Daniel, but if he were surprised to find him still waiting, his face revealed nothing.

That, too, was Apache. Not *taibo.*

The man sat on the edge of the bunk.

"Melody . . . Rivera." Daniel spoke the name in a measured voice. It made him uncomfortable, speaking of the girl who was no more. He brought his hand up to his hat, touched the hawk's feather stuck in the headband. His *puha*. His protection.

The prisoner looked up.

"Did you kill her?" Daniel asked.

The man spit again, missing the slop bucket. "Folks here say I did. And hanging suits me to a T. I got nothing to live for. Not any more."

This Daniel considered, but before he could speak, the man snapped: "Just get the hell out of here, boy. I got nothing to say to white men, and certainly nothing to say to a chubby Comanche buck dressed like some *indaaligande*."

He didn't need to understand Apache. He knew the word's meaning. *Taibo*. Pale Eyes. White man.

A gust of wind from somewhere blew out the candle, but Daniel could still see enough from the light coming through the door the jailer had left open now that his eyes had adjusted.

He had never been very good at this type of thing with Pale Eyes—asking the hard questions. Talking to Comanches came easily. Even with the Kiowas, who had a peculiar singsong way of talking, he was able to ask questions or just carry on a conversation about almost anything. But interrogate a *taibo*? Try to put them at ease and get answers out of them? That was uncomfortable

73

for Daniel Killstraight. He remembered a few times when he even had felt uncomfortable speaking to Deputy Marshal Harvey P. Noble, and he considered Noble a friend.

But this man seemed more stoic, more taciturn, than anyone from any race Daniel had ever encountered.

"If I brought you the makings for your smokes," Daniel said, "and coffee . . . would you speak to me then?"

The man shook his head, swung his legs up on the bunk, lay down, and rolled over, his back now to Daniel, his face staring at the hard stone walls.

"The only thing you can bring me, bub," he said, "is a rope."

When Daniel stepped inside the jail office, the wiry Mexican closed the door behind him. Police Chief Mark McLyler now sat behind the desk, holding a steaming cup of coffee. Another cup, also steaming, rested on the edge of the desk near a stool. McLyler pointed at both cup and stool with his free hand.

"How about some coffee for the prisoner?" Daniel said.

McLyler sighed in resignation. "Miguel," he said, "bring Groves some coffee." He sipped his own. "Maybe that'll shut him up."

Grumbling under his breath in Spanish, the jailer went to the stove to fill another cup, and

Daniel settled onto the stool. McLyler shot a finger toward the front door. "Miguel brought in your grip," he said.

Daniel saw the carpetbag resting on the floor. School Father Pratt had given it to him when Daniel left the Carlisle school. It was not a large bag by any means, but Daniel had little to carry, even on such an extended trip. It was made of a paisley fabric of black and silver, but Rain Shower had decorated it with the design of a hawk's feather on the front, using trade beads she had bought at the trading post and porcupine quills she had plucked, dyed, and plaited herself—the old way of The People. Daniel quickly looked away from the grip.

"*Gracias*," he managed to tell the jailer, who snorted, opened the heavy door, and disappeared in the cell chamber with coffee for the man McLyler had called Groves.

When the door closed, the policeman leaned forward, grinning. "So what do you think of our *Apache* prisoner?"

Daniel sipped the coffee. It was black, and bitter. Like most of The People, he preferred his coffee sweetened with plenty of sugar, but he had learned to adapt. As a tribal peace officer, he didn't get rations—some silly rule the government had made—and sugar was expensive at the trading posts, especially for a Comanche drawing only $8 a month.

"His name is Groves?" Daniel said, ignoring the sarcasm of McLyler's question.

"He damned sure isn't Cochise or Victorio."

Daniel asked: "How did you learn his name?"

McLyler practically slammed his coffee cup on a train schedule. "Damn it all, Killstraight, you beat all. Do you know that? You come here, and you don't even know the prisoner's name. You don't know the facts of the case. You don't know anything. You just thought we were holding an Indian prisoner, and, God forbid . . . you knew an Indian could not be guilty of breaking a sixteen-year-old girl's neck near the tracks west of town."

Daniel waited. He said nothing.

The chief shook his head. "And it turns out that the prisoner isn't even an Indian," McLyler said.

Daniel sipped coffee, then said: "He's Apache enough."

"Only he's as white as I am."

"My mother was Mescalero," Daniel admitted. "But I am Nermernuh."

"Ner—what?"

"It is our name. To you *taibos* we are Comanches. Among ourselves, we are The People."

"Well, I don't need to learn how to speak Comanche. How many cowboys did you say were part of this lynch mob?"

"Four left Rincon," Daniel said. "I do not know if more will come."

"When did they leave?"

"Yesterday afternoon."

"Do you know their names?"

Daniel sipped coffee.

"You are a peace officer," McLyler reminded him. "Damned deputy sheriff is out of town, so I'm in charge of the prisoner. And even though I know Groves is guilty as hell, I don't want him hanged like that. And I know you don't."

Daniel thought about that a moment. Then he placed his coffee cup on the desk, rose, and moved to his grip. The door to the cells opened, Miguel came through, and said something in Spanish to the young chief. Daniel caught some of the words, but McLyler certainly was more fluent than Daniel. Too bad, Daniel thought. As a kid, he had learned some Spanish from The People's dealings with the *comancheros*, and he still retained some of that. Most of it, however, was gone, forgotten, replaced at Carlisle by Latin lessons and the edict: *You-must-always-speak-ENGLISH!* The school mothers had tried to beat the Comanche out of him. Tried, but failed.

"Go home and have your breakfast, Miguel," McLyler said. "Give my best to your wife. Before you come back, fetch Roberts and Frazer . . . and bring that shotgun of yours with you. And see what you can find out about Moran." McLyler added under his breath: "Damned, worthless deputy sheriff."

Miguel was gone by the time Daniel had retrieved his Old Glory tablet and returned to the stool. He flipped the first page, then gave the names. "Jimmy, Charley, Vince, and Frank. Frank and Vince work for the Four-Five-Connected Ranch. Charley and Jimmy are, or were, with the Hanging Slash-W."

That seemed to relax the lawman. He should have enough time to prepare for the cowboys. McLyler lifted his coffee, and finished the brew.

"Now," Daniel said, "could you tell me about Groves?"

The police chief shrugged. "Francis Groves," he elaborated. "Well, he showed up here with nothing but a saddle and his smell four days back. Said his horse had died somewhere between Lordsburg and here. A complete stranger. Stayed at Perue's stables. Told Perue his name . . . about his horse . . . He hasn't told anyone else much of anything as far as I know."

He paused for breath, and Daniel took the opportunity to ask: "No lawyer?"

"He hasn't asked for one. And it's not my job to hire one for him. Anyway, we had a big Fourth of July celebration in town, and Groves was seen with Melody Rivera that evening. He was also seen to be well in his cups. I mean he was roostered. A railroad man named O'Shaughnessy found Melody's strangled body the next morning. He also found Groves right beside her, drunk,

78

had pissed in his pants, passed out. It didn't take much to figure out who had done the dirty deed."

Daniel let McLyler speak without interruption. As the chief went to the stove to refill his coffee cup, Daniel asked: "Did anyone see the murder?"

"Didn't have to," McLyler answered. "Besides," he continued, "if someone had seen the killing, don't you think they would have reported it, tried to stop it? This isn't a bad town, Killstraight. People here are civilized."

He thought of the man at the depot, the one who had told him: *What do I look like? A damned clock?* He said nothing, just considered what McLyler had said as the police chief returned to his seat.

*What to ask next?* Daniel wondered, wishing Harvey P. Noble and Hugh Gunter were here to help him. They were good lawmen, and even better detectives than Daniel could ever hope to be. Quanah Parker could have helped him, too. Quanah knew how *taibos* thought. But Daniel was in a strange town in a strange territory without any friends, or help.

"You know nothing else about Groves?" he finally asked.

"Someone said he lived with the Apaches for a while. Chiricahua. But that's obvious. You can tell just by looking at him. Or smelling him."

Which explained why the cowboys in Rincon had thought the girl had been murdered by an Apache, and not a white man.

"Who told you that?" Daniel asked.

"Burly Mexican named Jemez," McLyler said, and Daniel immediately wrote the name in his Old Glory tablet.

"That's all the name he has?" Daniel asked.

"That's all he calls himself. Rides for Matt Callahan. He and Groves had a bit of a dispute at the Harvey House."

*Matt Callahan's name. Again.*

"What kind of dispute?" Daniel pursued.

"They knew each other in Sonora. No blood shed. No fists thrown. No pistols pulled. That's all I know. Why are you so damned curious, Killstraight? You know that bastard's guilty."

"What brought him to town?" Daniel ignored the question. "Groves, I mean. Not Jemez."

McLyler shrugged. Sipped coffee. Then said: "Well, this is one of those someone-heard-someone-else-say kind of things. You understand?" After Daniel's nod, McLyler continued. "He's making his way to Saint Augustine, Florida." The chief laughed. "That's a far piece to be going, especially now that he's afoot."

But Daniel knew why. So did McLyler. After Geronimo's surrender a few years back, the citizens of the Territory of Arizona had demanded that all the Chiricahuas be shipped to that Florida prison. Where Daniel's own father had been sentenced to go in 1875.

"And what of the girl?" Daniel asked. This time he did not say her name.

"Sixteen years old. Isn't that all you need to know?"

Daniel thought about this, then said: "I don't know what you mean."

"I mean sixteen-year-old girls don't deserve to be strangled . . . to have their necks broken!"

"No one does," Daniel said calmly, after the chief settled down.

The People did not fear death. They did not fear the dead. Yet to die by hanging, with a broken neck, that did scare them. How could they wander through The Land Beyond The Sun with their head hanging loosely on the shoulders? How could this half-Mexican girl?

*Francis Groves is guilty,* Daniel told himself. Only he kept thinking back to what Groves had told him back in the cell.

The door opened, and two men entered. One was bald, sunburned, wearing denim trousers, work boots, a muslin shirt, carrying a railroader's cap in his big hand. The other wore duck pants, collarless shirt, buttoned vest, and a bowler. Daniel spotted the tin shields pinned to the chests of both men.

"Hank Roberts, Jasper Frazer," McLyler said, "this is Sergeant Daniel Killstraight. Of the

Tribal Police." The last part was said mockingly, but Daniel didn't lose his temper.

Roberts was older, big, not solid, but fat, jowly, unshaven, with rheumy eyes. His nod revealed no friendliness.

"Apache police?" Frazer, the younger man, asked. He sported a well-groomed brown mustache, and didn't appear to be much older than Daniel. He also wore a brace of revolvers—ivory-handled, nickel-plated Colts facing butt forward from a well-oiled black belt seated high on his waist.

Daniel had never seen anyone wear a rig like that, except on the covers of some penny dreadfuls.

"Comanche, and Kiowa, too," McLyler answered for Daniel. The police chief was standing now, fetching his hat, speaking as he moved about the office. "Listen, boys, we might have some trouble later today . . . maybe tomorrow. Some cowboys from around Rincon got word of Melody's death. One of them is Vince Ford, who you probably know was sweet on Melody."

"Who wasn't?" the older man, Roberts, said with a snort.

McLyler turned, frowning, and walked up to the two policemen. He lowered his voice to a whisper, and, as they talked, Daniel wrote down Vince's last name in his note pad. The lawmen knew Vince Ford, even though McLyler hadn't evidenced any recognition when Daniel had brought up his name earlier. He added to his notes on Melody Rivera: *Everybody sweet on.*

Then Mark McLyler was saying his name, so Daniel turned, closing the tablet. The two newcomers flanked the police chief, who held Daniel's valise. Inviting him to leave. Daniel recalled Harvey P. Noble's joke: *Here's your hat. What's your hurry?*

Daniel finished the coffee, set down the cup, stood, and moved toward the three men.

"Come on, Killstraight," McLyler said. "I want to show you something." At the last moment, he set Daniel's grip back on the floor of the jail. "You can pick this up later," he said. Daniel left his Old Glory tablet and pencil on the desk.

# CHAPTER SEVEN

Early morning, and the sun already was blisteringly hot, the wind dry and harsh. Daniel preferred the heat and humidity of Indian Territory, the tall grasses of the Big Pasture, and the timbers along Cache Creek. He preferred The People.

Another train had pulled into the depot. He couldn't see the station, but thick clouds of black smoke rose above the tops of the brick and stone buildings, and the railroad's rolling stock that had been transformed into businesses.

A stable, full of burros and mules—a café, smelling of coffee and stewed apples—a barbershop—a lawyer's office. No saloons. He and McLyler were in the respectable section of Deming proper.

Uncertain of their destination, Daniel walked silently alongside the equally taciturn police chief. People, *taibo* men and women, passed them on what passed for boardwalks, but few spoke. Some didn't even nod a good morning, didn't even attempt to hide the stares they cast at Daniel Killstraight.

So Daniel directed his attention to the business signs.

McKeyes & Washington
Real Estate Agents
Insurance-Conveyancing-Notaries Public

A sign in front of a grocery:

JUST ARRIVED!
Dwight's Cow-Brand Soda
Makes perfect biscuits

A schedule on a slate board for the stagecoach line from Deming to Palomas, Mexico, had once read: Leaves 7:00 a.m. Friday. Only the 7:00 a.m. had been chalked out and replaced with Noon. And somebody had put a question mark after Friday.

"We've got two schools, one private, another public. We've got four hotels, including the American. Best you'll find between El Paso and Tucson."

It took a moment before Daniel realized that McLyler was talking to him.

McLyler pointed out a building across the street. "Two churches, and they're building one for the Mexicans, the Catholics. Two newspapers." They passed a stone building, and Daniel glanced at the large gold letters painted on the frame window. This was the *Advance*, not the *Headlight*. He would like to meet the publisher of the Deming *Headlight*. Now there was a *taibo* with a sense of humor The People would enjoy.

"The mayor and the councilmen keep talking about forming a city club, getting us a library, an opera house, things like that." He stopped, turned, and stared at Daniel.

"This place has had a mean past, but that's what it is, Daniel . . . history. Men got killed here. Deming was rough, just a few years back. There's no denying that, but men get killed in every town on the frontier . . . and back East, back in civilization. Women get killed, too."

Daniel stared at his moccasins. He thought of Rain Shower.

McLyler was still talking about women getting killed in New York and Kansas City and Chicago and Charleston, then, just as quickly as he had launched into his monologue, he stopped and resumed walking. Daniel followed.

By this time, he knew where he was. He saw the depot, the train already pulling out, moving eastward. He wondered if Ladislaus Radegunde, the big brakeman, was on it. The American Hotel and the Harvey House were bustling with activity. Somewhere, a bell rang.

They crossed the railroad tracks, passed more saloons, cribs, gambling dens, all practically deserted at this time of day, then moved through the colored section of town, then came a section of dugouts and hovels. Finally Police Chief Mark McLyler stopped. He pointed to a door, or what passed for a door. It was canvas wrapped around juniper poles. A black bandanna had been nailed over the top frame.

*Their sign of mourning,* Daniel thought to himself.

"This is where Melody Rivera lived," McLyler said. "So why don't you go inside now, Sergeant Daniel Killstraight? Why don't you meet with Missus Rivera, Melody's mama, and her younger brother Toby? Why don't you go inside, Killstraight, and tell them that Melody deserved to die."

"I never said that," Daniel said, the Comanche in his voice so strong McLyler took two steps back.

"You think Groves didn't do it."

Daniel looked at the door, the wretched little hovel. Even this far south, this close to the Mexican border, Daniel knew it got cold here in the winter. That hot, dry wind could turn brutally frigid, and a canvas door wouldn't keep out the cold. *Taibos* often mocked him for living in a white man's house that kept horses, saying a man must be poor to live like that. But they did not know poor.

He turned to McLyler. "Show me where her body was found."

The policeman snorted, sighed, threw up his hands, and swore. But eventually he said: "Come on."

They took a different route, moving west, then south back toward the railroad tracks. They were on the outskirts of Deming, and turned to walk on the north side of the tracks, heading to Deming proper along the Southern Pacific's right of way. A few *jacales* and hovels and huts and tents began appearing on the north side of the tracks as they neared the city. On the other side of the tracks, Daniel saw switches and boxcars and flatbeds. They reached a mountain range of trash piles, took a few steps past the garbage, and McLyler stopped, turned, and pointed to the tallest heap of refuse.

"There," he said.

Daniel looked. "Where . . . exactly?"

Swearing under his breath, McLyler moved closer to one of the large piles of débris, pulling a handkerchief from a trouser pocket, pressing it over his mouth and nose. He pointed toward the bottom, closest to the tracks, dirty airtights, faded newspapers, rags, broken bottles. The handkerchief came away from McLyler's face. "She was here, in a seated position, spread-eagled. Leaning against the pile." McLyler spit the distaste from his mouth, inhaled deeply and quickly, and the handkerchief returned to his nose and mouth.

Daniel stepped closer, kneeled, and studied the heap. He tried to picture the sixteen-year-old girl.

"Can we go now?" McLyler asked.

Daniel rose. "I'd like to look around," he said. For what, he had no clue.

The young police chief cursed again, shoving the handkerchief deep into his pocket. "What makes you so damned certain Groves is innocent? He hasn't said he didn't do it. Hasn't said a damned thing, hardly."

He wasn't sure if a *taibo* would understand this. *Hell,* Daniel thought, *I don't know if I understand it myself.*

"I asked the prisoner," Daniel said, choosing his words carefully, "if he killed her. He said something about people believing he did it. Said he'd like to hang . . . that hanging suited him to a T, those were his exact words. He said he had nothing to live for."

McLyler spit again. "That's not a proclamation of innocence, Killstraight."

"Then why not just say . . . 'Yes, I am guilty. Hang me.' . . . why not just confess?"

The policeman's head shook. "It sounds close enough to a confession to me. And it will to a judge and jury."

"But not to an Indian." Daniel could read the sudden curiosity in McLyler's eyes. "Apaches do not lie. He could not say he killed the girl. Because he didn't."

Now a sense of righteousness replaced McLyler's curiosity. "You keep forgetting, Killstraight, that Francis Groves is a white man."

89

"Not any more," Daniel countered.

"Hell!" McLyler was turning, leaving. "Stay here at this stinking heap as long as you want. I'm going back to the jail. In case those cowboys show up. Or, God help me, Moran." He crossed the tracks, turned down an alley, but stopped before he disappeared between two adobe structures.

"But you might do yourself a favor," he called out, "and go talk to Missus Rivera and Toby!"

He poked through the trash pile—the airtights from tomatoes and peaches, and the bottles and the paper. He didn't know what he was looking for, wouldn't have known a clue had it sliced through a finger. And there was a pretty good chance of that happening. The cans' edges were sharp, the broken bottles even sharper.

Leaning back on his haunches, Daniel stared. Again, he tried to picture the body of Melody Rivera, strangled and her neck broken.

In the old days, before Quanah had led the last of the Kwahadi to the soldier fort, The People were expert trackers. Even a holy man like the late Isa Nanaka could have found something here, despite the fact that the murder had occurred days earlier. Daniel had no idea how many *taibos* had wandered through here, destroying sign, maybe even evidence. Then again, Daniel didn't know what he was looking for. Besides, he was no Isa Nanaka, no Quanah. Even his friend Ben Buffalo Bone could follow a deer trail. Daniel would likely get lost on a stroll through the woods. He wasn't a product of the old days, when The People ruled half of the Southwest. He was a product of the Carlisle Industrial School, a reservation Comanche.

Behind him came the sound of a man clearing his throat. Daniel tossed a busted beer bottle onto the refuse, and stood, turning around, wiping his fingertips on his trousers. To his surprise, he found the jailer, Miguel, standing near the tracks. Daniel looked at the old Mexican's right hand. It held a notebook.

Daniel blinked. Not just any notebook. It was an Old Glory tablet. It was Daniel's.

The Mexican spoke in rapid Spanish, stopped himself, held out the tablet. "I think you need this maybe so."

Uncertain, Daniel walked away from the garbage heaps until he stood just a foot away from the old jailer. Their eyes met. Miguel held out the tablet, which Daniel took. The old man even had brought Daniel's pencil.

"Did Marshal . . . ?" He stopped. It would take some getting used to. Police chiefs instead of town marshals. "Did Chief McLyler ask you to bring this to me?"

"No, *señor*."

He tried to read the man's dark face, but he saw

nothing. He looked back at the piles of rubbish, up and down the tracks, toward town, toward the desert, then back at Miguel.

"You don't think Groves killed the girl, either," Daniel was guessing. "Do you?"

"I knew the girl's family," he said. "I would like the . . . the right person punished."

"What makes you think Groves is innocent?" Daniel suspected no one else in Deming thought that.

"I feed this *hombre* every day. Breakfast. Dinner. Supper."

"It has only been . . ." Daniel shrugged. "What? A few days?"

"It has been long enough." For the first time Miguel grinned. "You made up your mind after . . ." He mimicked Daniel's guttural voice. "What? Three minutes?"

"Then why not tell McLyler?"

Miguel shrugged, said something in Spanish, then: "There is no love lost between my people and the Apaches."

Daniel removed his hat, wiped his brow. "As Chief McLyler points out to me, Francis Groves is a white man."

"No. He is Apache."

Daniel had nothing to say about that. He agreed with the jailer.

"Apaches killed many of my people," Miguel said. "They took many captives, including the sister of my mother's mother. And her two children. The father of my mother's mother's sister, he was tortured. What they did to him, this I will never tell. It was unholy. It was savage. If this renegade white man dies, I will feel no sorrow for his passing. But if he dies, and did not do this bad thing, then that itself is a bad thing."

Daniel flipped open the Old Glory. He looked back at the old man. "You will help me?"

Miguel shrugged. "The Apaches have troubled my people in recent times. But I am old enough to remember your people, too. There is no love lost between my people and yours, either. Maybe we would hate the Comanches even more than we hate the Apaches, but the Apaches are closer. But, *sí*, I will help you."

Daniel determined that Miguel was an honest man. It was a start, finding someone he could talk to and believe. It was important since he wouldn't be receiving any sage advice from Deputy U.S. Marshal Harvey Noble or words of wisdom—or sarcasm—from the Cherokee, Hugh Gunter. No Ben Buffalo Bone or even Agent Joshua Biggers, either. Miguel would have to do.

"I need to talk to the man named O'Shaughnessy," he said to Miguel. "He works for the railroad. He's the one who found the girl's body. He also found Groves."

He turned back toward the garbage. Thought of the notes he had written. Studied the debris area once more. Groves had been found right beside the dead girl. Literally? Figuratively? McLyler hadn't mentioned that when he had pointed out where the girl's body had been discovered. Then again, Daniel hadn't asked.

"O'Shaughnessy. Do you know him?" Daniel said.

Miguel shrugged. "I do not know him. Where he lives, what he does for the Southern Pacific . . . none of this I know. But I know what he looks like. And I know what saloons, what brothels, the railroad men frequent."

Not much, but a bit of progress. Daniel opened his note pad. "The girl's death," Daniel next asked. "There would have been a coroner's inquest?"

"*Sí.*"

"Who was the doctor?"

"Doctor Commager. His office is three blocks from the American Hotel. In an old boxcar."

"About Groves," Daniel said, after writing down the doctor's name and location of his office. "Were you working when they brought him to jail?"

"*Sí.* After the arraignment."

*An arraignment. Civilization has certainly reached Deming. But . . . ,* Daniel paused in his thinking. He knew the circuit judge was not in town. They were waiting for him to arrive so they could hold the trial.

"Who was judge at the arraignment?"

"Squire Fuller. He is the justice of the peace."

"When they brought him in . . . brought Groves in, I mean"—Daniel glanced at his notes—"was he . . . still . . . ?"

"He was drunk. *Muy*. Still, *sí*." Miguel grinned.

"Had he wet himself? You know . . . ?"

"He smelled worse than this trash. I did not get close enough to him to learn what made him stink so."

Daniel looked at the sky. No clouds. Just a pale, hot blue. From the sun's position, he guessed it was about 10:00 a.m.

"He had a white bandage across his head," Miguel added.

But Daniel was thinking: *Ten in the morning . . . The doctor . . . Commager . . . should be in his office. Unless he is on call. And Squire Fuller? He'll likely have an office in the courthouse, city hall, or whatever it's called.*

He blinked, looked again at Miguel. "Who had a bandage on his head?" he asked.

"Your *amigo*, Francis Groves."

"Groves is no friend of mine. No friend of anyone's." Daniel was quick to distance himself from the suspected murderer, the *taibo* turned Apache. "Wait . . . Groves had a bandage?"

"*Sí*."

With a leathery right hand, Miguel stretched three fingers across his forehead, and around the

95

head, above the ears. "He ripped it off . . . the bandage . . . day before yesterday."

"Where did he get it?"

Miguel shrugged. "I did not ask. He did not say."

*Groves won't tell me, either,* Daniel thought. *Even if I ask.*

Closing the notebook, sliding the pencil above his ear, Daniel said: "All right. We will try to find the railroader tonight. Who should we visit first, the doctor or the squire?"

"You must visit these men yourself. Alone. I have to go to the jail. My shotgun. Remember?"

Daniel gritted his teeth. He cursed Vince Ford and the other boys from Rincon. He had almost forgotten about them.

"All right. Where does the squire work?" he asked Miguel.

"In the City Hall."

"Doctor's place is closer then, right?"

"*Sí.* But there is someone else you must see first."

The old man was pointing, and Daniel knew where he meant, who he had to see. Mrs. Rivera, the mother of the murdered teen, and Toby, the younger brother of the dead girl.

# CHAPTER EIGHT

He knocked on the juniper door frame, then stepped back.

Inside, voices spoke quietly in Spanish. He caught the aroma of cooking beans. He looked up. There was no chimney, but smoke rose above the thatched roof, probably from a window.

The canvas door was lifted. A black-haired, dark-eyed, bronze face appeared. The boy did not speak.

Daniel tried the little Spanish he knew. "*Hola*," he said, "*¿Habla usted inglés?*"

A woman's voice called out from the dark interior, and the boy turned, pumped out a few fast words, then turned back to Daniel. "Yes. What is it that you wish?"

Daniel showed him the tin shield. "My name is Daniel Killstraight. I . . ."

The boy interrupted him, eyes clouded with suspicion. "You are *policía*?"

"In the Indian Territory, *sí*."

"Ah. Then you are Apache." He spit out the words with utter distaste.

"No." Daniel tried to smile, but one would not form. "I am Comanche. You are Toby, is that correct?"

"Yes."

"First, let me say how sorry I am to have learned of your sister's passing. It is . . ."

"You have no reason to be sorry, Comanche," Toby interrupted. "You did not know Melody."

Daniel tensed upon hearing the dead girl's name, and touched the hawk's feather in his hatband again.

Toby kept talking. "I have not seen you in Deming before, Comanche. So I think that you came to save your friend. I have nothing to say to you."

Just seeing the kid's face, his dirty white shirt, it was hard to tell how old Toby Rivera was, but Daniel doubted if he had reached his teens. Maybe ten. Maybe twelve. Already sporting an attitude that would get him in many fights in the years to come. Daniel looked closer at the boy. His nose had been broken. He had already been in a fight or two.

"He's not my friend." Suddenly Daniel laughed. "I don't have a friend in this whole damned town."

"You won't find a friend here, either, Comanche."

The canvas door closed with a snap since it could not be slammed.

Well, he couldn't blame a Mexican—or even a half-Mexican—for having hard feelings. His own father had led warriors of The People along what was known as The Great Comanche War Trace, all the way from the Wichita Mountains in Indian Territory and across western Texas and down into Mexico. They usually had returned with plenty of horses and other plunder, along with Mexican slaves, and scalps. Toby might not be old enough to recall those raids in the past, but his mother would remember.

"All I seek to learn is the truth," Daniel said to the dirty canvas. "That is my sole agenda. The truth. If Groves murdered your sister . . ."

The canvas lifted again, and Daniel stopped talking, mainly because he didn't know what to say. He was now looking at a fat but young Mexican woman, still attractive in spite of the bags under her eyes and her disheveled hair and her old pink cotton dress and apron. Behind her the boy was shouting. The woman turned her head and barked something at him. Her voice was not so pretty. Toby fell silent. The woman looked back at Daniel. She did not speak.

"*Señora*," Daniel said. "*¿Habla usted inglés?*"

"No," the woman said, her accent heavy.

That stopped him. In the old days, The People could speak to other Indians, and *taibos*, with their hands. Daniel could still do some sign language, but he seriously doubted if either he or Mrs. Rivera knew enough to keep up a conversation. He tried to remember the Spanish he had long forgotten.

The woman turned away, but held the canvas open. She shouted at Toby, and the boy yelled back. They went back and forth, back and forth, until finally the woman said something that changed Toby's mind, and, within moments, he was standing next to his mother.

"What is it that you want, Comanche?" he said bluntly.

"Tell me about your sister," Daniel said.

Toby turned, spoke in Spanish to his mother. She smiled grimly, and pulled the door open wider, but the boy stepped in front of his mother, blocking the entrance.

"No Comanche will set foot in my home," he said. He pointed at what might have passed for a brush arbor, toward the back of the hovel. "We will speak outside," he said, then turned, whispered to his mother, and led Daniel to the shaded area.

She passed the tin plate to Toby, who reluctantly gave it to Daniel. The bean filled tortilla smelled wonderful. He was about to set the plate on the ground between his moccasins when he glanced at Mrs. Rivera, saw the look on her face, and, instead, placed it on his lap. He ate. Actually he devoured the food, wiping his mouth with his sleeve when he was done and putting the empty plate on the ground. He wanted water to wash down his dinner, but did not ask. Once he had retrieved his Old Glory and pencil, he turned to a blank page.

"Your daughter was sixteen?" he confirmed.

Toby translated, and Mrs. Rivera nodded, then she stood up and dashed inside the hut, leaving Toby staring at Daniel with malevolent eyes. The woman returned quickly, lifting the hem of her dress as she hurried back. She handed Daniel a tintype. He thanked her before studying the image.

It wasn't a great photo, the image small, scratched, and blurred. A place like Deming, Daniel imagined, did not attract the best photographers—unlike Fort Sill and the reservation in Indian Territory. It seemed as though Quanah was always posing for photographs, and just about every summer some Easterner would ride his wagon across the reservation to take pictures of Comanches and Kiowas with his cumbersome black box.

Young. Bright eyes. Long black hair hanging over her shoulder, draping down the front of a print dress to her small breasts. A shawl covering her shoulders. A small crucifix around her neck. Daniel looked more closely. He could see the resemblance with Melody's brother, but even more of the mother.

Clearing his throat, he returned the tintype to Mrs. Rivera. "She is . . . she was very pretty," Daniel said, and he meant it.

Those words, Toby did not translate, for Mrs. Rivera was already dabbing her eyes with a wadded handkerchief. "When was that photograph taken?" Daniel asked.

"Last year," Toby said. "Paid twenty-five cents for four of them. That one's Mama's. I got one, too. And Melody."

"That's three," Daniel said.

"Yeah. She gave one to a fella."

"What fellow?"

The kid shrugged. His mother asked him something, and Toby answered. When Mrs. Rivera looked back at Daniel, she too merely shrugged.

"A beau?" Daniel asked.

"I reckon."

"But you . . ."

"Lots of fellas here liked her, Comanche. She was the most popular girl at every dance, every social, every Fourth of July."

"Including the one a few days ago," Daniel said flatly.

"That's right."

"Did you go to the picnic?"

"This country was once mine, Comanche. Once was part of Mexico. I have no reason to celebrate your independence."

Daniel smiled. "It's not my independence, either. I am not thankful on Thanksgiving."

*Almost,* Daniel thought. He had come close to getting Toby Rivera to smile.

Mrs. Rivera continued to stare at the tintype, still dabbing her eyes with the cotton handkerchief.

"Your sister's tintype?" Daniel asked. "Where is it?"

He spoke again to her mother, waited for her reply, then told Daniel. "At the undertaker's. It was on her coffin. We haven't gotten it back yet."

"The undertaker was . . . ?"

"Commager," Toby said.

"I aim to see him directly," Daniel said. "I can bring it back, if that is your wish."

The boy's eyes glared, then he spoke to his mother, whose eyes shone brightly as she leaned forward, reaching out, taking Daniel's left hand in both of hers, saying: "*Sí. Sí. Muchas gracias. Sí. Sí.*"

"Did your mother go to the dance, the celebration?" Mrs. Rivera had. "Did she see your sister there?" Of course, Daniel was told. They had gone together, but Mrs. Rivera had been more interested in the pie contest, while Melody had gone straight to the dance.

"How was she dressed?" was Daniel's next question.

Sadness returned to the mother's face. She stared at the tintype, speaking directly to it.

"The same dress, the same shawl as she had worn in that picture," Toby translated. Then he added: "We are not rich, Comanche. She had but one fine dress. Which is more than my mother owns."

Now came the hard part. Daniel wrote in his pad, taking his time, not wanting to bring up the man being held in the jail. But he had no choice.

"What do you know of this man Groves?" he said at last.

"He murdered my sister," Toby answered.

Ignoring the response, Daniel went on: "Groves arrived in town less than a week ago. When did he meet your sister?"

"At the dance," Toby said.

"Not sooner?"

"I told you."

Daniel looked at Mrs. Rivera. He should ask her. Make Toby translate. The mother lacked the bitterness, the hatred that Toby carried in his heart. Yet Daniel could not bring himself to push that subject.

The mother began speaking rapidly to her son, showing him the tintype. Mrs. Rivera pointed at Daniel, and Toby sighed, spoke softly to his mother. He stared at Daniel briefly before finally saying: "My mother asks if, when you go to see the *gringo*, Commager, you can also get from him my sister's crucifix along with the tintype."

Daniel held out his hand, and the mother showed him the tintype. He looked closely at the photo, examined the crucifix around Melody's neck.

"It is not much," Toby said. "Not worth stealing." As if that was Daniel's intention. "It's nothing but German silver. On a rawhide cord."

"Of course," Daniel told Mrs. Rivera, ignoring the kid's hard stare. "I would be honored to return these items to you." Then, just so the mother would understand, he added: "*Sí. Que me . . . honor.*" Listening to the conversation in Spanish between Toby and Mrs. Rivera had brought back some words of the language with which he had been slightly familiar as a child. He wasn't sure if he had gotten the words right, but he must have been close, because Mrs. Rivera had leaned forward again and patted Daniel's hand, smiling, muttering a quiet thanks.

"If I'm not home," Toby reminded Daniel should he return, "you are not to step inside my home, Comanche."

Daniel had taken enough of the kid's attitude. "Did any of your sister's beaus visit your house?"

"No," the kid snapped.

"Figures," he said. He rose, and, as best he could, he thanked Mrs. Rivera for her time and again expressed his condolences. Toby waited impatiently, eyes full of hatred.

That's when they heard the hoof beats of horses.

Both mother and son were on their feet, staring as six riders approached, slowed their mounts,

105

and walked the final few rods into what passed as a front yard for the Rivera family.

The horses were fine mounts, not the typical cow ponies Daniel was accustomed to seeing on the Big Prairie. Four of the riders definitely were cowhands. Wiry men, bony but solid, with sun-tanned, scarred faces, wearing leather leggings, jingling spurs, wide-brimmed hats. They also wore revolvers high on their waists.

"*Señora* Rivera . . . Toby." The one who spoke was not a cowhand, but he looked just as hard. Heavier, but not fat. The hair hanging to his collar was the color of gun metal, but his mustache remained pitch black, and his eyes were that cold blue Daniel had seen all too often among the *taibos*. He wore no chaps, only a linen duster already coated from what must have been a long ride. His store-bought hat still retained the crease in the crown, not the shapeless, battered affairs topping the heads of the four cowhands.

"Didn't mean to intrude," the leader of the bunch said to Toby. "Tell your ma I didn't have a chance to speak to her after Melody's funeral. Or before. I just came to pay my respects. See if y'all needed anything."

Daniel no longer looked at this man who was speaking, having a fair inkling that he was Matt Callahan. Instead, he focused on the sixth man, who didn't have the appearance of the average cowhand. This one looked larger than a bull. He wore a dusty sombrero, covering a giant head. His salt-and-pepper beard stretched to his chest; his greasy hair, streaked with gray, hung well past his shoulders. Scars marked the big man's forehead, nose, and cheek. His muslin shirt was without buttons, and his pants, dark leather adorned with pewter buttons featuring the design of Mexican eagles, were the *calzoneras* favored by the Mexican *vaqueros* and more than a few Comanches on the reservation these days. His moccasins were well worn. One gloved hand gripped the reins and saddle horn, the other was affixed to the hilt of a machete on his left hip. The butt of a revolver jutted out of his waistband.

The big man grinned, revealing a mixture of teeth—a few broken, two capped gold, one black, and several missing.

"*Hombre*," the big man said, and continued in Spanish, too fast, too mangled for Daniel to understand.

"Jemez," the gray-haired leader said sharply, "I am speaking to Missus Rivera." His accent was Southern, a dripping drawl. He had removed his hat.

The woman bowed, invited the riders into the house for beans and tortillas.

"Melody was a charming girl," the leader said. "I feel your loss, ma'am. Our loss, ma'am. Always considered her almost a daughter. I will see that the scoundrel responsible for your beautiful girl's death hangs." His eyes left the woman as Toby translated his words and settled on Daniel.

Matt Callahan stared hard. "And you are?"

"Comanche," Toby said. "An Indian *policía*."

"*¿Policía?*" That caused the giant named Jemez almost to double over in his saddle. "Him?"

"That's enough, Jemez." Callahan swung off his blood bay gelding, handed the reins to the nearest rider. Great clouds of dust flew from his duster as he swatted it. The rancher stopped a few feet from Daniel, those cold eyes looking him up, then down.

Callahan wasn't as big of a man as Daniel had envisioned him. At least not compared to Jemez. He was sturdy, and probably six feet tall without the high-heeled boots on his feet. Solid, hard, tough, he towered over Daniel, but Daniel saw him, as he did most of The People, as short and fat, not quite the cutting figure.

"You got business here, mister?" Callahan asked. He did not extend his hand.

"I am done, *señor*," Daniel said. He tipped his hat toward Mrs. Rivera. "*Señora*," he said, and managed to unlock a little more Spanish trapped in his memory. "With your permission, I take my leave. Truly, I am sorry for the loss of your daughter."

He turned, began walking away, but did not get far before Jemez called out to him. Turning,

Daniel saw the big man had unsheathed the machete, running a dirty thumb across the blade. The Mexican grinned. "Jemez thinks that if your hair was longer, *niño*, it might pass for an Apache's. A scalp like that would fetch a hundred *pesos* for Jemez."

# CHAPTER NINE

"That's right," Dr. Walter Commager told Daniel. "I'm coroner . . . undertaker . . . doctor in general . . . drunkard in particular . . . and I also cut hair." He wiped his hands with a white cloth that smelled of alcohol, looked up over the wire spectacles low on his nose, and said: "Who the hell butchered yours?"

Daniel cocked his head. "Sir?"

"Your hair, boy. Worst atrocity I've ever seen."

The black hat returned to Daniel's head.

Doc Commager laughed. "No offense, Sergeant Killstraight. Interesting name you got there. So you found me at last. What is it that I can do for you?"

Commager's office was housed in an old boxcar. Two curtains split the room into thirds, the office in the middle, and two rooms for the patients. The curtain to Daniel's right had been drawn back, revealing a long table, tin buckets underneath, no blankets or sheets, not even a pillow. Leaning against the wall were two pine coffins. Empty.

The doctor grinned. "That's my room for the dearly departed. That's where I do my undertaking. But you look healthy enough. A bit on the fat side. Might cut down on the sweets you eat."

He was one to talk. Commager had seventy pounds on Daniel. The top of his head was bald, spotted with freckles—or maybe they were age spots—but gray hair sprouted from the sides, over his ears, to his collar, and stretched down his chin in the fashion of those old Dundreary whiskers. Commager pushed up his spectacles with his left hand while tossing the cloth into a porcelain sink with his right.

"You got business, right, Sergeant?" Commager fished a cigar from a coffee cup. "No jurisdiction, I warrant. But business. So let me guess. It's about our most recent hostility."

Daniel decided he might have preferred talking to Toby Rivera. At least he knew where he stood with that one.

"The daughter of *Señora* Rivera," Daniel said.

The fat doctor's head bobbed. "Figured. Well, that was part of my undertaking and coroner duties. Like I said, I'm undertaker and coroner and doctor. I'm also hungry." He grabbed a long, frayed, green velvet coat off a hook on the wall. "Nothing like talking about dead folks over dinner. Come on, Sergeant. You don't look like a body who turns down a free meal."

He didn't wait for Daniel's answer, and was out the door, moving mighty fast for a fat man. Daniel had no choice but to run after him, closing the door to the boxcar behind him.

They covered the few blocks, stopping only to

let a mule-drawn stagecoach pass, then headed toward the Harvey House.

Daniel caught up to the doctor at the door, and tugged at the sleeve of his velvet coat. "They won't serve me," he quietly advised him.

"The hell they won't," Commager said, and stepped inside.

A young girl, her auburn hair held by a black hairnet, immediately greeted the customers. Perhaps Daniel's age, or maybe even a year or two younger, she wore a starched black and white dress with a high collar shirt. Black shoes. Black stockings.

"Good day, Doctor," she greeted.

"Alice." Turning back to the door, Commager pitched the cigar onto the dusty street. He had never even lit the smoke. "This young man is Daniel Killstraight. He's a sergeant. Sort of a detective, I guess you'd say. And he's a bona-fide, scalp-taking, white-girl-loving, horse-stealing, mean, ugly, dirty, thieving Comanche Indian. Tell L.J. I won't take any guff from him. We're here to eat your wonderful grub, and to talk private-like over a right delicate business."

Her green eyes were blank, but she nodded politely, and said: "Right this way, Doctor." She even grinned at Daniel. "You, too, Sergeant."

They were seated at a table with a view of the main street, but far from other customers.

Another girl in the same black uniform took their orders—steak, potatoes, biscuits and gravy, peas, hot tea, and a slice of pecan pie for the doctor; coffee and ham biscuits for Daniel. After their drinks arrived, and the waitress left, the doctor said: "Nice girls. Fred Harvey won't let them wear make-up, not even jewelry. Wants them to be respectable. Wants them to marry and have a family. A big family that will travel a lot. And stop at Harvey Houses." He pointed across the street. "Girls stay in that building there. Dormitory, I reckon you'd call it. Two to a room, overseen by the meanest, man-hating bitch of a matron you'd ever hope to find." He blew on the cup of tea, tested it, set it back onto the saucer. "But the food's good. And the girls are pleasant to look at. How's your coffee?"

Daniel was stirring in the four cubes of sugar he had dropped into the black brew. Without answering, he opened his Old Glory.

The doctor leaned back, laughed again. "All business, eh, Killstraight. All right. Fire away."

Daniel sipped some coffee first, and it was excellent. Took a breath. Exhaled. Sighed.

"Let me help you out." The doctor sipped tea. "Melody Rivera was dead. When she got to me, by my guess, she would have been dead eight, ten hours. So she was killed, most likely, not long

113

after midnight. That would be the wee hours of July the Fifth."

Alice led a group of businessmen past them, and Daniel waited until they were being seated at a table out of earshot of them. Another sip of coffee for courage. "How was she killed?"

"Strangulation," he said. "That's what killed her. Then her neck was broken."

"Not the other way around?" Daniel asked.

"Why in hell would you strangle somebody whose neck you just broke?" Doc Commager laughed, but Daniel found nothing funny.

"Why would you break the neck of someone you just killed?" Daniel asked.

"Because you're a brute. Because you hated the person you just choked to death." He brought the tea cup to his lips, drank. "I'm also something of a detective myself, Sergeant. Been doing this work a long time. You learn about killers. Most of them aren't bad people. They just get riled. Most, in fact, know the people they kill. Even love them. Not much difference between hate and love, Sergeant. At least in my experience . . . as a coroner."

Daniel drank more coffee. This was the question he didn't want to ask. "Was she . . . ?"

"No," Doc Commager shot out before Daniel could finish. "She was not."

On the page where he had written his notes on Melody Rivera, all he wrote now was *No*. He had

114

another question, one that had come to him when he was at the Rivera home, but one he could not ask there. "I was told that the girl who was murdered was only half-Mexican. But her mother is Mexican and . . ."

"And the last name's Rivera?" Doc Commager laughed. "Seventeen, eighteen years ago, there wasn't nothing here but a stagecoach stop and some really tough people. And Missus Rivera. Wasn't no preachers, neither. So no nuptials. Place wasn't so civilized back then. Hell, I wish I'd been here during them times. Didn't get here till 'Eighty-Two myself. Anyway, the Rivera gal hooked up with an Irish muleskinner. Who wound up getting caught in Doubtful Cañon by Apaches. Never took his last name. That's the story I've heard, anyway. That what you want to know?"

"I guess." Daniel sipped more coffee.

"Right on time," Doc Commager said, looking up. "As expected." He leaned from his seat, extending his meaty hand, saying: "Hello, L.J."

The man standing beside them was thin, handsome for a *taibo*, tall, erect, also dressed in black and white. He shook hands with the doctor, who introduced the newcomer. "Sergeant Daniel Killstraight, meet L.J. Vanderhider. He runs the Harvey House here."

To his surprise, the tall man held out his hand for Daniel to shake. "Sergeant Killstraight," he said, his accent revealing his Texas roots. "The Harvey House welcomes you to Deming, Territory of New Mexico."

It was not the reception Daniel expected.

He stuttered out a lame response. "T-the c-coffee . . . it's . . . it's real fine."

"Thank you," Vanderhider said. "And I hope you'll find your dinner just as excellent."

"I'm sure he will, L.J. Be seeing you."

A definite dismissal. But Daniel quickly flipped a few pages in the Old Glory and looked up. "Mister Vanderhider?"

The tall Texan turned back, still smiling. "Yes, Sergeant?"

"There was a disturbance here . . ."—Daniel checked his notes—"a few evenings ago. Between Jemez and the man named Groves."

Vanderhider just stared.

"Jemez," Doc Commager explained. "Matt Callahan's biggest cut-throat. And Groves, now residing in what passes for a jail in Deming." He thrust one of his chins toward Daniel. "The sergeant is doing some investigating."

"But"—Vanderhider switched his stare to the doctor—"I thought this renegade white man killed that girl."

"Indians are peculiar folks, L.J.," the doctor said. "They want to make absolutely certain that the right man swings."

Vanderhider surprised Daniel again. He moved

116

to the nearest empty table, took a chair, and slid it across the shiny floor, then sat down between Daniel and the doctor. He leaned forward, elbows on the table, fingers intertwined, thumbs under his chin.

"First," Vanderhider said, "it was not what I would call a disturbance. We do not allow any raucous, uncivilized behavior in the Harvey House. Mister Harvey would not tolerate such an act." His head tilted at one of the waitresses. "For the girls' sake."

"What happened?" The doctor beat Daniel to the question.

"The renegade . . . I mean . . . this man Groves, he came in for supper. This would have been the night of the Third."

"Was he alone?" Again the question came from Commager.

"No. G.K. Perue was with him."

Commager snorted. "That figures."

"They were almost finished with their meal when this Mexican brute, this Jemez, came in. With three other men employed by Mister Callahan." Vanderhider looked to Doc Commager. "I swear, Walter, I don't see why Matt Callahan has to hire men of that ilk."

Doc Commager shrugged. "The Four Gates Ranch has always been a tough place to work. And this country's a tough place to live."

The restaurant manager considered this, but

117

said nothing further. He looked at Daniel. "They all had been drinking. My hostess said she could smell liquor on their breath even before they opened their mouths."

"Hard to do," Doc Commager quipped.

Ignoring the doctor, Vanderhider continued: "As they were being led to their table, Jemez saw this man Groves, and he went directly to him."

"And?" Daniel and the doctor asked at the same time.

"They talked. Well, Jemez did most of the talking, insulting talk, laughing. This man Groves just tried to finish his supper."

"So they knew each other?" Finally Daniel had gotten a question off before Commager.

Vanderhider said: "That much was clear. And then . . ."—Vanderhider's head shook—"Jemez reached inside his shirt and pulled out this pouch. He pulled on the cord, reached inside, and out came . . . a scalp."

Daniel stopped writing. He looked at L.J. Vanderhider.

"That's when this man Groves stood up. And that's when I stepped between the two men. I told Jemez that he was drunk, that he was disturbing my place of business, and he was to leave at once. I told him that Perue had been coming to the Harvey House since 'Eighty-Three and that I take care of my guests." Vanderhider smiled.

"And he left. He and the others. They just filed out the front door. That was all there was to it. Not a disturbance."

"Thanks to you," Doc Commager told the manager.

"Don't be an ass, Walter," Vanderhider said. "I've known you too long. I simply was doing my job, which is to protect these young girls." He winked at Daniel. "And to protect my career. Fred Harvey would have me out on the streets if I let fisticuffs break out in this place."

Doc Commager laughed, and finished off his tea. "You're a good man, L.J. That satisfy you, Sergeant?"

Nodding, Daniel began writing in his Old Glory. He heard the doctor say: "Good, 'cause here comes dinner." Then Vanderhider dragged the chair back to its proper spot, and said: "Enjoy your dinner, gentlemen." Next a girl's voice asked: "Which one of y'all got the ham biscuits?"

Daniel looked up from his notebook, nodding slightly at the waitress. He had one more question for Vanderhider who was walking back to the counter, so Daniel called out: "Mister Vanderhider!"

The manager returned as the waitress set down the plates, asking if they needed anything else and saying she would return with more tea and coffee. When she was gone, Vanderhider said: "Yes, Sergeant. What else is there?"

"You said you slid between Jemez and Groves? To prevent a brawl?"

"Yes," Vanderhider replied. "I've run restaurants in Houston and New York. I never allowed fistfights in any of them."

"That means you were close to them."

Doc Commager chewed on his steak, but promptly laid knife and fork on the tablecloth.

"Yes." Vanderhider nodded. "I could tell there might be trouble between those two."

"You were close enough to hear what they said?"

The doctor laughed, almost choking on his steak. He managed to swallow the meat, and wiped his mouth with the napkin. "Damnation, Killstraight. That's good deduction, son. Damnation, I'm getting dumb in my old age."

They both stared into L.J. Vanderhider's eyes.

"I only got there right before Jemez withdrew the scalp," Vanderhider said. "He, Jemez, said . . . 'How much you think a scalp like this would fetch in Mexico?' He then said . . . 'It being a scalp from a squaw.' That's all I heard. Except for this Groves cursing Jemez, and G.K. Perue telling him to calm down. Then I was shouting at both of them. Other customers were coming to their feet. And then . . . Jemez and Callahan's other riders left. This Groves sat down, didn't eat anything else. G.K. paid the check. That's all there was to it."

"Good job, L.J." Doc Commager went back to his steak.

They ate in silence. Daniel wolfed down the ham and biscuits, finished two more cups of coffee. He didn't resume his questioning until the doctor was eating his second slice of pecan pie.

"Did you know her?"

"The Rivera child?" The jowly head shook. "No. I'd seen her around."

"She was popular, wasn't she?"

"Friendly, I reckon. But no strumpet, Sergeant. And let me make this clear now. I don't rob cradles, young man."

Daniel looked at his notes. Frowned. "Could a man like Groves have broken her neck?"

"It's not that hard to do, Sergeant." He took the last forkful of pie, kept on talking. "She had been hit on the back of the neck. With a club. Rifle stock. A bar from the railroad tracks. Who knows? Anybody could have broken her neck, Sergeant. And anybody . . . man or woman, for that matter . . . could have strangled her. She wasn't big."

Daniel nodded, then noticed something else he had written. "Groves," he said. "His head was bandaged when he was brought to jail."

"I did that, too." Doc Commager grinned. "In my patient room. Had a knot on the side of his noggin. About the size of a walnut. Above the left ear. Right about here." He indicated the place on his head.

"How did that happen?"

"Hit his head, you dumb Indian." He winked to let Daniel know he was kidding. Daniel found no humor in the rebuke, even if it had been said in jest, and Doc Commager seemed to realize his mistake, his lack of etiquette.

"Sorry, son. Can't help but being a smart aleck. He was found by the railroad tracks. . . ."

Daniel shot out: "Which side?"

"You are a detective, son. Town side."

"Not by the trash heaps?"

"Other side. So he could have slipped, hit the rail or a cross-tie."

"Or someone," Daniel said, suddenly excited, "could have hit him upside the head, knocked him out."

"You're fishing, Daniel." The doctor grinned. "You looked around these parts, son? Desert's a mighty poor place to go fishing."

The old doctor was right. Daniel was making assumptions. Leaping to conclusions. Jumping at theories. Hugh Gunter and Harvey Noble had warned Daniel against doing just that. Collect the evidence first, not theories.

"You done eating?" Doc Commager asked.

Daniel nodded.

"Best get back to my office, then. A pleasure eating with you, son."

Daniel liked the fact that the doctor had stopped calling him sergeant, and now called him son. Sergeant had sounded facetious. Son seemed sincere.

"Missus Rivera asked if I could pick up the tintype of her daughter," Daniel said. "And . . ."

"Let's go get it." The big man was sliding out of his chair, tossing down some coins for the food and the tip. "I'll allow you have more folks to question before suppertime."

"Yes, sir," Daniel said.

They walked to the door, started to step outside, when L.J. Vanderhider stopped them.

"Sergeant Killstraight," he said, lowering his voice while easing the two men outside, onto the boardwalk—a real boardwalk—in front of the Harvey House. "I did remember one thing. One thing this man Jemez said to Groves."

Pencil in hand, Daniel waited.

"Jemez called him . . . Walking Man."

# CHAPTER TEN

Squire Fuller turned out to be about as informative as Toby Rivera. Daniel learned that Mickey O'Shaughnessy had found the girl's body while bringing a hand cart from the Gage station. The girl was dead, neck broken, lying in a pile of trash. Groves had been found unconscious on the other side of the tracks. Still in his cups, Groves had been roused by two city policemen. Said he couldn't remember anything that had happened since he had arrived at the 4th of July dance. Other than drinking a lot. Doc Commager had testified that it appeared to him that the girl had been strangled, then her neck had been broken. She had been dragged to the garbage, dumped there. Since Groves had been seen talking to the girl, and leaving the dance with her just before midnight, there was enough reasonable suspicion to hold the man for murder, pending the arrival of the circuit judge.

That was it.

Enough, Daniel thought, to get Francis Groves convicted by a Deming jury, and hanged by the neck until he was dead, dead, dead.

The rest of Daniel's questioning had gone like this: "Someone said Groves was making his way to Saint Augustine, Florida."

"Not to me."

"How many people were at this dance?"

"I wasn't there, so I couldn't tell you," Fuller said, looking annoyed.

"Did it come up in the inquest?"

"Why should it?"

"How many people saw Groves leave with the girl?"

"Enough."

"More than one?"

"One would be enough."

"More than ten?"

"Ten would be enough, too."

"What was said about the knot on Groves's head?"

"What knot?"

"Do you remember a bandage over Groves's head?"

"Oh, that."

"Was that brought up in the inquest?"

"A bandage. That's not evidence."

"Who testified at the inquest?"

"I'd have to check my notes."

"I have all day."

"You're one uppity red devil, boy. All right. Mickey O'Shaughnessy. Walter Commager. María Rivera. Mark McLyler. Hank Roberts. Jasper Frazer. Moran . . . no not Moran. But Matt Callahan. And G.K. Perue."

"O'Shaughnessy found the body. Commager

was the doctor. María Rivera, I'm guessing, was the mother of the dead girl. Is that right?"

"Yeah."

"McLyler is the chief of police. Roberts and Frazer then must have been the policemen."

"Yeah."

"Why did Matt Callahan testify?"

"He saw them leave together. And the word of Matt Callahan, by the way, is as good as the word of twenty preachers."

"And G.K. Perue?"

"She saw him leave, too."

"She?"

"That's right. She. She also said that Groves was drunker than a skunk, and that he didn't return to the livery to sleep that night. We're done here, boy. I haven't had my dinner. Don't be here when I get back."

Looking over his notes, Daniel realized that maybe he had gotten something out of the squire, after all. At least he wouldn't look like an idiot when he went into G.K. Perue's livery stable and found out G.K. was a woman.

That was his next stop.

After getting directions from a vendor on the street selling tamales, Daniel headed to the livery, glad that Doc Commager had treated him to dinner. By now, it was after noon, and the sun had turned blazing hot—and it had been hot enough that morning. He smelled G.K. Perue's livery stable before he saw it, the aroma of horse manure and sweating horsehair reminding him of his home.

Nowhere near as fancy as Hickox's livery and blacksmith shop in town, Perue's stables and barn lay on the eastern edge of town among the small adobe businesses. The poorer part of town, Daniel figured, if you didn't count the north side of the tracks. From inside, came a horrible, nasal voice singing over the clanging of hammer and anvil.

Oh, I'm a good old Rebel.
Now that's just what I am.
And for this Yankee nation,
I does no give a damn.
I'm glad I fought ag'in' 'er.
I only wish we won.
I ain't askin' any pardon
For anything I done.

The hammer slammed on a horseshoe, sparks flew, and the big smithy turned around.

Daniel wouldn't have known G.K. Perue was a woman if Squire Fuller hadn't warned him, and yet he began to wonder if the squire hadn't set him up, told him that Perue was a woman when in fact Perue was a man.

She—or he—probably topped two hundred

pounds and stood better than six-feet-two. Her hair was a hideous orange and gray, plastered by sweat. Perue wore a smithy's apron, scuffed, dung- and dust-covered boots, and a yellow bandanna, soaking with sweat. The smithy plunged the horseshoe back into the coals, and tossed the hammer on anvil. Then, pulling off heavy work gloves and stepping toward Daniel, G.K. Perue smiled a toothless smile.

"Been a-wonderin' when you'd show up here, Sergeant Daniel Killstraight. My name's G.K. Perue, and I'm a female iffen you ain't already noticed." Her calloused right hand swallowed Daniel's, and the grip almost made him wince.

"How do you know my name?"

She snorted, spit, and moved away from the heat, motioning for Daniel to follow. They moved out of the barn, and toward the corral, where G.K. Perue dropped the gloves on the dirt, kneeled, and plunged her head into a water trough. She came up, shook herself dry, getting Daniel wet in the process, and leaned against the juniper fence.

"Shucks, boy." Perue fished a tin of snuff from the back pocket of her jeans. "Ever'body in Demin' knows who you is. I figgered you'd be murdered by now. You surprise me, Killstraight. You've survived more'n twelve hours, I reckon, in this here burg."

"Did the brakeman tell you?"

"Brakeman?" She filled her bottom lip with

a mountain of snuff. "You mean Radegunde's in town, that sorry cur? No, I ain't seen that skinflint, but warrant he'll show up at some point 'afore too long, worthless rapscallion that he is. No, boy, you's the talk of Demin'. You want a stall, I suspect."

Daniel thought. He might be staying the night in the jail. Would Mark McLyler trust him to help guard Francis Groves?

"I'm not sure," he said.

"Not sure you'll be livin' come nightfall." She turned, spit into the trough, and told an approaching paint horse to get the hell away from her. The gelding must have understood, because it turned and walked to the opposite end of the corral with a half dozen other horses. "That's practical."

"Why wouldn't I be alive come nightfall?"

"Boy, is you that dense? It's 'cause you's a red savage Injun, boy. Hell, you's Comanch'. And top things off, you seem to think that a certain gent called Walkin' Man didn't do the dirty deed he's already been condemned for."

He had come, he decided, to the right place in Deming. He had found the one person who could, and perhaps *would,* answer some questions for him. Daniel opened his notebook. He looked at G.K. Perue for permission, and when she snorted, shook her wet head, and laughed, he fetched his pencil from over his ear.

"You *is* a detective. Hell's bells, I thought folks was just a-funnin' me. All right, Mister *Police Gazette*, do your business."

"Why is he called Walking Man?"

She moved from the trough to the shade, against the barn, sitting on a bale of hay, motioning Daniel to sit on another bale on the opposite side of the open door.

"That's what the Apaches called him," she said. "And scouts for Crook's boys, too. You ain't talked to him?"

"I talked," Daniel said. "He didn't."

"Well, he wasn't such a quiet sum-bitch when he arrived here."

"Walking Man?" Daniel prodded.

"He was a civilian scout for the Army over in Arizona Ter'tory." Perue spit. Everybody in Deming, Daniel decided, had to spit. "He'd lived with the Apaches, so he made a good scout. Plus, he spoke that Apache lingo, so the Army could use him to translate for the Apache scouts."

"Apache scouts?" Daniel asked.

"Yep. Ol' Crook, he got the bright idea. Figured it took an Apache to track an Apache. So he got some of 'em bucks to do the job. Worked out pret' good for the Army, and us white folks, too. 'Course, didn't turn out so fine for Gen'ral Crook. He got his arse fired, more 'r less, and Nelson A. Miles come in to reap the glory. But even Miles learned that Crook was right. It was the Apaches who tracked down Geronimo, got them to fin'ly surrender and make this part of the country safe for white folks."

He had to digest this, and it sickened him. He knew the Apaches had surrendered, had been imprisoned in Florida, but he hadn't known that the Army had used Apache scouts. Using Indian scouts was one thing. In the campaigns against The People more than a decade ago, the Army had employed some Delawares and Pawnees as trackers and scouts. Mostly, however, they had used Tonkawas, dreaded enemies of The People.

A vision came to him, and he remembered sitting in the lodge somewhere on the Staked Plains, and his mother warning him: *If you don't do what I say, Oá, the Tonkawas will come. And eat you.*

Tonkawas. Cannibals. He hated them. Feared them.

Yet the Tonkawas, the Pawnees, they had been enemies of The People. It made sense to Daniel that the Army would use them, but to use Apaches to track down other Apaches. He could never think that a Comanche would be so low as to hunt another Comanche—to help a *taibo*. The various bands of The People did not always agree with each other, and even came to bitter disputes, but they would never stand against one another, never betray another Comanche.

There were Apaches on the reservation near

Fort Sill, but not Chiricahuas. Not yet, anyway. There had been talk about giving them some allotments—just to get them out of the malaria-ridden dungeons of Florida.

"You look a mite off your feed, Daniel Killstraight. A little green around the gills . . . as green as an Injun buck can gets, I reckon."

Daniel carefully chose his words. "I had not heard this," he said. "That Apaches were used to hunt their own kind."

"Well, sonny, you needs to know that Geronimo wasn't so popular with his own kind. Oh, some worshiped him, but quite a few Cherry Cows and other bands despised that murderin' bastard. But iffen it makes you feels any better, you should know that when the Army sent all of 'em Cherry Cows back East, they sent the scouts with 'em."

She chuckled, then spit again. "That's our Army, our gov'ment for you. Help us out, and we'll cheat you anyway." She ran her massive fingers through that ugly mess of hair. "What else you wants to know?"

"What else did Groves . . . this . . . Walking Man tell you?"

"Mister *Police Gazette*, I ain't no scribe for *Harper's Weekly*, so it ain't that Walkin' Man tol' me his whole sad life story." Chortling, she stood, went back to the trough, plunged her giant right arm into the water, and withdrew a jug. As she made her way back to the hay bale, she withdrew

132

the stopper and had a long swallow before sitting.

"Care for a snort?" Perue asked, smacking her lips.

"No, thank you." From Perue's breath, Daniel could tell that the liquor inside the container would likely blind or kill.

"Good. Walkin' Man wasn't nigh as polite as you. All he tol' me was that he was tryin' to get to Saint Augustine 'way back east. Says that's where his people was, what was left of 'em."

Daniel thought a moment. "The Apaches," he said, "surrendered almost three years ago."

"Fourth of September. My birthday." She had another pull from the jug.

"That's a long time."

Perue sniggered, almost spitting out some of the vile whiskey. After she set the jug between her boots, she wiped her mouth, and said: "Well, he was preoccupied for a spell. Spent a couple of years in Yuma for bustin' up a dram shop in Tucson. A white guy said somethin' 'bout Apaches."

"What did Jemez say?"

Her face turned granite. The mock friendliness disappeared from Perue's voice. "What do you mean?"

"At the Harvey House," Daniel said. He slipped the pencil above his ear, hoping that, if he wasn't taking notes, it would relax Perue. "You were having supper with Walking Man. Jemez and some of Matt Callahan's men came in. He . . . Jemez, I mean . . . took out a scalp."

Perue drank. This time, she didn't set the jug on the ground. In fact, she had another pull—a long swallow—and looked at Daniel without speaking for several seconds.

"L.J. Vanderhider has a big damned mouth," she finally said.

"You want to tell me what happened?"

"Hell, nothin' happened. Jemez come in. He says . . . 'As I live and breathe, if that ain't Walkin' Man.'" Another snort. "You gots to understand that me and Walkin' Man had been doin' ourselves some considerable drinkin'. Figured we'd put some food in our bellies so we could drink some more. But Jemez and them Callahan boys, they was drunker than we was."

Daniel waited.

"Jemez comes right to our table. Asks where has Walkin' Man been keepin' hisself. Asks how was things down in Yuma. Then he says that business has sure slowed down a mite, and that's when he reached inside his shirt, pulls out this pouch. He says to Walkin' Man . . . 'How much you think a scalp like this would bring down in Sonora?' Oh, it's an Apache scalp all right. And then Jemez, he says . . . 'It bein' a squaw's scalp an' all.'"

Another drink.

"Sobered us both up pret' quick, it did. Walkin'

134

Man, he's up and at Jemez, who's reachin' for that brush cutter of his'n, but Vanderhider gets between 'em, and I grabs Walkin' Man's arms, pin 'em back. And Vanderhider politely asks Jemez and his crew and me and Walkin' Man to go some place else."

Pretty much, Daniel thought, the same as Vanderhider had told him.

"So you went . . . where?"

"Back here. Tied us on a damned fine drunk."

"And Walking Man said nothing else?"

"Nothin'. He went as silent as a dead horse."

Daniel scribbled a few notes. "When did Walking Man meet the girl who is no more?"

The whimsical look returned to Perue's reddening eyes. "The girl who is no more?" She cackled. "Boy, her name is . . . er, was, I mean . . . her name was Melody Rivera. Oh, that was the next evenin'. We slept till noon, I reckon. Piddled around here, then went to partake of the festivities. That evenin', Walkin' Man decides to go to the dance. And he meets that high-minded little bitch. Her sashayin' and all. Damned whore. She was dancin' with ever'one and ever'body. The Callahan kid. McLyler. Ever'body. Comes up to Walkin' Man, and damned if he ain't smitten. Tells me she reminds him of his daughter. Daughter! Never knowed he had one. An' afore you knows it, he's tellin' me . . . me! . . . that he's gonna walk her home. So I tells him to go to blazes, and I leave. Got drunker than Hooter's goat."

Daniel looked at the smithy. He made a wild stab. "You liked Walking Man, didn't you?"

She waited a while before replying. Took a drink. Spit. Looked at the sky. "Boy," she finally said, "I like anybody who'll drink with me. Sure you won't have a snort?"

"Sorry," he said. "I'm not partial to spirits."

"Suit yourself."

"What happened next?"

"Nothin'. Oh, McLyler roused me next morn, tellin' me that that fella had killed the Rivera bitch and what all did I know about it?"

"What did you know?"

"Nothin'." Another pull. The jug was empty. She tossed it away, and it splashed in the trough. Awkwardly she pushed herself to her feet. "C'mon, Mister *Police Gazette*. Reckon you'll want to see that bastard's stuff."

Not that Francis Groves, also called Walking Man, had much stuff. Daniel found the old McClellan saddle and a Springfield .45-70 still sheathed in the Army-issue scabbard. The carbine might have been Army-issue, as well, but the brass nail heads forming an arrow in the stock would have been frowned upon by any bluecoat officer. A poor excuse for a bedroll, still rolled out, stretched across the stall. The saddlebags were practically empty, too. Inside, Daniel found two flour sacks, one containing a few pieces of jerky that felt hard enough to break molars, the other containing one stale biscuit tougher than the jerky. A pair of socks, more holes than wool, and then . . . He pulled out the tintype, gently wrapped in three silk bandannas. Daniel brought the image into better light.

"Hell's fire." G.K. Perue's voice, right behind him, startled Daniel. He turned, glaring, as the drunken livery owner said: "That's the Rivera bitch."

# CHAPTER ELEVEN

"No," Daniel said, angry, but keeping his temper in check. He looked back at the tintype, saying, even before he examined the girl closer: "It isn't." However, he could definitely see the resemblance.

The tintype he held pictured two women, the older one looking away from the camera, looking shy. Daniel remembered the handful of Kiowas and Comanches who would refuse to let an itinerant photographer take a photograph of them, fearing the image would steal their shadows, their souls. Come to think of it, Daniel had never had a photograph taken of himself, except for some of those class pictures School Father Pratt forced upon the Indians at Carlisle.

Most likely the older woman was the mother of the younger, and it was this girl who held the attention of Daniel and G.K. Perue.

Recalling the tintype of Melody Rivera, Daniel mentally compared the two girls. They were probably around the same age. Instead of a crucifix, this girl wore a necklace, decorated with what might have been an abalone shell. This one also wore what appeared to be a dress of doeskin, heavily beaded at the top, painted diamonds on the sleeves from which long fringe flowed. Her hair was longer than that of the older woman, her eyes less weary. She was, it seemed, trying not to smile. She was quite attractive—for an Apache.

Yes, these two women were absolutely Apache, but Daniel could see how Melody Rivera would have reminded Walking Man of his daughter, and how G.K. Perue might have mistaken this Indian girl for the dead girl from Deming.

He held the tintype toward Perue. "The daughter," he said. "Walking Man's daughter. I guess the other woman is her mother. . . ."

"Walkin' Man's squaw." Perue turned her head and spit.

The way she said it sickened Daniel. Gently he rewrapped the tintype, put everything back in the saddlebags—including his Old Glory tablet—and rolled up the bedroll.

"This," he said, "should go to the police office to be held there." He picked up the saddle, too. "I won't be staying here tonight, but thank you for the invite."

She seemed even larger, stronger, when she put both hands on her hips. "I ain't so sure you should leave with that there stuff. It ain't your'n."

"You can come with me to the police station and jail," he said. "To make sure I deliver it."

"Walkin' Man owes me money."

"That's between you and Groves. Or Chief McLyler."

She snorted. "Hell, boy, I's gots work to do,

a hoss to shoe. I'll see McLyler soon enough, I reckon."

She let him pass, and he moved out of the stall, moved around the fire, but stopped at the door, setting Groves's tack on the hay. G.K. Perue had put on her gloves, and was back, pulling a horseshoe from the coals, dipping it in a water bucket. Steam shot skyward with a loud hiss.

"Miss Perue . . . ?" He didn't know what else to call her.

"It's missus, Mister *Police Gazette*." She didn't look at him, just put the shoe on the anvil, and grabbed a hammer.

"You said that after . . ."

The hammer clanged loudly.

". . . after Walking Man told . . ."

*Clang!*

". . . you that he would see the . . ."

*Clang!*

". . . girl home . . ."

*Clang!*

". . . that you left . . ."

*Clang!*

". . . and came back here."

*Clang!*

The hammer fell on the anvil. She moved to the horse, forced up his left forefoot, saying—"What of it?"—as she placed the shoe against the hoof.

"Well, how could you have testified that Gro— . . . that Walking Man left with the girl?"

140

She turned, letting the horse's leg down, holding the horseshoe at her side. "I never said that," she said.

"You didn't see him leave?"

"No." She went back to the hammer, and, as the hammer crashed against the horseshoe, Daniel tossed the saddlebags and bedroll over his left shoulder, got a better grip on the saddle, hoisted it, and walked into the hot afternoon, the noise of the smithy's hammer echoing in his head.

Squire Fuller was not pleased to see Daniel standing in the open doorway to his office.

"I told you not to be here when I got back from my dinner," he snapped, dipping a pen in an ink dish and then signing a paper.

"I wasn't," Daniel said. "I am here now."

Groves's saddle, bedroll, and bags were set on the floor at his side.

Cursing, the justice of the peace leaned back in his chair, and wiped his brow with his right hand. "I once figured sending you bucks to those boarding schools was a good idea. Make you white. Take the savage out of you. But, by grab, you're almost too white for me now."

Going to *taibo* schools was not his idea, Daniel thought, but kept quiet.

"What the hell do you want now, boy?"

"You told me that G.K. Perue testified that she saw Groves leave the dance with the girl."

141

"That's correct."

"Perue says she didn't."

"Didn't what?"

"Say that. She told me she didn't testify that she saw him leave. She left before."

"Like hell."

"You want to tell G.K. Perue that she's a liar?" Daniel grinned.

The justice of the peace didn't. He just dribbled his fingers on the desk top for a moment. "Well," he said, "we are at a conundrum, Killstraight." Then Squire Fuller picked up the paper he had signed and blew on the ink, before looking back up. "You're still here?"

"There would have been a stenographer at these proceedings?" Daniel asked.

"Damn." The paper slid back onto the desk top. "What the hell do you know about stenographers?" Before Daniel could answer, the squire was waving his hands, conceding defeat, standing, and heading toward the glass-cased attorney bookshelves against the outer wall. "All right, Killstraight. All right."

While Squire Fuller looked through the papers, Daniel opened one of Groves's saddlebags and retrieved his note pad. The justice of the peace found the papers, walked past Daniel, and laid the stack on an already cluttered table. He flipped through a few pages, pointed, stepped back.

"See for yourself, Killstraight."

Daniel moved beside the squire, who placed a finger on the side of the page. The penmanship was beautiful.

COURT: State your name, occupation, and place of residence.

WITNESS: G.K. Perue. Run a livery and blacksmith shop on the east part of town. Live and work here in Deming.

COURT: Where were you on the night of the Fourth of July?

WITNESS: Me and him went out a-drinking. Then we decided to go to the Independence Day ball.

COURT: By him, you mean, Francis Groves?

WITNESS: Yep. That's him.

COURT: How long were you at the dance?

WITNESS: Not long. Thirty minutes. Maybe forty. Thought there'd be some liquor to slake our thirsts, but there weren't none.

COURT: What happened then?

WITNESS: The dead girl come by. Well, she weren't dead then. [Laughs.] Melody Rivera come by, and him, Groves yonder, he said: "My God. It's Liluye."

COURT: Liluye?

WITNESS: Yeah. That's what he said. I tells him, nah, it ain't Luly or Lewallen or nobody but Melody Rivera.

COURT: What happened then?

WITNESS: Then he said she looked just like his daughter. Hell, I didn't even know he had no daughter. But he goes over and starts talking to her. And, boy-howdy, did that rile up Matt Callahan some. And our snot-nosed police chief as well. Kind of got bent out of shape that Melody started talking to him and not them. And I reckon I got irritated my ownself.

COURT: What time was this?

WITNESS: Didn't have no watch. Late, I reckon.

COURT: Did the girl and the stranger dance?

WITNESS: Nope. Just talked is all. Then they left.

Daniel turned the page, but the rest of the testimony was just confirming when Groves had arrived in Deming, that he had stayed in a stall at Perue's place, that he drank a lot of whiskey, hadn't come back to the livery that night. He flipped back the two pages and read again.

" 'Then they left,' " he said out loud.

"Satisfied?" Squire Fuller asked.

Daniel's head shook, far from satisfied, but he thanked Squire Fuller for his time, and picked up Groves's gear. The saddle he dropped off at the jail, leaving it with the policeman named Roberts, and walked to Doc Commager's office, studying the notes he had taken that day.

*Then they left.* That could mean they had left for the Rivera home, but it was vague, and no one had asked for clarification on the statement. Certainly Fuller and the court believed that to mean that G.K. Perue had seen Groves or Walking Man with Melody Rivera. G.K. Perue, however, said she hadn't seen them leave.

Matt Callahan, on the other hand, had testified that he had seen Groves take Melody Rivera home. Yet, from Perue's testimony, Callahan had seemed upset that Rivera even talked to Groves. So had Mark McLyler. And then there was G.K. Perue herself.

Everyone Daniel had met who had known Melody Rivera had nothing but the fondest of memories of the dead girl. She was an angel. She was friendly. She was no strumpet, just a nice kid. Everyone, that is, but G.K. Perue. To the smithy, Melody Rivera was a sashaying little whore. A bitch. G.K. Perue had hated Melody Rivera.

A chill went up Daniel's spine. From what he had seen, G.K. Perue was certainly strong enough to knock out Francis Groves, strangle a sixteen-

145

year-old girl to death, and then, in a murderous rage, break her neck.

He found himself back outside the boxcar that served as Doc Commager's office. The front door remained open, to allow a draft, Daniel supposed, for the heat had become even more oppressive. Inside, he heard the doctor chatting with a woman. Daniel sat on the dirt, leaned his back against the boxcar's wall, and read through his notes.

As usual, nothing seemed clear. Oh, he had theories. G.K. Perue, or Matt Callahan, or Mark McLyler, jealous of the attention Melody Rivera had showed this stranger in town, had followed them as Groves escorted the girl home. Then one of them had knocked out Groves, and murdered the Rivera girl.

Right. But how does a detective prove it?

There was another theory, too, and it would be easier to prove. Francis Groves, alias Walking Man, killed Melody Rivera. Dragged her body to the trash heap. Stumbled over the railroad tracks until, in an alcoholic haze, he fell, hitting his head and knocking himself out.

A woman walked out of the doctor's office, jumping at the sight of Daniel, then hurried toward the American Hotel and the crowd of people in that general direction before Daniel could apologize.

"It's not polite, Sergeant," the big doctor said as he stepped outside, "to give one of my best customers an apoplexy."

Daniel started to apologize to the doctor, but Commager was wiping his brow with a rag, saying: "How was your visit with Squire Fuller? Come inside, son. It's no cooler, but the sun isn't as bright."

This time, Daniel sat on the patient's table, sipping water from a glass, while Walter Commager, getting comfortable in a chair, propped his big feet on a trash can and drank what appeared to be straight alcohol or some kind of medicine.

"G.K. Perue's a big woman," Daniel said.

"Good detective work." Doc Commager laughed, set the bottle on the floor, and grabbed a copy of the *Headlight* to fan himself.

"Big enough to strangle a girl."

The fanning stopped. "I don't think so."

"You don't think she could?"

"Oh, physically, sure. G.K. Perue's a drunk, a tough woman, stronger than most men. But I don't see her murdering a child."

Daniel flipped through his notes. "A child who, in front of me, she called a 'high-minded bitch,' always 'sashaying,' always dancing, and a 'damned whore.' "

The fanning resumed. "And I'd lay odds that she was drunk when she said it."

"She was."

"People say lots of things when they're in their cups," the doctor said.

"Including the truth, or at least how they really feel."

Doc Commager placed the newspaper on his lap, and found the bottle again. "For a young man who does not partake of ardent spirits, you seem to know a lot about what liquor does to a man . . . or woman."

"I've seen enough drunkards on the reservation."

The doctor took another drink. "You should try it sometime."

"I think not."

The doctor was saying something else, but Daniel was studying his notes, flipping ahead to the last page, then back again. Doc Commager had stopped, waiting for Daniel's attention to return. After several minutes, Daniel became aware of the quiet, and looked up at the doctor.

"Discover something interesting?" he asked.

"Squire Fuller said that Perue testified that she saw Groves leave with the girl, but she told me she never said it. I read the stenographer's account, and she said they left, but it's not clear if she actually saw them leave together."

"You seem to forget, Sergeant, my boy, that I was at those proceedings. Matt Callahan said he saw them leave together, and there was no doubt about that."

"Yes, I read that part in the transcripts, too. But the rancher was a bit jealous of Groves, too."

"On his son's account, more than likely. Callahan loved that girl like a daughter. His boy, Jules, was infatuated with the girl. The boy's not right in the head, you know, but harmless."

Daniel had not considered the son. He remembered the AT&SF brakeman speaking of the simple-minded kid, how strong he was. Harmless? Maybe not, as strong as the boy was said to be.

"Was the Callahan boy at the dance?"

"I gather that Jules was."

"Could the kid . . . could Jules Callahan . . . ?"

Doc Commager's pointer finger wagged sideways and he clucked his tongue. "Remember what I said about fishing, son."

"Police Chief McLyler was jealous, too," Daniel said.

The doctor's feet met the floor. "Who told you that? Perue?"

"Yes, and here's something Perue also told me. When Groves told Perue that he was walking the girl home, she told him to go to blazes. Then she left. That's what I was looking up, checking to make sure I remembered it right. She told Groves to 'go to blazes.' Because Groves was going to walk the girl home. Maybe Perue did see him leave. Maybe she was lying to me."

But Doc Commager wasn't interested in Perue

or the girl or what she had allegedly said. He said: "McLyler."

"You know something, Doc?"

Grunting, the doctor climbed to his feet, put the paper and bottle by Daniel's side. "I'm too old and too wise to go fishing, young man, without the proper bait. You got a place to spend the night?"

"Jail," Daniel said. "Most likely."

"Well, it's time for my *siesta*. Not that I'm kicking you out, you see, but I'm kicking you out."

"That's fine, Doc. I appreciate everything you've done. But . . . I told Missus Rivera that I would get back her daughter's tintype. And her crucifix."

"Certainly, certainly." He moved to the center part of the office, went to a desk, opened a drawer, and his head jerked up. "What crucifix?"

At first, Daniel stared blankly. Then he went back to his Old Glory, finding the note he had made. He recalled the tintype. There was no mistaking that.

"She was wearing a crucifix on the night she was killed," Daniel said.

It was the doctor's face that now went blank. He swung around, reached into a cabinet, came out with a leather-bound book. When he looked up, he cleared his throat. "Son, I examined the dead girl. There was no crucifix on her body."

For what seemed an eternity, they looked at each other, trying to figure out just what it meant. Daniel recovered, began scribbling in his Old Glory. Doc Commager resumed his warning about speculating.

"Don't go barking up the wrong tree, Daniel." It was the first time the doctor had called him by his *taibo*-given first name. "That girl's body was dragged across the railroad tracks. A crucifix could have fallen off. Probably did, in fact."

Daniel considered that, but only briefly, then asked: "Did the body have bruises, scratches, cuts on her head?"

"Just strangulation marks, contusions . . . that's a hifalutin word for bruises . . . on her throat. And one on the back of her neck."

"So the killer probably grabbed her by the arms," Daniel said. "Her feet would have banged over the rails. Less likely for the crucifix to come off that way."

The doctor's big head shook. "You forget that her neck was broken. Likely with a club or some such. A blow like that could definitely have snapped a little chain."

"It was on a rawhide thong," Daniel said.

"You're still fishing, son. Most likely that crucifix came off at some point during the crime."

Doc Commager was probably right, but Daniel was one of The People. A fighter. To the end.

"Or," Daniel said, "it could have been stolen. That . . ."

Doc Commager's big head shook. Daniel set down his pencil. "It was no robbery, Daniel. A person doesn't steal a crucifix and leave behind fifteen dollars in coin and script. That's what we found in that bag Groves was wearing."

Daniel remembered the ration pouch. A thief would have more than likely taken that as well. Still, the crucifix was out in the open, enticing. Except . . . Daniel sighed, realizing his theory was being destroyed. Even Toby Rivera had said the crucifix wasn't worth much. He closed the Old Glory and returned the pencil atop his ear.

"All right," he told the doctor. "I won't go fishing. But the tintype?"

"Certainly." The doctor reached back into the drawer with his right hand. He withdrew it, shifting and pulling the drawer all the way out, before reaching inside again. Out came papers and pencils, an empty bottle and some tins, and two more leather-bound journals.

When Walter Commager looked up, his face had turned a ghastly white.

"Good God," he said. "That tintype . . . it's missing."

# CHAPTER TWELVE

Shaking his head, Doc Commager looked one more time in the drawer. Daniel waited.

When the doctor looked up, he kept shaking his head. "I am certain that I put it in this drawer. I know I did."

"A thief?"

The doctor's head shook. "A thief would have taken medicine, money . . . but a tintype?"

"When did you put it in that drawer?"

"During the funeral." He waved a large hand. "I know it sounds strange, but we move fast this time of year because of the heat. Inquest. Then the funeral. Both here."

"The inquest wasn't held in the courthouse?"

"I had to point out the bruises on the victim."

"With her mother and brother present?" This Daniel practically shouted.

"Good God, lad, no. María Rivera testified at the courthouse with everybody else. Then the judge, stenographer, Chief McLyler, and the prisoner came here with the jurors. I gave my spiel, and everybody filed out. Ten minutes later, the family and friends and a priest came in for the funeral. There is no Catholic church yet in Deming, Daniel. That's why the funeral was here. And the coffin was closed. Didn't want to upset the poor mother or her son any more than they already were."

Daniel stared, completely bewildered. *Taibos* thought The People had odd customs. A funeral in a boxcar? Where the doctor had just pointed out what had killed the victim?

Doc Commager found another bottle. Reading Daniel's expression, he swallowed, coughed, corked the bottle, and said flatly: "This is New Mexico Territory, Daniel. There is nothing normal here. Nothing abnormal, either. It's our own little world. Always has been. Always will be."

Daniel thought for a moment. "Missus Rivera did not ask for the tintype after the funeral?"

Again, the doctor's head shook. "She was upset, son. Everybody was. Hadn't been a killing in Deming, a murder, that is, in three months. A few accidental deaths, sure. Happens in a railroad town. But no woman had ever been killed, especially not a sixteen-year-old child. We had the funeral, and the coffin was carried to the Catholic cemetery."

"You would have removed the tintype before the coffin left this place, of course?"

"Of course."

"And you put the tintype in the drawer immediately."

This the doctor had to consider, but only for a few seconds. "Yes," he said. "The priest was folding up the cloth we had placed over the coffin. He handed me the tintype as the pallbearers lined up, and I put it in the drawer. They carried the body out. The family and other mourners followed. I didn't attend the graveside services."

Daniel tapped his pencil on the tablet. "Who was this priest?"

"Dominic something. Holds Mass on an empty lot on the eastern edge of town. That's where the church is going up, and the weather usually allows services to be held outside."

"The pallbearers?"

"Cowboys from the Four Gates."

Daniel looked up. He had heard that name before, but hadn't thought much of it, until now. "Four Gates?"

"Matt Callahan's ranch. Four Gates. It's a huge spread, but in country like this it takes a lot of acres for one cow and calf to survive. Story goes, one gate leads out north toward the mountains around Kingston. Eastern gate points to Mesilla and the Río Grande. Southern gate is just this side of the Mexican border. And the western gate is among the *playas* before you hit Lordsburg. But Matt Callahan will tell you all them gates lead straight to hell."

"Did you recognize the cowboys?" Daniel asked.

"I don't know the names of most cowboys in

155

these parts. Just know they ride for Callahan."

Daniel recalled what he had heard about the Callahan spread. The rancher hired tough men, and a lot of those men had been kicked out of Arizona Territory for some crime. It wouldn't take much imagination for a cowboy like that, an outlaw of sorts, to steal . . . He stopped. Why would a cowboy steal a worthless tintype? He couldn't shake that thought, so he asked: "Was one of those cowboys a big, brutal-looking Mexican? Thick beard and mustache, black hair turning gray? Carries a machete?"

Doc Commager grinned. He took another snort from the bottle, which he then corked and slipped inside a coat pocket. "Daniel, even in Deming, New Mexico, most people don't bring machetes to funerals or to a coroner's inquest."

Daniel sighed.

"But Jemez was here," the doctor continued. "I do know him. Everybody in Deming knows him. There've been quite a few I've had to patch up for tangling with the monster. Didn't think about it. Yes, Jemez was one of the pallbearers. He's always with Matt Callahan."

So Jemez could have stolen the tintype, Daniel was thinking. But then he was back to the same theory-ending question: why steal a tintype? He started to close the Old Glory, but thought of something else.

"Matt Callahan," he said. "He stayed for the funeral?"

"Yes."

"Who else?"

The doctor closed the drawer, and sat on the edge of the desk. He had to think. "Well, I'd say a dozen or so Mexicans from north of the rails. Folks I don't know. Friends, I'd guess, of María and her family. Chief McLyler. Squire Fuller. I guess Fuller just stayed to be polite. Me. Editors for both newspapers. That might have been it, but I could be mistaken."

"Miguel?" Daniel asked. "The jailer?"

"He wasn't here for any of the testimony. Or the funeral. Why ask about him?"

Daniel answered only with a shrug. "Perue?"

The doctor snorted. "Testified in the courthouse. Then probably went to the nearest bucket of blood to seek oblivion."

Daniel flipped through the Old Glory. "Mickey O'Shaughnessy, the railroad employee who found the body?"

"Courthouse," Commager said. "Then he was gone."

"The two policemen, Roberts and Frazer?"

"They took Groves back to the jail after the inquest." Doc Commager stood, ready to get to his *siesta*. "I think that's all. You'd have to ask María Rivera about those Mexicans. I just don't know them."

Daniel closed the notebook, thanked the doctor, and headed through the door. Outside, he waited, deciding where to go next. The doctor stepped out, pulling the door behind him, fished out a key, and locked the door.

"Good luck, Daniel." He patted his jacket, making sure he had not forgotten his bottle. "I'll see you around."

"Thanks, Doctor." They stepped in opposite directions, but Daniel stopped, turned, and called out the doctor's name.

"Yes, Sergeant Killstraight?" Doc Commager's face showed a whimsical, but somewhat frustrated, expression.

"How about Callahan's son?"

"Jules?"

Daniel was remembering what the AT&SF brakeman, Ladislaus Radegunde, had told him about Matt Callahan's son. About thirty years old, but a simpleton. A powerful kid who had pinned Radegunde in less than five minutes. Daniel had never seen the young man, but if Radegunde's opinions were accurate, a kid like that could easily have overpowered both Francis Groves and Melody Rivera.

"No." Doc Commager's head shook. "No, Jules wasn't there. For the inquest or funeral."

"He was at the dance," Daniel said. "Why wouldn't he have testified?"

Doc Commager was already sweating. He

leaned against the boxcar's side. "Daniel," he said softly, "Jules has the mind of a child. Callahan probably didn't want him to testify, put him under that kind of stress. And I'd have to think that was why the boy wasn't at the funeral, either. He loved Melody Rivera deeply . . . or as deeply as a kid like that can love anyone. You understand?"

Daniel nodded.

The doctor pushed himself off the boxcar wall, straightening. "No, I don't think you do understand. You're fishing again, Daniel. But if you go after Jules Callahan, you'll be the one who gets chopped up into fish bait. Trust me." With that, the doctor turned on his heels, and headed home.

Daniel decided to go back to the railroad tracks, back to the trash piles, back to where Melody Rivera had been killed.

Once there, he tried to find exactly where Groves had been found unconscious. Thinking he had found the right spot, or at least close, he began his search. For what, Daniel wasn't sure. The crucifix? Perhaps.

Kneeling, he felt around the ground, stirring up the dirt. No telling how many *taibos* had been around here since the murder, how much sign they would have destroyed. The wind tugged at his hair, stung his face with blowing sand. The wind, too, would have wiped out sign. His fingers pressed against the sand. If he found the crucifix of the dead girl, that would shatter his theory that this had been a robbery. He looked up and around.

An adobe building, a storage shed probably for the Southern Pacific or maybe the Atchison, Topeka & Santa Fe, was nearby. No windows on this side. One large door. Four barrels, no tops. From their proximity to the roof, he figured they were to catch rain water. He knew the drains were called *canales*. The barrels were situated underneath the *canales* and they were huge. A thief could easily have hidden behind one, waiting. It had been dark. Groves had been drunk.

Daniel studied the big piles of trash. Thirty yards, he guessed from where he stood.

"Why?" he asked out loud, and shook his head. "Why would a thief strangle a girl to death? To shut her up, keep her from screaming? But then why break her neck, too? Out of rage?"

But a thief, Daniel decided, would not have dragged the corpse over the railroad tracks and tossed her into the trash pile. The dance, the Independence Day ball, had been going on just a few hundred yards from here. All too easy for the killer to have been spotted, even caught. A thief, a petty robber, would not risk that. Abandoning that theory, he kept looking at the giant mounds of trash. This had been no robbery. Doc Commager had to be right. The crucifix had probably been lost during strangulation or when the corpse was dragged over the railroad tracks. For all Daniel knew, the crucifix lay hidden under some piece of garbage, an airtight or sack of Dwight's Cow-Brand Soda.

"Why?" Daniel asked himself again. His eyes bore into the trash. Why would anyone drag a dead girl to a pile of trash? The body wasn't hidden. Not where it had been found. The dance was winding down, and people would have been leaving, heading home. It just made absolutely no sense. No one in his right mind . . .

He felt the presence behind him. There was no shadow because the sun was in his face. Turning, trying to stand, he caught only a glimpse of the fist that slammed into his head, knocked him onto the railroad tracks.

His ears rang. He felt blood running down his left cheek, but pushed himself to his feet. A giant boot stepped on his Old Glory tablet, twisting, turning, driving it into the sand. The other boot stepped on the Faber pencil, snapping it in half.

"You talk a lot," he heard the voice say. "For a damned Injun. Jemez thinks you ask too damned many questions."

Daniel's tongue skimmed over his teeth. All still there. When the form stepped toward him, Daniel stepped back.

Daniel's revolver, an old relic—like most of

the equipment, even the uniforms, issued to the Indian policemen—had been left back in the *taibo* house in Indian Territory. There had been no reason to bring a Remington .44 from Indian Territory. He hadn't even carried his skinning knife, just a folding Barlow knife—and that he had left in the grip back at the jail.

Jemez slid the machete out of its sheath, began waving it back and forth, left and right, left and right, grinning all the while.

"The *rurales*," Jemez said. "In Janos. They pay one hundred *pesos* for the scalp of an Apache man." He stepped closer. "Fifty for a squaw or child."

Daniel moved back, toward the water barrels.

He remembered his introduction to Jemez earlier, at the Rivera *jacal*. Daniel said: "Thought my hair was too short now for an Apache."

"Jemez thinks you were in mourning. *Rurales* will think the same."

The big killer didn't know he had spoken the truth. He brought memories of Rain Shower back to Daniel. He hated this Mexican with a giant knife for reminding him of his loss.

"But," Jemez continued, "*rurales* always try to cheat a poor businessman like Jemez. They will say you are no buck, just a *niño*."

"I am no Apache."

"*Sí*. But the *rurales*, Jemez thinks, will not know this." He brought the machete up.

162

Daniel thought about reminding the brute that the Apaches were gone, that there was no more trouble, and that the *rurales* no longer would pay for a scalp. But he knew that would not be fitting for a Comanche to say. That would be begging. He removed his hat with his left hand, waving it as Jemez did the machete.

"That is why," Jemez continued, "Jemez will bring your head to the *rurales*, instead. It will prove that you are Indian." He grinned his ugly smile. "And not just a Mexican."

The big man crouched, began easing toward Daniel, his eyes as sharp and deadly as his machete.

"A hat against a machete." Jemez laughed. "Jemez thinks he knows who will win this fight."

Then he moved like lightning, the blade whistling as it passed. Daniel just managed to jump back in time, sucking in his breath, realizing how he had almost been disemboweled. Before that thought had barely registered, Daniel was jumping back again as the blade tore cloth. Again. Again.

The next time, the blade missed, and Daniel slapped at the Mexican's face with his hat. It struck, and, to Daniel's surprise, Jemez screamed, lost his balance, and fell on his backside.

Daniel stared at his hat as if he had unlocked Excalibur.

"Jemez will kill you for that, Comanche!" the

Mexican beast roared, as he pushed himself back up.

He was just a few feet from Daniel. So Daniel kicked with his moccasins, sending sand into the big man's face.

Again, the brute roared, dropping his machete, bringing both hands to his eyes, rubbing, spitting, cursing.

He remembered the story from both the missions on the reservation and the School Mothers at Carlisle. To his surprise, the words rang in his memory as clear as they had all those years ago.

> And David put his hand in his bag, and took thence a stone, and slang it, and smote the Philistine in his forehead, that the stone sunk into his forehead; and he fell upon his face to the earth.
>
> So David prevailed over the Philistine with a sling and with a stone, and smote the Philistine, and slew him; but there was no sword in the hand of David.

He remembered another story, too, one told among The People. About a grandmother who had been surprised by a black bear. And how the grandmother, holding only a buffalo horn spoon, had chased the bear out of the camp, across the river, and into the mountains. The heroine of that story, still told at campfires and in lodges, had been Daniel's grandmother, the mother of Marsh Hawk.

He knew, however, that he had not smote this giant, had not chased this bear away. So he stepped closer, and kicked Jemez in the nose.

The giant went down. Daniel saw the machete, kicked it, watching it sail to the railroad tracks. He moved toward it, hoping to reach it, but Jemez was on his feet now, blood pouring from his nose, saliva being spit out of his mouth.

Jemez shook off the cobwebs. Blood soaked his mustache, his beard. His face had turned crimson, not from blood, but rage.

"Jemez kills you for this," the big man hissed.

As the brute charged, Daniel knew that Jemez was likely right.

# CHAPTER THIRTEEN

Daniel swung his hat like a saber, missing, the momentum spinning him. That's when Jemez rammed his shoulder into Daniel's side. Air fled Daniel's lungs. His hat flew into the dust. He grunted upon impact. The outskirts of Deming turned blurry. He felt himself being driven backward, the big Mexican's arms wrapping around his midsection. Felt the life being squeezed out of him.

He slammed against something. An immoveable force. By that point, Daniel couldn't see anything, but guessed that Jemez had driven him back against the adobe storage shed. He smelled dust, blood, sweat. Heard his own groans, a loud ringing in his head, heard Jemez grunting, cursing.

Daniel's left arm was pinned by his own weight, and the pushing, bull-strong Jemez, against the adobe wall. It felt as though the thick adobe bricks would give way in a moment, and he and the scalp hunter would go crashing through the shed's walls. He couldn't move his left arm, but his right remained free. He punched, but had no strength, and not much room. He grabbed a handful of Jemez's beard, pulled, but his fingers slipped on the blood pouring from the Mexican's nose. He knew he was losing strength, focus, and consciousness. He grabbed again for that bloody mane.

Suddenly Jemez screamed out in pain, and Daniel felt the pressure ease. He was free, falling, hitting the ground, slamming against the adobe walls, sliding onto his side. It hurt like he had been hit by a locomotive, but he knew he had to get up. Had to open his eyes. Jemez was somewhere, cursing, probably coming at Daniel now. His eyes opened, but sweat and dust blinded him. He pushed himself up, fell, got up again. In a sitting position, his hand found a stone near the wall, and he gripped it.

"Come on," Daniel said in the language of The People. "Come on, you fat Mexican, and I will kill you."

Jemez shouted out something in Spanish.

Daniel's vision was slowly coming back, and he could make out a blurry shape that had something in his hand, and Daniel knew the giant had found the machete. Jemez came nearer, but a voice stopped him.

"One more step toward that Indian, you Mex bastard, and I'll lay you out again. Only this time, you'll be dead."

Jemez stopped.

Still gripping the stone, Daniel pushed himself to his feet. He spit out sand and saliva and probably a fair amount of his own blood. Now, he saw another shape, just to Jemez's right, and he also held something in his hand.

"Drop the machete, you fat bastard. Or I drop you," said this second figure.

Then, another voice, not as threatening, not as loud, Southern instead of sharp, but forceful: "Jemez, do like the railroader says."

The third man sat atop a horse.

Daniel slid back down the wall. He no longer saw blurry shapes. Just blackness.

*His eyes open to find Rain Shower kneeling over him, smiling. She says:* "Marúawe. Unha hakai nuusuka?"

*He answers:* "I am well." *Almost asks . . . And how are you? Only he remembers that Rain Shower is dead.*

Maybe I am, too, *he thinks.*

*Her smile disappears.* "It is not your time to make the journey to The Land Beyond The Sun," *she tells him.*

"Why are you here?" *he asks.*

"To help you," *she says.*

*He says:* "Ura."

"You need not thank me," *she says.* "Why don't you return home? My brother Ben Buffalo Bone misses you. My sister, my mother, everyone misses you."

"I miss you," *he tells her.*

*Tears fill her eyes, but they do not escape, do*

168

*not run down her cheeks. She brings a wet silk rag to his face, wipes off the blood, presses it against his forehead. The coolness helps. He closes his eyes, takes in her scent.*

*"There is work to do here," she says. "When you are finished, you must return to The People."*

*"Yes." His eyes remain shut. He fears if he opens them again, Rain Shower will be gone. "I think this Walking Man is innocent. I don't know how to prove this to these* taibos. *And, yes, I know I must return home. But . . ."*

*"You are right," she says.*

*"About what?" he asks. His right hand raises. It touches her arm. Good, he thinks, she is still here. She has not left me . . . again.*

*She does not answer. Instead, she tells him: "Your journey will be hard."*

*"Everything," he tells her, "is hard for The People." His eyes open. She is still there, holding the rag against his head, still smiling. "It is hard for me. To be without you."*

*A finger touches his lips.*

*"Walking Man will help you," she says.*

*He feels her remove the wet rag. He wants to sit up, be closer to her. He knows she is leaving. The finger moves from his lips.*

*"He does not even want to help himself," he tells her.*

*"He will."*

*She is standing.*

*Not wanting to see her leave, he closes his eyes.*
*"And I," he hears her say, "have never left you.*
*I will never leave you."*

Daniel's right hand gripped the arm, felt the wet bandanna, but the arm was too big, too strong, to be Rain Shower's. His eyes fluttered open, and the arm pulled away from his grip. He watched a big man in a railroader's cap stand, plunge his hand into one of those barrels, and come back out holding a sopping wet bandanna.

The big man squatted back down. This time, he held out the dripping rag to Daniel.

"You all right?" Radegunde asked. The odor of whiskey was strong on the brakeman's breath. His eyes were bloodshot, too.

Daniel answered first in the tongue of The People, then shook some clarity back into his head, and nodded. "I'll live."

Accepting the proffered bandanna, Daniel brought it to his face, and looked beyond the big railroad brakeman. Jemez sat on the rails, holding a rag to his head. His nose and lips still seeped blood, but it was his head that troubled him now. Daniel looked again at Radegunde. The big man was looking at Jemez, too. Radegunde held a crowbar in his left hand.

"He won't bother you no more," Radegunde said, and looked back at Daniel.

The crowbar made that clear to Daniel. Or

170

maybe there was another reason. Daniel remembered the third man. Mounted on a big, blood bay gelding, sat Matt Callahan. His hair seemed shorter, no longer touching his collar. He had gotten a haircut. Maybe that's why he had ridden to Deming. For that, and to pay his respects to María Rivera.

Daniel draped the wet bandanna over his shoulder, reached up to find some semblance of a grip on the adobe wall, and gingerly began pushing himself to his feet.

Radegunde helped him. Bracing himself against the shed, he waited for the dizziness to pass, studying Matt Callahan while the railroader fetched Daniel's black hat. Radegunde kept the crowbar handy, but Jemez was no longer a threat.

Although it still wasn't exactly clear to Daniel, he had a pretty good idea what had happened. Radegunde had slammed that crowbar atop Jemez's skull. That had dropped the big Mexican, but it must have been Matt Callahan who had finally stopped Jemez.

"Thank you," Daniel said. "Both of you."

Callahan took a cigar from his mouth. "You weren't doing bad yourself, Comanch'."

The brakeman handed Daniel his hat. Taking it, Daniel slapped the dust off the brim, reshaped the crown, but left it hanging from his left hand.

"You should control that beast of yours,

Callahan," Radegunde said. "He probably would have killed this fella, if I hadn't come along."

"I came along, too," Callahan told him.

"Yeah, but I don't think you would have stopped that Mex from killing this kid."

"He's older than a kid. And he's Comanch'. Twenty years ago, fella his age would have had forty scalps hanging from his lance. Mostly women's."

"Makes no never mind to me what he is. He's got a pass to ride the Atchison, Topeka, and Santa Fe. That means somebody thinks highly of him."

Callahan took another puff on the cigar, blew smoke into the hot air. "If I was you," he told the brakeman, "I'd keep that crowbar handy. Jemez doesn't like getting nigh brained to death."

"I need no crowbar to whip the likes of him."

Callahan let out a mirthless chuckle. "You couldn't even whip my kid in a wrestling match. Anyway, next time, I might not be around to save both your hides."

Footsteps sounded, and all four men turned as Police Chief Mark McLyler rounded the corner, holding one of those Chicago nightsticks in his left hand. He was sweating. Must have run all the way from the city hall.

"What's going on here?" the young policeman asked.

"Nothing, Mark." Callahan smiled. "Nothing

at all. Not now." He shifted the horse closer to Daniel. "You've been asking a lot of questions, I hear. Lot of questions."

*For which I have gotten few answers,* Daniel thought, but held his tongue.

"That gent in the jail, that white man turned Injun, he was found right here." Callahan pointed. "The body was right yonder. He was the last person to see that young girl alive." Callahan waited.

"Next to last," Daniel said. "The man who killed her was the last."

Callahan's blue eyes hardened. Then, with a grim smile, he backed up his horse, put the cigar in his mouth.

Daniel took the wet bandanna from his shoulder, wiped his face once more, then returned it to the brakeman.

"You think somebody else killed Melody?" Callahan asked after a moment.

"Yes," Daniel said. "I do."

"Who?"

A sigh escaped Daniel's lips.

"Got any ideas?" Callahan asked.

Just to say something, Daniel pointed a finger at Jemez. "Him," he said, "for one."

That produced a chuckle from Callahan. He tossed the cigar onto the dirt, didn't bother to stomp it out, and picked up his reins. "Jemez," he said, "get your horse where you left it by the

Mimbres Saloon. We're leaving." He pulled his hat down tighter.

Daniel, Radegunde, and McLyler watched the big Mexican get up and walk, holding his sombrero in his left hand, still keeping his right against his head, his face already beginning to bruise. Daniel felt proud of himself. Felt like a Comanche warrior. Even if he had almost gotten himself beaten to death.

"My boy Jules," Callahan said to Daniel, "was fond of that dead girl, Comanch'. So was I. I think you're wrong, but prove it to me, to Mark here, to the circuit judge. You prove that that mongrel in the Deming jail is innocent. You find the right killer. You do that, and I'll pay you five hundred dollars. You heard me, Mark." He looked at Radegunde. "You, too, mister. You're my witnesses. Five hundred dollars."

Daniel could think of nothing to say.

"He'll need to hurry," McLyler said. "The circuit judge arrived this afternoon."

Daniel's heart sank.

"He set a date for the trial?" the rancher asked.

McLyler's head shook. "Got some minor things to go through first. It'll be a day or two before we get a jury picked."

Then a day, maybe two, for a trial. That's one thing Daniel had learned about Pale Eyes justice. They didn't waste much time when they finally got inside a courtroom.

"Imagine I'll be summoned," Callahan said, and nodded at the police chief. "Well, you know where to find me." He started to turn the blood bay around, but stopped, looking down at Daniel. "Like I said, Comanch'. Five hundred dollars. If you bring me the right killer. But I think the right man is already behind bars. And I know you're dead wrong about my man Jemez. He didn't do it."

"How can you be sure?" To Daniel's surprise, it was Radegunde who asked that question.

"Easy," Callahan said. "Jemez would have taken the girl's scalp. Sold it as an Apache's across the border."

"Do either one of you want to explain to me just what the hell happened?" Mark McLyler asked after Matt Callahan had ridden off with Jemez.

"Nothing happened," Daniel said.

"Your face tells me otherwise, Killstraight." McLyler stepped closer to Radegunde. "And I could arrest you right now for drunk and disorderly conduct."

Grinning, the brakeman brought up the crowbar, rested it across his shoulders behind his neck, hands gripping it on both sides. "Sure, MacLiar. Arrest me."

"Get out of here." McLyler hooked a thumb.

Radegunde laughed and lowered the crowbar, which he tossed to the side of the shed.

"Come with me, Killstraight," Radegunde said.

175

"I told you about G.K. Perue's livery. She'll put you up in a stall."

Daniel's head shook. "No, thanks. I've met G.K. Perue."

Radegunde stepped back. "You already been there?"

Daniel nodded.

"Did she mention me?"

Daniel moved to find his Old Glory. Picking it up, he brushed off the dirt, watched the sand sift onto the ground. Jemez's big boots had ripped out some pages, but these Daniel folded and stuck inside the tablet. He left the broken pencil in the dirt. "She said something. I don't remember what." His head was beginning to pound.

Back on the reservation, Daniel might go visit a holy man, who would dig a long trench, in which a fire would be built until the heat began to crack the ground. Coals would then be raked out, and sage spread over the hot ground. The holy man would then pour water over the thin layer of sage, and when the steam began to rise, Daniel would have been placed inside the trench, wrapped in blankets, and the headache would be sweated out of him. Or he could sniff *natsaakusi*, and the sneezing medicine might rid him of this headache. It worked a lot quicker than the pit and sage treatment. *Natsaakusi* also cured hiccups.

"G.K. knows you're in town," McLyler told Radegunde. "Best get to your wife."

Daniel almost dropped the tablet. "Wife?"

"Well," the brakeman said sheepishly. "Not in no legal way. Or church way. She's more like a . . ."

"Concubine," the policeman said.

"Wouldn't call her that, neither. But I best get to see her. You come, Killstraight. Ain't a bad place to spend the night, and it's cheap."

"Jail's cheaper," McLyler said.

Radegunde started for the crowbar he had tossed away. "You ain't arresting him, MacLiar."

"Don't get yourself in more trouble," the policeman warned the brakeman. Then added: "I'm not arresting him. But we might have need of him." He stared grimly at Daniel, and Daniel knew why—Vince and those cowboys from Rincon.

"I'll be fine," Daniel told the brakeman. "Go see your . . . wife."

"All right." Radegunde breathed in deeply. Trying, Daniel guessed, to find some courage to face that rough woman at the livery. Radegunde walked down the rails, and started to turn the corner.

"What about that?" Daniel called out, and, when the brakeman turned, Daniel pointed toward the crowbar.

"Ain't mine," he said. "Don't go walking around town with no crowbar. MacLiar wouldn't like it. And I don't need it to whip the likes of

177

that Mexican." With that, he disappeared around the corner.

"Let's go," McLyler said, but Daniel was walking in the other direction. He gripped one of the water barrels and looked around until he saw the crowbar. Thinking: *Commager said that Melody Rivera's neck had been broken by a club, or the stock of a rifle.*

McLyler stepped to Daniel's side. The two men studied each other, then looked back down at the crowbar, both thinking the same thing.

# CHAPTER FOURTEEN

Inside the cramped, dingy jail, Mark McLyler handed Daniel a blue cobalt bottle. On the side read: *The West Electric Cure Co.* And stenciled around the small bottle's lip: *Electricity in a Bottle.*

"It's safe," McLyler said. "Good for headaches and earaches and everything else."

It was not *natsaakusi*, but, after ten minutes, Daniel's headache was easing. And he was still alive.

The two policemen, Hank Roberts and Jasper Frazer, were there, and old Miguel sat in the corner, cradling a massive double-barrel shotgun in his lap. The stove made the jail even hotter, but kept the coffee warm. Daniel had helped himself to a cup. Now he read over all the notes he had taken today.

"You don't think those boys could make it all the way from Rincon by tonight, do you?" McLyler asked.

Daniel looked up. The People knew how to ride horses, how to push their mounts, how to cover great distances quickly. But four *taibo* cowboys? Across that furnace?

"Tomorrow," Daniel said. "At the earliest. Or the day after. Or . . ."—he shrugged—"never."

179

McLyler swore, then shouted out: "Where in hell is Moran?"

Moran. Daniel had forgotten all about the deputy sheriff.

Frazer shrugged. Roberts said: "No one's seen him since the night of the killing."

That got Daniel's attention. "You mean the deputy hasn't been seen in almost a week?"

"Don't go working up some damned theory about Moran," McLyler said. "Something happens in town . . . something like this . . . and our faithful servant decides it's a good time to go collect taxes."

"I don't know," Roberts added.

"I do." McLyler ended the conversation.

Daniel dropped any thought of the *taibo* sheriff's deputy he had never met. He looked back at his notes, realizing suddenly that he had been in Deming less than one day. It was only about this time yesterday that he had even heard of a dead teen-aged girl named Melody Rivera or a town called Deming.

He thought of his vision of Rain Shower, and he thought of the dead girl. He slid the coffee cup onto the desk, and laid the Old Glory beside it.

"I would like to speak to the prisoner again," Daniel said.

McLyler sighed. "Suit yourself. But you'd likely have a better conversation with a stone wall."

• • •

The white man known among the Chiricahua Apaches as Walking Man lay on his bunk, his legs crossed at the ankles, head propped up by a filthy pillow, hands behind his head. He stared at the ceiling. He stared at nothing.

Daniel had dragged a stool from the office. He set it on the hard floor, then sat down in front of Groves's cell.

The *taibo* did not acknowledge his presence.

Daniel had left his writing tablet on McLyler's desk, thinking that it would be better if Groves did not see him writing down what he said. If he said anything. But Daniel thought he would. Hoped he would. So he sat there, and waited.

Five minutes passed. Another ten. Groves did not move, just looked at the ceiling. Daniel looked through the bars, through the dim light, at the prisoner.

Fifteen minutes.

Groves, at last, shifted his ankles.

Daniel did not move.

Among the Pale Eyes, Comanches were thought of as wild savages, with no control of lust, of rage, of hatred. Daniel knew better. The People were humorous, and loving. They were also patient, extremely patient.

He waited.

Almost an hour passed, and still neither man had acknowledged the other.

The door to the outer office cracked open. Daniel didn't bother to turn or look, figuring it was either Miguel or McLyler checking on him. To make sure he was still alive.

When the door shut, Francis Groves, without taking his eyes off the ceiling, said: "You didn't bring a rope, boy."

Daniel said nothing.

"Or coffee," Francis Groves said.

Another ten minutes of silence. Then Groves uncrossed his ankles, and swung his legs over the side of the bunk. He sat, brushing the long hair off his shoulders, staring through the iron bars, eyes trained now on Daniel Killstraight.

"What is it you want?" Groves turned to spit into the slop bucket.

"You did not kill that girl," Daniel said.

Groves snorted. "You don't know a damned thing," he said.

"I know about you," Daniel said.

"You know nothing about me, boy."

So Daniel smiled. He shifted his legs at last, stood, knees popping, muscles sore. He had been sitting a long time. He was glad he didn't have to walk far, just to the cell's door. His hands gripped the bars, and, looking between them, he stared at Francis Groves.

He was mostly guessing. Daniel knew that. He could hear Hugh Gunter—or Doc Commager—giving him hell for churning out more theories than facts. But as he talked, Daniel realized, that, no, he was not really guessing. Not any more.

"You are Walking Man," he said. "This is not your first time in jail."

"Yeah." Groves let out a mirthless laugh. "Figured you boys would learn about my stay in Yuma."

"No," Daniel said. "Before that."

Even in the pale light, Daniel could see the *taibo*'s eyes harden.

Maybe that part about the jail had been a guess, but Daniel knew that the rest of what he was about to say had to be the truth.

"You hired on with the Army in Arizona Territory as a scout. Mainly because you spoke the language of the Chiricahua Apaches and could translate to the bluecoats what the wolves were saying." Wolves. Maybe that was a bad word choice, but that is what The People called all of the Indians—the Pawnees, the Delawares, and those horrible Tonkawas—who betrayed the other Indian peoples by tracking them down for the bluecoats. Daniel didn't stop, though, knowing instinctively that he couldn't stop, couldn't correct himself, and that he definitely would not apologize to this *taibo*-turned-Apache.

"Only, you did not just speak the language. You were Apache. You became Apache. Because you married an Apache."

Both of Groves's fists clenched.

183

"I do not say that you took an Apache to bed, like many *taibos* have done. She was not your . . ."— he remembered McLyler's word—"concubine. She was your wife. You had a daughter. A very beautiful daughter. You lived with your people, and your people were Chiricahuas."

Groves stared, his fists still tight balls.

He pointed at the ration bag hanging over Groves's shoulder. "You lived with your people, the Chiricahuas, even on the reservation at . . . San Carlos." He hoped he got that name right. The Mescaleros had mentioned the reservation in Arizona Territory. "And you lived with them when they left the reservation."

Suddenly Groves sang out: "What were their names?"

Daniel blinked. He hadn't expected this. He wet his lips, feeling that headache beginning to return.

Groves continued: "You think you know so damned much, tell me. What were their names?"

He had the daughter's name written down in his notes, but couldn't remember it, and probably couldn't pronounce it correctly. But he didn't have to.

"Among The People," he said calmly, "we do not speak the names of those who have gone to The Land Beyond The Sun."

Groves fell silent. The words seemed to have numbed him. Daniel took a deep breath, exhaled.

He had been talking for some time, and he was far from finished.

"It was a good life," he said. "Until the Mexicans came."

Groves stood, but did not move away from the bunk.

"Among The People, my people, the Indians you call the Comanches," Daniel continued, "we did not hate the Mexicans. We did not like them, but they provided us many things. Horses and slaves. Maize and cattle. Weapons. I do not think we even considered the Mexicans. But the Apaches . . . yes . . . you have much reason to hate the Mexicans. And, they, I imagine, have reason to hate you. But to do what they did . . ." Daniel's head shook.

Groves was sitting back down, his head in his hands, looking at the floor.

"Shut up," Daniel heard Groves say.

But Daniel did not obey.

"One hundred *pesos* for the scalp of an Apache man. Fifty *pesos* for the scalp of an Apache woman." He would not use the *taibo* word squaw. He would never call a woman a squaw. It was an ugly word. Given by ugly people. "Fifty *pesos* for an Apache child. The Mexican government put up this reward. To encourage men like Jemez to hunt down the Apaches. To kill as many of you as they could."

"Shut up," Groves said again.

"And they did," Daniel continued. "They came into your village, the village where your wife and daughter lived. They killed them both. They took their scalps. For Mexican money."

He couldn't be sure if he was getting everything in order, following the right chronology, but he must have been getting close. At least he was finally reaching Francis Groves.

"They called you Walking Man." He recalled some of what he had heard on the reservation near Fort Sill, by the Apaches living there. "Apaches are not like The People. We move with horses. Horses are our life. But Apaches, especially the Chiricahuas, love the mountains. Horses are good, certainly, but Apaches can cover more ground afoot. So could you. That is why they named you Walking Man.

"Geronimo left the reservation. To make war on the Mexicans, and the Pale Eyes. You rode for the Army. To scout. Maybe you wanted to be with your people again. Maybe this was your way. To find the Chiricahuas. And you, and the Apache scouts, did this. Under the command of the great *taibo* leader, Crook."

Crook, to Daniel's knowledge, had never fought against The People. They had had to deal with the bluecoat Bad Hand, who eventually had lost his mind and lost his career. Daniel wanted to think that The People had driven Bad Hand insane.

"Then Miles replaced Crook. But eventually this bluecoat found Geronimo. And Geronimo surrendered almost three years ago. And the *taibos* sent all of the Chiricahuas, even those who had helped the bluecoats, to Florida. They would have shipped you. But you were not Chiricahua. Not to the *taibos*. You were just like them. A white man."

"No." Groves was moving, slowly, toward Daniel. "I was not like them." He hissed the words.

"You got drunk. You fought in a saloon in the *taibo* town called Tucson. You were arrested. Tried. You were sent to Yuma."

Groves had reached the bars.

"You decided to rejoin your people, the Chiricahuas. So you began to ride to this soldier fort in Florida." Remembering his own father, Daniel felt his own eyes misting over, matching the sadness in those of Francis Groves. He had to pause, regain control. Somehow, he managed to do just that.

"Your horse died in the desert. You walked to Deming. Walking was easy . . . for a man named Walking Man. You found G.K. Perue, and you got drunk. That is something else you had become good at. Getting drunk. To forget. Forget your pain. But even the Pale Eyes whiskey cannot make you forget. And then you went to the Independence Day dance. You went with

187

this crazy woman to get drunk. Instead, you saw this Mexican girl. About the same age as your daughter was . . . when the Mexican scalp hunters came."

Grove's hands gripped the iron bars. The sadness had left Groves's eyes, was replaced with a murderous rage. Daniel had not backed down from a man like Jemez, and he would not quit now. "You saw your own daughter in this Mexican girl. And you saw how these Pale Eyes looked at her. Jemez was there. Jemez hunted Apaches for their scalps. For all you knew, he could have been with the party that murdered your wife and child. And Jemez, and others like him who seek scalps for *pesos*, was not particular. He would scalp a Mexican. And say it was an Apache.

"So you wanted to protect this girl, this girl who looked so much like your daughter. That is what you wanted to do. That is why you walked her home. Not to kill her. To save her." Daniel swallowed. "But you did not."

He leaped back, knocking over the stool behind him, almost crashing against the iron bars of the cell behind him. Somehow he kept his feet.

"You son-of-a-bitch!" Groves's fingers sliced like a mountain lion's claws through the air. "Damned bastard! I'll kill you. I'll kill you!" He fired out something else, words in Apache.

The door down the hallway opened, letting

188

in more light. Daniel, never looking away from Groves, said: "I'm all right. Leave us alone."

The door closed. Francis Groves, Walking Man, had not noticed.

"I'll kill you!" he howled, switching back to English.

"You failed her," Daniel said again. "You failed yourself. I do not even know why I try to help you. You did not love your Apache family. You are not capable of love. You hate everything. Including yourself."

Groves stopped. Tears poured down his face. "You . . ." Sobbing now. "You . . . don't . . . know . . . what . . ."

Now Daniel felt his Comanche blood boiling over. He stepped forward, and Groves took a defensive step back, away from the bars.

"Don't tell me what I don't know," Daniel insisted, his hands gripping the bars tightly, squeezing them so hard his fingers were turning white. "Look at me . . . damn your *taibo* soul. See my hair. It comes from mourning. Would you like to see the scars on my arms? I know exactly what it's like to lose someone. . . ." Someone he loved. Only Daniel could not say those words. He had not deserved Rain Shower. She should have married some other warrior. She should still be alive.

"If you loved your daughter, you son-of-a-bitch, if you loved your wife, you would have the courage, the decency, the honor to find the man who really killed that girl here. Or was she just a Mexican? Do you hate Mexicans that much? Were all of them scalp hunters?"

Daniel let go of the bars, grabbed the stool, threw it against the bars. It bounced off, landed on the floor, rolled across the aisle.

"I am done with you, Walking Man. You are a disgrace to everyone . . . Pale Eyes and all Indian peoples. I cannot help you. Hang. Go hang. See if you can find your wife, your daughter, when you wander across The Land Beyond The Sun with a crooked neck." He spit. People in Deming weren't the only ones with that talent. He walked away, heading for the door.

"Hey!" Groves called out.

Daniel kept walking.

"Hey!"

He was ten feet from the door.

"Killstraight!"

Daniel stopped. Turned. Waited.

Just loud enough for Daniel to hear, Groves said: "I don't know if I killed that girl or not." Then he stepped back to the bunk, sat down, buried his face in his hands.

Slowly Daniel walked back. He picked up the stool, righting it, setting it on the stone floor. And waited.

Groves seemed to tremble, and then he lifted his head, dropped his arms. He spoke softly. "I

don't remember anything. Just the girl. Just Li—
. . . just my daughter. I could have killed her, I
guess. I was drunk enough."

"Not that drunk," Daniel said.

"No." Groves shook his head. "Not that drunk.
I remember everything about her. She looked
so much . . . she was the . . . spitting image . . .
I . . ." He sighed heavily. "No, I don't think I
could have killed her." Groves fingered the bump
over his left ear.

"Do you remember anything else?" Daniel
asked.

"No. I just remember seeing her. Like it was a
dream."

"The judge is in town," Daniel said. "Your trial
will begin in a couple of days. That does not give
us much time."

Groves nodded. "Don't drink whiskey,
Killstraight. It'll ruin your life."

Daniel did not smile. "I don't. And I know."

"Where was she found? The girl?"

"Near the railroad tracks. You were hit on the
side of your head. Remember that?"

Groves's head shook.

"Anything? Any memory at all?" Daniel
pushed.

"No."

"Did G.K. Perue see you leave with the girl?"

"I don't remember."

"Jemez? Matt Callahan? McLyler?"

"I don't even know who those folks are. Except Perue. And Jemez."

"All right." Daniel stood. "I'll get you some coffee."

"Thanks."

He moved down the hallway, stopping when Groves called his name.

"The railroad tracks? That where she was . . . ?"

Daniel nodded.

"What side of town?"

"West. Almost out of town?"

This Groves pondered for a few seconds. Then he asked: "How many days ago?"

Daniel shrugged. He didn't even know what day of the week it was. "Four days, I guess. Maybe five." Daniel reached the door, opened it, could see McLyler and Miguel waiting, eyes curious.

"Killstraight."

Daniel looked back at Groves.

"I can find out who did it. But you have to get me out of here."

Daniel almost laughed. Even Quanah Parker did not possess enough *puha* to free Francis Groves, Walking Man, from the Deming jail.

# CHAPTER FIFTEEN

"Well," Mark McLyler said, "that was some conversation you had."

After pouring some coffee, Daniel asked Miguel if he would take the cup to Groves. The jailer grumbled, but took the coffee and disappeared down the dark corridor. Turning to face the smirking young police chief, Daniel asked: "Did you hear any of it?"

The chief's head shook. "Just a lot of cursing. And yelling. Did he confess?"

Daniel shook his head. "But . . ."—he decided to be honest—"he doesn't remember anything that happened."

McLyler nodded. "Same as he said at the inquest. Which was about all he said."

"How well did you know the victim?" Daniel glanced at his Old Glory tablet and a new pencil sitting on the desk, and went to the stove for some coffee for himself. He heard the change in the lawman's voice when he answered.

"She lived on the wrong side of the tracks for me," McLyler said. "I didn't know her at all."

Holding the coffee cup, Daniel turned to look the chief in the eye. "Yet you danced with her."

McLyler's eyes lost their friendliness, and blazed into Daniel. The police chief had been leaning in the chair, hands behind his head, rocking slightly, head against the wall. The front legs of the chair came down, and McLyler leaned forward.

"What are you saying, Killstraight?"

Daniel sipped coffee. Tried to be nonchalant. "That you danced with her."

"So?"

He shrugged. "I know little about how you Pale Eyes act. The People's dances are different." As a Baptist, Indian Agent Joshua Biggers frowned upon The People's dances on the reservation. There had been little dancing back at Carlisle, and what he had seen in the saloons and dance halls near Pittsburgh and Philadelphia, Daniel would not have called dancing.

"It was our nation's birthday." McLyler turned defensive. "A lot of people were there. I danced with a lot of girls. And that girl danced with a lot of men, a lot of boys. You think I killed her? Hell, man, I barely knew her."

Daniel took a sip of coffee, set the cup down, lifted his pencil, and flipped open the note pad. "But during the inquest, G.K. Perue said . . ."— he searched through his notes—"that when the Mexican girl began talking to Groves, it riled Matt Callahan and you." He did not say that Perue called McLyler "our snot-nosed police chief."

"Because Groves was drunk." McLyler was hot

now, ears turning redder by the minute. "That's a girl, a young girl, and it seemed like this Groves was forcing himself upon her."

"Then why not arrest him?"

"For being drunk? Jail's not that big. Not on the Fourth of July."

"No. Not for drunkenness. But for forcing himself upon her."

McLyler's head shook. "I didn't mean that literally. He was just . . . just . . ."

"Talking to her?"

McLyler sighed. He began rubbing both temples. "Well, he was a stranger. And . . ." He looked up at Daniel, his eyes no longer defiant. "Well, you've seen him."

Daniel nodded. He understood. A man "gone Injun." Isn't that what the *taibos* called it? Pale Eyes would frown upon that kind of thing. Talking to a young girl, even if that girl happened to be Mexican. It was all right for a white man to take an Indian girl, but not the other way around. Melody Rivera was pretty. And she was talking to this stranger, this Walking Man. This stranger, who, in everything but his blood, was a Chiricahua.

"Did you see Groves leave with the girl?"

"No." Another sigh. "I left. She danced with him. They started talking. I got a little riled, probably because Callahan and his son and a lot of people were getting hot. So were plenty of those Mexican boys from north of the tracks. I left. Went home."

Daniel thought: *So if a fight broke out, if Francis Groves got beaten senseless, you would not have been there to witness the fight, would not have been forced to act like a police chief.*

Miguel returned from the cells, and shut the door. Daniel did not ask McLyler anything else. He sat in a chair, and reread the notes he had taken, pulled out the dirty crumpled pages Jemez had torn out of the tablet with his boots, and uncreased them.

An uncomfortable silence descended on the jail.

L.J. Vanderhider and one of his Harvey House girls personally brought supper to the jail that night for all of the lawmen, which made Daniel quite pleased that he had not spent the night in one of G.K. Perue's horse stalls. It wasn't a feast of *cuhtz*—back when The People had buffalo to eat—but it beat eating pemmican.

The riders from Rincon did not arrive that night. Daniel hadn't expected them, but he did respect Chief Mark McLyler for taking no chances. The young lawman stayed in the jail, along with Miguel, who seldom lowered his shotgun. The two police officers, Frazer and Roberts, traded duties, one waiting outside the jail, the other patrolling the streets. Daniel waited inside.

Before dawn, McLyler suggested that Daniel get some sleep in one of the empty cells, but he declined the invitation, figuring he couldn't sleep in the dark, smelly *taibo* jail, anyway.

L.J. Vanderhider did not bring them breakfast. Instead, the peace officers and Daniel sipped coffee and chewed on jerky.

Sitting behind his desk, eyes bloodshot, beard stubble on his face, Mark McLyler pointed at the older policeman, Roberts, and said: "Earliest I'd expect those boys to get here would be late this afternoon." He shot a glance at Miguel. "That sound about right?"

The old jailer shrugged. "*¿Quién sabe?*"

The younger officer, Frazer, the one with the brace of fancy revolvers, spit a stream of brown tobacco juice into a bucket that served as a spittoon. "Criminy, Mark, if you knew them boys wouldn't be here till today, maybe tonight, maybe tomorrow, why the hell did we stay up all night?"

"Because the deputy sheriff's still not here, and I'll be damned if I'll let any prisoner get lynched." The lack of sleep had shortened McLyler's temper. He turned to Miguel. "You go home, Miguel. Get some sleep. See your family. Just be back here sometime after dinner."

The door opened. Everyone jumped.

In walked a sober-looking man in a gray frock coat, black cravat with a pearl-topped stickpin, and wearing a wide-brimmed straw hat. The hat came off as he stepped inside, his smile revealing crooked, tobacco-stained teeth.

"Mark," he said casually, and Daniel, seeing everyone else relax, did the same. "I have some summons for the trial, courtesy of David Barber."

"Already?"

"Barber's like a mad dog. Sinks his teeth in something like this, he won't let go." The man looked more like a cadaver than a living being, the flesh on his bony face hanging like a sick, sick man. He turned, covering his mouth as he coughed, and looked back at Daniel.

"Don't believe I've met your acquaintance," he said. He did not smile.

"Judge, this is Daniel Killstraight," McLyler said. "He's visiting us from Indian Territory. He's what they call a peace officer around Fort Larned."

"Sill," Daniel corrected.

"Sergeant Killstraight, this is Judge Embry."

The judge's nod dismissed Daniel, and he reached into his coat pocket, pulling out some papers, which he thrust in McLyler's direction. "Nobody seems to know where Deputy Moran has hauled his arse to. So I'll leave it to you to bring me a panel of jurors. Good jurors, Mark. Men who can reach a decision without any foofaraw. We'll start the big trial day after tomorrow. Get them petty ones off my docket tomorrow."

McLyler stared at the writs. He looked up at the judge. "Judge Embry, we have something of a situation here, sir. There might be some cowboys heading to town. Coming, maybe, to lynch our prisoner."

The judge waved his hat, then set it on his head. "Good," he said. "Save the county the expense of a trial. Wouldn't mind getting out of your fine town as soon as humanly possible. Silver City's my next stop, and it's a mite more pleasant than this blight on humanity." And he walked out the door.

Daniel walked through Deming with an irritated Jasper Frazer, the morning already a scorcher. When they reached the depot, Frazer snapped at Daniel—"Stay here for a second!"—and walked over to a chubby gent wearing a funny cap and barking orders at a group of Negro workers. Frazer bulled in front of the fat man, started talking, but they were too far away for Daniel to hear what was being said. The man with the cap turned, pointed past Daniel, and, turning, Frazer walked back.

"He's this way," Frazer said without slowing down.

Daniel followed.

They found Mickey O'Shaughnessy on the other of the side tracks, laughing with a couple of other men who were sitting atop a hand cart.

"Hey, Irish!" Frazer snapped as he crossed the tracks.

O'Shaughnessy turned. He was a big man with red hair, a peachy face covered with hundreds of freckles, a railroader's cap held at his side in a big left hand.

"Copper," the Irishman said. "And what can we do for you today?"

The two men sitting on the hand cart chuckled.

Frazer handed him one of the papers. "That's your summons, Irish. Be at the courthouse."

"Bloody hell, I was just there."

"For the inquest. This is the trial."

"That was fast," said one of the men on the cart.

"Just be there." Frazer turned, and crossed back over the tracks, not saying a word to Daniel.

This time Daniel didn't follow the hot-headed policeman. He had come to find Mickey O'Shaughnessy. Daniel crossed over the tracks.

"And what in bloody hell can I do for you?" the big Irishman said, staring as if trying to figure out just who Daniel was.

Daniel stopped, opened his tablet, found his pencil. He didn't answer the big man's question, instead said: "I was hoping I could talk to you a bit about how you found the body of the girl."

"Newspaper reporter?" O'Shaughnessy grinned. "Hell, yes. It would be a pleasure to see me name in print."

Daniel saw no need to tell O'Shaughnessy he wasn't a reporter. The railroader was walking past Daniel, motioning for him to follow. The two other men jumped down from the hand cart and went along, too. As tall as these workers were, with long legs and the gait of one of Ben Buffalo Bones's uncle's racehorses, Daniel knew he would have trouble keeping up with these men.

He was almost out of breath when they reached the trash pile. As he leaned over, trying to catch his breath, O'Shaughnessy was already pointing at the largest pile.

"She was right here," he said, smiling at his two friends. "Knew she was dead the moment I saw her." He winked. "Hadn't been drinking that much . . . no, not by a damned sight. Seen her, and I say to meself . . . 'Jesus, Mary, and Joseph, that girl's dead.' That's what I said."

"Where were you when you first noticed her?" Daniel asked.

"Across the tracks yonder. I see the Injun lover first. You're Mexican, right? Didn't catch your name? Come up from Janos, did you? Didn't know they had newspapers in Mexico. Well, I was coming from Gage's . . ." He hooked a thumb behind him, indicating west. "Pumping that cart, hard I was, hoping to be able to catch Tip before he closed his place. And that's when I seen it. Right about yonder."

Daniel stopped writing. He looked at the trash pile, then where O'Shaughnessy was pointing. "I was right about there."

"But . . ."—Daniel wet his lips—"you couldn't have seen the girl's body. Not if she were there." Pointing.

"Mickey can see through trash," one of the workers said.

"On account he is trash," the other one said.

They all laughed, including O'Shaughnessy.

"No. 'Twasn't her I seen," O'Shaughnessy said. "It was the Injun lover. Lying right over yonder, dangerously close to the rails, in fact. That's why I stopped. I saw him. Figured he had a wee too much Irish whiskey or London porter. So I stopped, grabbed him, pulled him away from the rails, I did, and slapped his face a mite, trying to bring him to, you see. That's when I looked up. That's when I seen her."

O'Shaughnessy crossed the tracks, stopping at the spot where he said he had found Groves's unconscious body. "He lay here. Had a train come along during the night, he would have been laying here." He pointed in the opposite direction. "And here." Pointing. "And here. And here. And there. And over there."

The railroaders chuckled.

"Like this." O'Shaughnessy dropped to his knees, and lay face down.

Groves had been walking west then. Which

202

made sense, Daniel guessed, if he was taking the Rivera girl home.

"Was Groves injured?" Daniel asked, even though he knew the answer.

"Groves? Oh . . . that's the Injun-lover . . . the damned scoundrel who murders young Mex girls." O'Shaughnessy touched the side of his head. "Right here. Big knot on his noggin, quite a bit of blood."

"Damned fool killed the girl," one of the workers said. "Dragged her body to the trash. Staggering, probably tripped over the rails, hit his head."

The theory everyone in Deming seemed to believe.

"Aye," the other worker said. "Would've been just, if a train had happened along."

Yet Daniel stared, turned west, and shook his head. "He was facing this way," Daniel said. "Yet the blow was on this side." He touched just above his left ear.

"Could have rolled over," one of the railroaders said.

"Wish he would have swallowed his tongue," his companion chimed in.

"Well, he was drunk," O'Shaughnessy said.

Daniel made a beeline to the trash pile. The railroaders, suddenly curious, followed. He turned and looked southeast toward where Groves had been found.

"You ain't a newspaper reporter, are you?" one of the railroaders asked.

"Hell, I don't think he's even Mex," the other man said.

O'Shaughnessy frowned. "You're not saying I'm a liar, are you?"

"Not at all. You're as truthful as anyone I've found in Deming."

"Horse shit," one of the railroaders said.

All three laughed again.

"He kills the girl," Daniel said. "There." He pointed.

O'Shaughnessy nodded. "Right. I saw the sign. Well, Moran seen it. Said it was plain as day. Murder happened about yonder, fifteen yards or thereabouts from where that Injun lover was lying."

Sign? No one had told Daniel about any sign.

"Did you find a crucifix?"

The worker reached up to his neck, pulled out one on a silver chain. "Like this? Me mother give it to me."

Daniel's head shook. That wasn't the one from the tintype. It was large. And gold. Toby Rivera had said his sister's was German silver. "No, not like that. I mean the one belonging to the dead girl."

"No. Just saw her body. In the trash."

"Like she was dumped there?" Daniel said.

O'Shaughnessy's head shook. "No, I wouldn't

204

say that. To me, it was like she was laying there. Like Christ himself on the cross. You know what I mean? And she was half sitting. Except her head."

The railroaders—callous souls—even laughed at that.

Daniel said: "Let's say Groves killed the girl there." He pointed to where the struggle would have been, where the girl who was no more had been murdered. "Then he takes her body across the tracks, lays her down, spreads her arms, leaves her in this mountain of garbage."

The trio nodded.

"Then he crossed the tracks. That way." Pointing.

"Aye," O'Shaughnessy said.

"That's what happened," one of the railroaders said.

"But he's walking back that way." Daniel pointed west. "Why not cross the tracks here? Or just walk west from here? Why change the route?"

"Because he's drunk," one of the men said.

"Aye," O'Shaughnessy and the two agreed, nodding. "Just what are you, me lad, if you don't write for some newspaper?"

Instead of answering, Daniel thanked the railroaders for their time, and turned down the tracks. Another theory had started developing in his mind, one he wanted to test out on Doc Commager.

# CHAPTER SIXTEEN

It's after midnight, and the Independence Day dance is winding down. After Melody Rivera delivers farewells to her friends, she joins Francis Walking Man Groves, who has agreed to escort her home. The residents of Deming watch them depart. No one likes seeing that.

Walking Man and the girl, who strikingly resembles Groves's dead daughter, walk toward the railroad tracks. They turn west, on the south side of the tracks. In this part of town, where there are no streetlights, everything is pitch dark. The girl has to lead the way. They pass the shed, and as they pass, the killer sneaks out from his hiding spot. He wields a crowbar, raises it, and smashes it against Groves's head.

Groves falls, unconscious. For all the killer knows, he has killed this man. The girl screams, but no one hears, and she turns to run, but the killer is fast. He reaches her, grabs her, puts his hands around her throat. Enraged, he chokes her to death, but even that does not satisfy his need. He picks up the crowbar, and smashes it against the base of her neck.

Daniel's throat felt dry after the long explanation of how the girl was killed. He sipped the cup of water Doc Commager had handed him. Looking up at the fat doctor, he waited for the Pale Eyes medicine man to speak his mind.

"Interesting theory," Commager said, "but you're still fishing."

Daniel smiled. He had expected the doctor to say exactly that.

"On which side of Groves's head was the injury?" Daniel already knew the answer.

Commager had to think. The fat man closed his eyes. "Left," he answered at last, touching the spot above his own ear.

"If they were walking west, which is the way they would be heading to the Rivera home, the railroad tracks would be on his right side. And . . ."

"I see where you're going, Daniel, but if he killed the girl, carried the body across the tracks, and was walking back to town, he would be facing the east. . . ."

It was Daniel's turn to interrupt, even though The People considered such behavior rude. They always let a person finish speaking first, no matter how long, no matter how much they wandered, but Daniel had lost his patience, and he really wanted his theory to be right or, at least, accepted as possible. . . .

"Why would the killer walk back to town?" he asked. "Why run the risk of being seen?"

Commager shrugged. "Perue's livery stable is east of town. That's where he was staying."

Daniel nodded. "Yes, but if you or I had just killed someone, we wouldn't make a beeline back to our home. Not down a street that would soon be filled with people leaving the dance. Most killers I've met don't want to be seen."

The fat doctor grinned. "But," he countered, "by his own admission, not to mention in testimony by every official the next morning, Groves was drunk." He lifted his hand to stop more protest, but Daniel had no intention of interrupting the doctor again. "Like I said, Daniel, it's a good theory. But if this got brought up in trial, our solicitor, the honorable Mister Barber, he would gut that theory like that fish you keep trying to catch. Without bait. Or any damned water."

Nodding, Daniel accepted the rebuttal. Then he said: "Groves was facing east, according to O'Shaughnessy, when he was found."

"And?"

"The knot was on his left side. Away from the tracks."

Commager said nothing, letting the image settle in his mind. "It's still just a theory," the doctor said after a long while.

"I know."

Silence.

Finally Commager smiled and said: "It's early for my *siesta*, but I'm thinking I might need one. Or a drink." The doctor's head shook. "All right,

Daniel. I see where you're going, but I know Davy Barber pretty well, and I know that cadaver of a judge, Ichabod Embry. They're smart, and they know the law, know how to handle a jury, how to skewer a witness they don't like. Theories are well and good, but you can't just throw these ideas out there and expect the court to allow it. It's like I've been telling you, you must have evidence. Don't go fishing."

"I am Comanche," Daniel said. "We don't eat fish."

The doctor's grin widened, but his head shook. "I don't know what I'm gonna do with you."

Daniel flashed a smile back at the doctor. "You can tell me that my theory makes sense?"

"In theory," Commager said, "most theories make sense. But courts don't care much for just theories. But here's one for you."

Daniel nodded.

"The killer's hiding in the dark, right?"

Daniel expected the doctor to say that it was a half moon, but on the night of the 4th, the moon would have barely been at the quarter stage— and there are no streetlights on that side of town. This, however, was not what Doc Commager brought up.

"Why would a robber be waiting there? It's not a well-traveled section of our fair city, and, meaning no disrespect, most people walking that way aren't worth robbing."

Daniel's head bobbed. That was a good argument, but Daniel had another theory. "I don't believe robbery was the reason behind the killing."

This surprised Doc Commager. "Then what happened to the girl's crucifix?"

He shrugged. "Who knows? It fell off during the attack, or when her body was being dragged to the trash. Maybe it's in the trash. It would be difficult to find."

"Then why kill the girl?" Commager asked.

Daniel continued his theory.

After the girl has been killed, the murderer lifts her body and carries it to the trash pile, leaves her there. In the killer's mind, if she was the kind of girl that would associate with a man like Francis Groves, then trash is what this half-Mexican, half-Irish kid was. Just trash. He even takes the time to sit her up. Poses her body like Jesus Christ hanging on the crucifix.

Finally the killer throws the crowbar across the tracks, and hurries away.

The killer knew that everyone in Deming will think that Groves killed the girl. He was a stranger, a brutal white renegade who lived with the Apaches. He was drunk. He was the last person seen with the girl. They will say that he strangled her, broke her neck, then tumbled against the rails, hitting his head, accidentally killing himself. Saving the county the expense of a trial. He is guilty.

Everyone will believe this.

Even when it turns out that Francis Groves is still alive, everyone still believes him guilty. He will hang after a trial . . . or, perhaps, a lynching. It's not what the killer wanted, or expected, but it will suit him just the same.

"So she was killed because she danced with a stranger." Doc Commager was moving now, finding another bottle, drinking, gasping at the effect of whatever medicine he had found this time. He coughed, but did not cork the bottle. "Someone followed them, eh?"

Daniel's head shook. "No . . . waiting. He left before. While the girl was telling her friends good bye."

Another drink, another cough, but a wiry smile. "It's too bad you have not passed the bar in our fine territory, Daniel. I'd pay to see you square off against Davy Barber. All right, son, your theory is improving. But without facts . . ." He had a small pull, and this time corked the bottle and returned it to a drawer.

"Is it enough for an acquittal?"

The doctor no longer grinned. "Not with Embry holding court. And not in this town, this territory. You got an American jury, Daniel. Even if it was Mexican, there's still a lot of hatred for

211

the Apaches. And for a white man who has gone Apache . . ." His head shook.

"One more question for you, Doctor?"

"Just one? Hell, yes. Then I'll get you out of my office. You're probably scaring off my customers, kid. Lots of sick people in this part of the country. They need me." He belched.

"Say I'm right," Daniel said. "The man is waiting in the shadows. Groves and the girl walk past. The man sneaks out, raises the crowbar, smashes it against Groves's head." He paused. Commager motioned him to continue. "The wound on Groves's head is on his left side. Does that suggest anything to you?"

Commager thought, then shrugged.

Daniel raised his right hand over his head, brought it down. "What side would I likely have struck, swinging like that, at a man's back?"

It took a moment before it registered with the doctor. "By grab, Daniel. I see where you're going. You're telling me the killer's left-handed."

Still, Daniel knew it was just a theory. What he needed now was proof. That was why Daniel returned to the office of Squire Fuller.

"You again?" Working in his shirt sleeves, the justice of the peace shook his head. "I've warned David Barber about you, Killstraight. This whole deal is now in Ichabod Embry's court. You're his headache. And Barber's. Why don't you bother them, and leave me alone?"

Daniel let the *taibo* rant before politely asking: "May I see those transcripts again?"

Fuller pointed to the table. "Something told me you would be back. Left them right there."

So Daniel read closely, trying to find something that would prove his theory. A lie, or something else. He had suspects. Mark McLyler . . . Matt Callahan . . . Callahan's son Jules . . . the Mexican scalp hunter, Jemez . . . the fat smithy, G.K. Perue. All were at the dance. All were bothered or jealous of the attention the girl had given Francis Groves, and the attention Groves had given her. McLyler and Perue had even said they left the dance early.

Yet he could find nothing in the testimony that would prove anything he was thinking. Which did not surprise him. Pale Eyes did not always tell the truth, even when they swore to do just that on the Bible. He kept reading. Still nothing. Until . . . He rose, moved to the open door, and tapped on the wall.

Sighing, Squire Fuller looked up from a document he was reading. "What is it now, Killstraight?"

"There is something in these transcripts about Deputy Sheriff Moran being called as a witness, but he was unavailable. Why?"

"Embry opens court tomorrow. Can't you wait . . . ?" He didn't finish. Shaking his head, tossing the paper onto the desk top, he cursed slightly. "Moran's a good man. Solid. Capable. This wasn't his affair. The murder happened on the edge of town, but still under the city jurisdiction. Moran was there to help after the body was discovered. As for housing prisoners . . . city, county, federal, whatever . . . that's the sheriff's responsibility."

"What was he to testify about?"

"Talk about the body of the girl. He scouted for the Army during the Rebellion. Been in these parts a long time. He was the one who read the sign, said the girl was murdered a few yards from where we found the killer. He saw where the bastard had dragged the girl to the trash pile."

"So . . . where is he?" Daniel asked.

The justice of the peace shook his head.

Daniel considered what Squire Fuller had just told him. Police Chief McLyler had suggested that Moran was addle-brained, and had gone off collecting taxes instead of doing his job, but Fuller had just called him solid and capable.

"He rode out that morning," Fuller elaborated. "When Frazer and Roberts were taking the prisoner to jail and McLyler went to fetch the doctor, Moran rode off."

"Where?"

The squire shrugged.

The lawman had been gone almost a week. "No one's worried about him?" Daniel pursued.

"Glenn Moran can take care of himself."

Daniel considered this, but didn't know what to make of it. Looking across the room, he stared through the window. It was getting dark. Squire Fuller stood, picked up the paper he had been reading and stuck it in a tray in his desk, and then walked to the coat rack, fetching his jacket and hat.

"It's suppertime, Killstraight. I'd like to see my wife and kids. If you don't mind."

"Thank you," Daniel said.

"Just remember. Come tomorrow, you bother Embry. Not me. I got a wedding to officiate."

Daniel picked up his own hat, and headed out of the office, but turned to ask: "Do you happen to know if this Glenn Moran is left-handed?"

After thinking over Daniel's question for two silent minutes, Miguel the jailer finally raised his right arm.

"*Derecha*," he said.

Daniel nodded. Just as well, he thought. Trying to prove that a solid, capable deputy sheriff had murdered a girl, framed a stranger in town for the killing, then took off for parts unknown . . . Well, a theory like that would be sure to get Daniel run out of Deming on a rail. Yet at least he now knew Moran was right-handed. Squire Fuller hadn't known, or, at least, the justice of the peace had said he could not recall.

So Daniel found himself back in the jail for another night, guarding Francis Groves, waiting for the cowboys from Rincon—if they were still coming. Vanderhider again brought supper—roast sirloin *au jus*, whipped potatoes with beef gravy, asparagus, rolls, and Charlotte of peaches for dessert—and left immediately. The smell of the food made Daniel's mouth water, but he wasn't that interested in eating, although he took a plate. Instead, he watched.

Mark McLyler, Hank Roberts, and Jasper Frazer favored their right hands. Daniel frowned. Miguel was right-handed. Daniel looked at the food on his plate, decided to take it to the prisoner. He didn't ask for permission, just carried the plate across the room, opened the door, and walked down the dim, smelly corridor.

"Last meal?" Groves asked.

Without responding, Daniel slid the plate through the bottom of the cell door, but not before removing the knife. He didn't know what Groves had eaten since he had been jailed—probably nothing more than the proverbial bread and water, with coffee since Daniel's arrival—but the man ate with relish. Like he no longer had a wish to die.

Groves looked up, wiped his mouth with a shirt sleeve. "Ain't got manners," he said, swallowing.

Daniel smiled. "You're right-handed, too."

"Huh?"

Sighing, Daniel shook his head. "Nothing."

In a matter of moments, Groves had wolfed down the whole meal, then set the plate by the slop bucket on his bunk. Groves belched, shook his head, and said: "That's fine grub."

"Did you know the deputy sheriff?" Daniel hadn't planned on asking Groves anything. The question just popped out.

"What deputy sheriff?"

"A man named Moran." He had left his Old Glory in the office, and couldn't remember the deputy's first name.

"Here? In Deming?"

After Daniel nodded, Groves shook his head.

Daniel said after a long while. "Can't you remember anything that happened that night? Can't you remember walking that girl back to her place across the tracks? Or anything about the dance?"

Each question resulted in Groves just shaking his head.

"You playing nursemaid to me again?" Groves asked.

Daniel pulled up the stool, sat down, and sighed.

"I don't see why you even give a damn about me," Groves said.

Daniel had no response to that. The longer he stayed in Deming, the more he questioned himself. And the image of Rain Shower—the vision, or whatever it was—kept running through Daniel's head and he heard her saying: *Walking Man will help you.*

"Help you what?" Groves asked.

Daniel blinked. "What?"

Groves snorted. "You just said . . . I'll help you."

Daniel didn't realize he had said his thoughts aloud.

Groves moved up to the bars, putting his arms through them. It was growing darker outside, and the door to the office remained open, casting light down the hallway, illuminating the end of the jail.

"So help me," Daniel said. "Help me prove you're innocent."

Groves turned, spit. He was doing that again. Spitting on his life. "For all I know, Killstraight, maybe I did."

Which remained a real possibility Daniel accepted. Francis Groves could very well be the killer of the half-Mexican girl.

"Tell me," Daniel said.

"Tell you what?" Groves asked.

"Everything," Daniel said.

# CHAPTER SEVENTEEN

He blamed it all on the Rebellion. Before Abraham Lincoln and Jefferson Davis, North and South, blue and gray, and an ugly, numbing war came along, Francis Groves had a bright future before him as a store clerk in Dubuque, Iowa. Only as soon as news spread about Fort Sumter and Secession, the cry to preserve the Union rang out all across Iowa. So Francis Groves, then sixteen years old, joined up and was mustered into the 12th Iowa Volunteer Infantry.

Like most of the boys who enlisted, Groves thought of this march to war as something glorious. The boys from Dubuque and other Iowa towns and farms left for Benton Barracks in St. Louis late in 1861. There in Missouri, along the Mississippi River, they learned about death. Not from buck and ball or Rebel bayonets, but from measles, typhoid, pneumonia. Seventy-five soldiers died, never even seeing battle—seeing the elephant, as the saying went. Eventually the 12th joined Ulysses S. Grant and the war in Kentucky.

In Tennessee, Groves sort of saw the elephant, at Fort Donelson in the spring of 1862. A short while later, he learned just what war truly was on that first day at what the bluecoats called

Pittsburg Landing on the banks of the Tennessee River.

Southerners could fight, long and hard, and they had surprised the bluecoats before they even got a chance to sit down for breakfast. Francis Groves saw plenty of his Iowa friends fall that day. He would have died himself if the sergeant in charge hadn't ripped the sleeve off his shirt, jammed it atop a bayonet, and raised it high, waving it like the Stars and Stripes, yelling at the top of his lungs, above the din of battle: "Don't shoot! For God's sake, don't kill us! We surrender! We give up! Take us prisoners!"

Which is what the Confederates did. The next day, after more hard fighting, the Southern army withdrew back to Corinth, Mississippi, and Francis Groves walked with several other Iowa soldiers as a prisoner of war. Eventually they were marched down to Montgomery, Alabama, and found their new quarters.

Seven hundred bluecoats were locked inside an old brick cotton depot not far from a slow-moving Alabama River on Tallapoosa Street, right in the heart of Alabama's state capital.

At first, the depot still smelled of cotton, but soon it smelled much worse. The prisoners were crowded into that dungeon, only two hundred feet long and forty feet wide, along with the ever-present cockroaches, fleas, ticks, rats, gnats, flies, and mosquitoes. This far south, there was no spring. Summer temperatures had rolled in long before the 12th Iowa had landed at Pittsburg Landing, Tennessee.

Seven hundred men wearing only the clothes on their backs, if the rags could be called that. There were no blankets. Beds were the earthen floor, the rotting wooden planks. They roasted in this oven. They grew feverish. They sweated, then came down with the chills. The place stank of human waste, of the swamps nearby, of their own wretchedness. Before long, there was a new smell in the shed. The place stank of death.

"I don't know how many died in that pit," Groves told Daniel. "Maybe two hundred. Two hundred out of seven hundred. And we were only there six, seven, eight months."

In December, the survivors were shipped like cattle up north to Tuscaloosa. A month later, Groves and the survivors were paroled, and exchanged at Benton Barracks. By that time, Groves's health was pretty much broken, so he found himself discharged, invalided out of the Army, and he returned to Dubuque.

"They figured I'd contract consumption, be dead within a year," Groves said. "And I probably would have, had I stayed clerking in that mercantile. But I just couldn't see myself doing that any more. Couldn't see myself living in Dubuque. So I sold most of my traps, got me a new pair of boots, and just walked. Heard the preacher say that a lot of lungers were heading west . . . New Mexico Territory, the new Colorado Territory, and the even newer Arizona Territory. Good for the lungs. And nowhere near as boring as life in Dubuque. That's really what brought me to this country. Not my lungs. Not my health. It's just after all I'd seen in what little of that war I saw, Dubuque was just too damned boring a place to live."

He worked his way sometimes south, sometimes north, but always west. Clerking, farming, swamping saloons and livery stables, picking apples, churning butter. Or stealing eggs, corn, even liberating a mule in Indian Territory and crossing into Texas.

Toward the end of the war, he found himself in Denver City, Colorado Territory. He was there when Major John Chivington's boys brought their trophies from Sand Creek.

Daniel knew about Sand Creek, where Colorado volunteers had attacked a camp of peaceful Southern Cheyennes in eastern Colorado. They had massacred hundreds of them, mostly women, children, old people. It had been nothing short of butchery.

"Made me sick," Groves said. "Don't know what sickened me more, what those boys . . . some of them no older than me . . . proudly displayed as the spoils of war . . . I'm talking not just scalps, but ears, tongues and . . . and . . ." He had to stop to catch his breath, to keep the tears from falling into his beard.

Daniel didn't need to hear it from this *taibo*. He had heard from Cheyennes who had survived the attack. He knew. Everyone knew.

"After that, I was done with Denver, with Colorado," Groves said. "I'd seen what white men were capable of doing to other white men at Shiloh, and then at that hell hole in Montgomery. Now, when I had joined the Twelfth in Dubuque, I wasn't joining to free the slaves. Never even considered the Negroes. Hell, I wasn't even joining to save the Union. I was just joining to do something different. And all the time I was in Kentucky, Tennessee, Mississippi, Alabama, I still never really considered those slaves I saw. But when I saw what those butchers had done to babies and women . . . Indians, yes, but still women and kids . . . well, I don't know. Something inside of me must have snapped."

He left Colorado. Rode south. Over Raton Pass and into New Mexico, landing in Las Vegas for a while, then joining a bunch of white settlers bound for Prescott, Arizona Territory.

Around 1872, George R. Crook was placed in command of the Army in Arizona. The Yavapai War was heating up, and Crook hired Apache scouts to help the bluecoats. Throwing aside all that he had seen with the 12th Iowa Infantry, Francis Groves joined the 5th Cavalry.

He was there at the Salt River Cañon a few days after Christmas.

"We had the high ground, looking down into Skeleton Cave," Groves said. "I don't know . . . more than a hundred of us soldiers, some thirty Apache scouts. We had the Indians below surrounded, but they wouldn't surrender. So the officers start yelling at us to fire, fire, fire.

"Sergeant next to me, he cocks his carbine, grins, tells me to aim high. 'Hit the roof of the cave,' he tells me. Tells us all. So we did.

" 'It's like a hog killin'!' shouts this buck-toothed bastard beside me.

"And that's pretty much what it was. When we'd shot most of our cartridges, we rolled rocks down on those poor Indians below. Then, when it was all over, when the handful of those Indians still alive had surrendered, we went down."

Groves stopped talking for a long while. Daniel could hear the beat of his own heart, and the dripping of water in one of the cells near the office.

"It reminded me of Sand Creek," Groves said at last. "Only I hadn't been at that massacre. But I was at Skeleton Cave. Ever seen what a slug from a Spencer carbine can do to an Indian baby after ricocheting off a rocky roof?" He sighed. "War was pretty much over after that. The Yavapai, most of them, anyhow, surrendered at Camp Verde the following year. I served out my hitch, in the guardhouse for the most part. Wonder they didn't ship me off to Leavenworth. And having seen the results of Sand Creek and Skeleton Cave, I decided I was done with white folks. Went south. Started prospecting on my own. All that silver they've found around Tombstone . . . hell, I never got enough to buy me a decent pack mule.

"And then I found the Apaches." He laughed. "Well, they found me."

In the dim light, Groves smiled for a long time, not speaking, not sharing whatever he was thinking with Daniel.

"They found me," he said. "Had been bitten by a scorpion, was sick, out of my head. They could have killed me. Tortured me. Could have done anything, and I wouldn't have cared, but they took me into the Dragoon Mountains. Nursed me back to health."

Groves learned the customs of the Chiricahua, their language. He married a Chiricahua woman. In a few years, he was more Chiricahua than he was a white man. He lived with them in the Sierra Madres in Mexico, in the rugged mountains of southern Arizona. He even lived with them when they returned to the reservation at San Carlos.

And in September 1882, General George Crook returned to command the Army in Arizona. Crook sought out Francis Groves, now known among Indians and whites as Walking Man.

"Actually it was Al Seiber who came to my wickiup."

Seiber had served as Crook's chief of scouts during the early 1870s. A tough German, Seiber had fought for the North during the Rebellion, too, most prominently at Gettysburg. Like Francis Groves, he had headed west after the war, arriving in Arizona in the late 1860s.

"Crook said . . . 'To polish a diamond, there is nothing like its own dust.' He knew the best way to hunt down Apaches was to use Apache scouts. Seiber had told Crook . . . 'No one can find an Apache like another Apache . . . or Walking Man.' "

Groves's head shook.

"So you became a wolf for the bluecoats," Daniel said.

"Oh, it wasn't that hard." Groves had detected the disgust in Daniel's voice. "I'm sure all you Comanches love each other. You ever been married, Killstraight?"

Daniel saw Groves staring at him, but he could not look into the *taibo*'s eyes. He looked down at his moccasins, remembering too late that Rain Shower had made them. "No," he answered as a lone tear fell to the dirty floor.

"You will," Groves said. "And most of it'll be bliss. Was that way with me. But there will be disagreements. It happens in the best of families. And it happened among the Apaches."

In the spring of 1882, Geronimo and another Apache leader named Juh slipped onto San Carlos. They hunted down the Mimbreño Apaches led by Loco, who had recently always been pushing for a peace with the white men. They killed the chief of the reservation's Indian police. They led hundreds of Apaches, most of them Chiricahuas, off San Carlos and into Mexico.

"My wife, my daughter, my mother-in-law, many of my friends rode with Geronimo," Groves said. "But it wasn't their idea. Geronimo made them go with him. Would have killed them if they didn't. I was in Tucson when this happened. When I returned, found my family missing, I went a little crazy. Busted up the agent's place, blaming him, blaming all the white men. 'Course, I should have been blaming Geronimo and Juh. So they locked me in the stockade for a spell. When Crook sent Seiber to find me that fall, I was more than happy to join him, to join Mimbreños and other Chiricahuas. I was happy to go looking for my family."

Groves served under Captain Emmett Crawford's scouts, more as an interpreter for the bluecoats and Apaches. The Mexican and U.S. governments had negotiated an agreement that allowed soldiers in what was called "hot pursuit" to cross the border to hunt down

Apaches. Crook knew exactly how to impress the Apaches, even warmongers like Geronimo. Juh drowned in the fall of 1883, so then only Geronimo was left.

Later that year, Crook met with the renegade Apaches. It took a lot of parleys, but Geronimo finally agreed to bring in his people. Crook trusted Geronimo. He let the Apache gather his people, and take his time in bringing them across the border.

By the spring of 1884, to the surprise of white soldiers and civilians across Arizona—and maybe even Crook himself—Geronimo lived on the reservation. So did other warrior Apaches, men like Nana and Chihuahua.

Peace returned, ever so briefly, ever so tenuously, to Arizona.

In May of 1885, however, Geronimo got drunk on *tizwin*. Fearing he would be arrested, he led a small band back toward Mexico, back into the Sierra Madres. Crawford, the Apache scouts, and Walking Man went back across the border, hunting down Geronimo and his renegades.

In January, those soldiers and scouts were ambushed. Not by Apaches, but by Mexican scalp hunters.

"Damned Mexican sons-of-bitches." Groves balled his fingers tightly into fists. "Thought we were Geronimo's boys. Or maybe they knew who we were and just didn't give a damn. I mean, an

Apache scalp is an Apache scalp. Didn't give us any chance. Just opened fire. Crawford . . . God bless him . . . he jumps on a rock, waves a white handkerchief. He's yelling . . . '¡*Soldados norteamericanos*! ¡*Soldados*! ¡*Soldados*!' And the bastards shot him in the head."

An Apache scout named Dutchy pulled Crawford out of the line of fire. Dutchy then shot the bastard who had wounded Crawford. Walking Man put a bullet in the forehead of the commander of the scalp hunters.

"Eye for an eye. Only it wasn't. Emmett Crawford was ten times the man that the Mex was."

Crawford was still alive, but barely, when they got him behind the rocks. He never woke up.

A stand-off followed. Eventually the Mexicans went their way, and the Americans, after burying their dead, including Emmett Crawford, returned to Fort Bowie.

"Was Jemez one of those scalp hunters?" Daniel asked.

"Said he was," Groves answered tightly, barely audible. "I had a few run-ins with him in Sonora. Lordsburg. Tucson. In the Sahuaripa district. And then . . . here in Deming."

Daniel knew he should change the subject. Get away from scalp hunters.

"So you returned to America. And then?"

"You know the story." Groves's fists

229

unclenched. He reached up to finger his ration pouch. "Geronimo didn't have many warriors. Didn't have a chance. Time came when he's got both armies hounding him, scalp hunters. That spring, he meets with Crook and those Apache scouts. Decides to come in peacefully. Again. Crook tells the Apaches one thing, but the War Department won't agree to what Crook has told the Apaches. And you know as well as I do that the Apaches don't tolerate lies. Crook feels the same. But it doesn't matter. Geronimo gets scared again, thinks they'll hang him once they're back on the reservation. Because some damned whiskey-runner showed up, got the Apaches drunk, and scared the hell out of Geronimo. So he turned tail and fled. Which led the War Department to get rid of Crook, bring in Nelson Miles, who didn't have a clue about how things work in this country. Months pass, and then Miles brings back some Apache scouts. They meet. A truce is declared. Geronimo surrenders at Skeleton Cañon."

Groves shook his head, spit onto the floor.

"And in September, the Chiricahuas are sent to Florida. And so are the scouts."

"But not you," Daniel said.

"I was out of the Army by then. Done with scouting. I was looking for my family."

Daniel hated to ask the next question. "Your wife . . . your daughter?"

A long silence before Groves answered: "I never found them. Best damned white scout in the territory, but I couldn't find them. But, down in the Sierra Madres, I found an old friend of mine, big old boy named Jlin-Litzoque . . . means Yellow Horse . . . and he told me what had happened. He had found their bodies." Groves's sigh sounded more like a sob. "Sand Creek," he said. "All over again."

"I'm sorry," Daniel said.

Groves's head nodded slightly. He wiped his eyes. Sniffed. "My daughter's name meant Hawk Singing." He nodded.

Daniel thought of his father Marsh Hawk. Maybe that was why he had come here, to this place, with no real reason. Maybe his father's spirit had led him here, or perhaps Daniel's own *puha*.

"I have seen the tintype," Daniel said.

Groves smiled at some memory. "Taken right before her puberty ceremony. Dressed like White Painted Woman." The smile disappeared. The face cracked with pain.

"The girl who is no more . . . ," Daniel said, "she looked very much like your daughter."

"Yeah."

"We must find the one who killed her."

Groves nodded. "I can do it, Killstraight. Just get me out of here."

Daniel didn't know what to say, so he felt

231

relief when someone blocked the light coming through the doorway from the office and shouted: "Killstraight! Get your ass out here. And if you want to live, Groves, get away from that damned window!"

# CHAPTER EIGHTEEN

Every gun in the office, including Miguel's heavy double-barrel shotgun, was aimed at the thick, front door.

As Daniel stepped through the doorway into the jail's office, he heard the pounding outside the front entry. His first thought, his first fear, was that dozens of angry Deming residents were ramming the door to get inside to lynch Francis Groves. It didn't take long, however, for him to realize that the pounding on the door was not from a battering ram, but a fist.

"Damn it! Open up!" someone was yelling. "Open up! I got to see the law!"

Daniel didn't recognize the voice. Before moving, he glanced back down the passage toward the cells, then he pulled the door shut. That would make it even darker in the cells, which would make it harder for some assassin to put a bullet through Francis Groves's head.

"There's been a murder!" the voice outside the door cried.

The panic inside the cramped office seemed palpable. Someone had been killed. But was the man lying? Was it a trick to get the door open? Was there perhaps a mob waiting outside, ready to hang Francis Groves, and kill anyone who tried to stop them? Frazer glanced at McLyler, who lowered his revolver, and shot a worried look toward the older policeman, Roberts. Miguel continued to point both barrels of the shotgun at the thick door.

"Open up!" the voice yelled.

McLyler looked around the room, and said: "It might be a trick."

"Who gives a damn?" Frazer said. "Let them have that son-of-a-bitch."

"McLyler . . . you in there?" the voice shouted. "For God's sake, man, open up! Moran's dead. Do you hear me? Glenn Moran's dead!"

A long moment passed, before McLyler slid his Smith & Wesson into the shoulder holster, looked at Roberts, then Daniel. The police chief walked to the door, barricaded by a two-by-eight bar.

"It could be a trick, Mark," Roberts warned.

Although McLyler put his hands on the bar, he didn't lift it. Instead, he asked: "Who are you?"

"Vince Ford!" came the answer. "You know who I am, McLyler. I ride for Houston Jim Lynne's brand, the Four-Five-Connected."

Daniel frowned. The riders from Rincon had made good time. Vince and Frank, Charley and Jimmy had made it to Deming, covering those sixty miles in less than two days. A Comanche, Daniel thought, could have done it in one, but for a bunch of Pale Eyes with bellies full of Rincon's worst whiskey, it took a lot of skill on horseback, along with good horseflesh, to cover that distance across that desert.

"Damn it!" Vince yelled. "McLyler . . . I swear to God . . . we found Glenn Moran in an arroyo north of town. Deader than dirt, man. Shot down like a dog."

Had it been anyone else, Daniel believed, Mark McLyler would not have acted with such caution, but Vince Ford had liked the Rivera girl. Not only that, Daniel had warned the Deming lawman that Vince Ford was heading to town for his own brand of justice.

Without speaking, McLyler motioned Miguel to keep the shotgun trained at the door, and for Roberts and Frazer to move into the room's corners. The police chief glanced at Daniel, who had no weapon, and then said to the door: "Vince, I'm going to open the door. You can come in, but you come in slowly, hands over your head." McLyler, to Daniel's surprise, sounded strong, confident, despite the beads of sweat on his forehead, the nervous shaking of his hands. "When you come inside, you come in alone," he added. "If we see anyone with you, or anyone close to you, we'll blow you apart. Understand?"

"Christ Almighty, McLyler. What in the bitter hell has . . . ?"

"I mean it, Vince." The police chief lifted one end of the bar, shifted position to get a better grip, and, after a pause, hefted the two-by-eight out of its slots, then leaned it against the wall.

Daniel held his breath as Mark McLyler pulled the door open.

It was the cowboy from Rincon, all right. He looked worn out, dusty, and not as tall as he had appeared to Daniel the last time he had seen him. Daniel saw the he wasn't even wearing his shell belt and revolver.

As Ford came in and looked nervously at the weapons trained on him, Daniel looked past the cowboy, to the outside. He knew then the cowhand had spoken the truth. He was alone. For outside, all Daniel could see was darkness, the flaring lanterns across the street, and the outline of a horse at the hitching rail. One horse. At least, that was all Daniel could make out.

"Where are the others?" McLyler asked.

"What others?" Vince looked confused.

"Damn it, man!" McLyler slammed the door shut, causing Vince Ford to jump back. The lawman didn't bolt the door. He pointed vaguely, haphazardly toward Daniel. "We know you left Rincon with three other cowhands. We know you came to lynch our prisoner. It's a white man, Vince. Not an Indian, though he's more Apache now than he ever was white. So, where the hell are those friends of yours, Ford?"

Vince staggered farther back. He looked at Daniel, then at the guns aimed at him. His eyes remained uncomprehending. He looked at Daniel again, but Daniel detected no recognition in the bloodshot eyes.

"It's Moran, Mark." Vince faced the police chief. "We found his body at Apache Arroyo."

"Where are the others?" McLyler demanded.

"There ain't no others, Mark. I rode in here alone. Left Frank at the arroyo with Moran's body."

"He said . . ." Again McLyler gestured toward Daniel.

"Christ, Mark. I don't recollect this stranger. But, hell, yeah, I was drunker than a skunk when we found out about Melody. We all were. Yeah, I reckon I said I was coming here to string up the bastard who killed Melody. But I don't remember that. Don't remember much of anything. Just riding like hell. I liked Melody. She liked me. Hell, I got a tintype of her hanging above my bunk at the ranch." He stopped to catch his breath and his eyes traveled around the room. "But it don't matter no more. You got the killer locked up. I'll watch him hang. But you gotta believe me, Mark. I tell you, swear to God, we've found Moran's body."

There was silence inside the office. Just the wind, and the distant sounds of Deming—music, the organ-grinder, laughter probably from a saloon. A horse, Vince's horse, blowing after its pounding ride.

"Miguel," McLyler said.

The old jailer lowered the hammers on the shotgun, and walked to the door. It opened just enough for him to slip through, then McLyler closed the door again and stepped back to lean against it. "There were two others with you," he said. "Besides Frank."

Vince took off his hat, as if trying to remember. "How the hell . . . ?" He didn't finish, but shot another look at Daniel. "And who the hell is that?"

Daniel didn't introduce himself. No one introduced him.

"Mark,"—Vince raised his hands, moving them far from his waist—"I ain't even wearing a gun. Left it with Frank. He was damned spooked. You don't know what we found. You don't know about Moran."

The door opened ever so slightly, and McLyler moved away from it. Roberts and Frazer sucked in their breaths, brought up their weapons again, but it was only Miguel who slid inside, closing the door, shaking his head. "No one is out there," the jailer said. "He speaks the truth. He is alone."

McLyler cursed. Roberts and Frazer put away their weapons, and Frazer gave Daniel a bitter look, as if Daniel had lied about the whole damned situation. As if all of this was his fault.

Even McLyler sent Daniel a hard, suspicious

238

glare before he stepped around the cowboy, and said: "What the hell do you mean that Glenn Moran's dead?"

Vince Ford didn't remember Daniel. Daniel knew that whiskey robbed memories from both The People and the *taibos*. But the cowhand from Rincon hadn't forgotten that Melody Rivera had been murdered.

Along with Frank, Charley, and Jimmy, Vince had crossed the Río Grande, had ridden hard, but when they had neared the Hanging Slash-W range, Jimmy and Charley had had enough. They hadn't been as drunk as Frank and Vince, and they'd ridden hard just to tell Vince about what had happened in Deming.

Vince had sworn at them, long and hard, cursed them until the whiskey rebelled in his stomach, and he had slid from his saddle to throw up. By the time his stomach was purged, by the time he could sit up, could climb back into the saddle, Charley and Jimmy had ridden away.

"It was just me and Frank," Vince said.

So they rode to the nearest line shack, swapped their worn-out mounts for two fresh horses from a cowhand named Culver, and then made for Deming.

"I kept thinking about Melody," Vince said, his voice honest. "Kept picturing that photo I got of her. Hanging above my bunk."

"A tintype?" Daniel asked.

The cowboy shot an angry look at Daniel. "Yeah," he said. Then asked: "Who the hell are you?"

"He's an Indian lawdog," Frazer answered.

"What about Moran?" McLyler demanded, trying to keep Vince focused.

*Well,* Daniel thought, *now we know who got the fourth tintype from the girl who is no more.* It made sense. That's why Vince Ford had ridden all this way. Not to string up some Apache Indian, but because he had been sweet on the girl, and she must have liked him.

"We got to Apache Arroyo," Vince said. "God, I ain't had nothin' but jerky and some hot water since we left the line shack. Can I get a cup of coffee? Or something stronger?"

McLyler motioned to Daniel, the closest to the coffee pot, as he said: "Moran. Damn it. What about Moran?"

"He's dead."

Daniel listened as he filled the cup and brought it to Vince Ford, who was now sitting in a chair, hat on his knee. He was massaging his temples with his long fingers.

The stink had drawn them to Moran. Although dark, the moon shone bright when the clouds parted. Frank had gestured toward the arroyo, insisting that they should find out what was causing that horrible smell.

" 'The hell with that,' I told him. We weren't that far from Deming."

But Frank was older, wiser, and must have had a good idea what was causing that smell. He had eased his horse toward the arroyo, and reluctantly Vince had followed. When the horses had become skittish, they had dismounted, hobbled the mounts, and walked the few feet toward the edge of the dry creekbed.

" 'It's just a damned horse,' I told him. But Frank disagreed, and then he crossed himself. 'It ain't,' he told me. You see, Frank had spotted the dead man lying a few feet away from the dead horse. Coyot's had gotten to 'em both, horse and man. Vultures."

Daniel handed Vince the coffee, but Vince didn't drink, didn't even acknowledge the tin cup that was now in his hand. He just stared. Likely he didn't see anything in the room, not McLyler or his lawmen, or Daniel. Right now, Vince Ford was seeing a dead man and a dead horse in an arroyo in a dark desert.

After several minutes, the cowhand's Adam's apple bobbed. He closed his eyes, and shook his head. "Thought the poor bastard had just ridden over the edge, somehow. Horse wreck is all. Accident." A heavy sigh escaped Vince's lungs.

He looked up at Mark McLyler, almost apologetic. "But Frank struck a lucifer. And we seen his face. Moran's face. Varmints hadn't gotten to it . . . yet."

A long minute passed before Vince continued.

"There was a hole right here." Vince tapped his forehead, a little to the left of his right eye. "That part of his head was just black. Eyebrow had been singed off completely." Vince took a drink of the coffee.

"Shot," Roberts said softly.

Vince nodded. "Yeah. Real close. Frank found another bullet in his leg, and he looked to have been shot in his shoulder, too, but . . . that . . . well . . . the varmints . . ."

"And the horse?" McLyler asked.

"Don't know. Frank seemed to think the bullet through Moran's leg might have killed the horse. But we ain't scouts, trackers. And it was dark. Didn't read no sign. Besides, we'd seen enough. Moran had been shot. His damned brains blowed out by someone who must've just put a rifle barrel on his forehead and pulled the trigger. Like he was shootin' a skunk. So Frank and me, we drew lots. I won. Frank had to stay." He sipped more coffee. "I rode here."

"Any idea how long he'd been dead?" McLyler asked.

"Man can mummify out there," Vince said just barely loud enough for Daniel to hear. "But with them coyot's and vultures . . ." His head shook.

"Jasper," McLyler said to Frazer. "Get fresh

242

horses. We're riding to Apache Arroyo. You and me and Roberts." Frazer nodded.

The police chief then moved to Vince's side, and squatted to be at his level. "I'm getting you a fresh mount. Can you ride with us? Make sure we get to the right spot?"

Vince sighed. The cup trembled in his hand, but he nodded.

"I'll let Judge Embry know what's happening," McLyler said, and motioned Daniel and Miguel to the far side of the office. "Roberts will stay here," McLyler said softly to Daniel and the jailer, "till we come back with horses. Once we ride off, though, you two have to stay here and guard that sum-bitch." His head tilted slightly toward the cells.

"Shouldn't you wait until morning?" Miguel asked.

"I'm not leaving Glenn Moran out there any longer than necessary." Mark McLyler sounded twenty years older, and Daniel had to respect the lawman for his professionalism. The People would not have left one of their own to coyotes, ravens, ants, and vultures, either. McLyler sucked in a deep breath, held it several moments, then slowly exhaled. "But y'all need to be careful"—his voice dropped to a whisper—"in case Vince is lying. In case those boys are waiting for us to leave . . . so they can take Groves out of this calaboose without much of a fight."

# CHAPTER NINETEEN

Hank Roberts took the coffee cup from Vince Ford's hand. The cowhand didn't appear to notice. He just sat there, staring at the floor. Following orders, Miguel slipped the bar back across the door when McLyler and Frazer left to get the horses and talk to Judge Embry. Then it was just a matter of waiting.

Daniel moved to the desk, picked up his Old Glory. There was something he wanted to check, and it frustrated him when it took a while to find it. Once found, he walked to the cot where Hank Roberts sat feeding .44-40 cartridges into a shell belt.

The older lawman merely glanced at Daniel, then went right on forcing bullets into the belt.

"I have something to ask you," Daniel said.

The lawman pulled a brass cartridge out of the box, rolled it between thumb and forefinger, then looked up at Daniel. "Yeah," he said. There was no friendliness in his voice, but Daniel hadn't expected that.

"Two days ago Chief McLyler said it wasn't so unusual for the deputy"—Daniel was careful not to say the dead man's name—"to go riding off collecting taxes or something. And you said . . . 'I don't know.'"

"So?" Roberts stopped rolling the bullet, but appeared to be fascinated by it as he held it in his hand, not looking at Daniel.

Daniel asked: "What did you mean?"

Roberts shifted, readjusted the gun belt, and pushed the big cartridge through the open slot. "Nothing."

Daniel remained quiet and merely looked down at Hank Roberts. Waiting.

It worked. Roberts tossed the belt aside, and closed the box of shells. "Mark wanted that deputy's job," Roberts said, finally looking into Daniel's eyes. "He didn't get it. Moran got picked. So Mark don't think that much of Glenn, but Glenn ain't a bad guy." The police officer's eyes fell away from Daniel. Roberts sighed, and said: *"Wasn't* a bad . . ."

"He was there that morning?" Daniel said, prodding just a bit. "When the girl's body was found."

Roberts nodded. "Yeah, Glenn looked around."

"He read the sign," Daniel said, filling in what he already knew. "Saw where the girl had been killed . . . where her body had been dragged to the trash."

Another nod from Roberts as he wet his lips. "Yeah. Everybody said the drunken renegade had done it. Glenn wanted to make damn' sure. Squire Fuller come by. And that big Mex. So while we were carting that bastard, there"—he nodded to the cell-block—"Glenn hung around. Checking on things."

Daniel said: "Squire Fuller said the deputy sheriff just rode off. Did he . . . ?" He paused, understanding what Hank Roberts had just told him. "What big Mex?" he asked then, though he had a good idea of the answer.

"Big cut-throat who rides for Matt Callahan."

"Jemez?"

"Yeah."

Daniel thought about this. "Was Callahan still in town? His son?"

"I don't know. Didn't see them. And I ain't their keeper."

Daniel thought about what Roberts was saying. "But it was Jemez? You're sure it was him?"

Roberts snorted. "You don't mistake that big hoss."

Daniel hadn't expected this—that Jemez had remained in town. Jemez went everywhere with Matt Callahan. At least that was the impression Daniel had gotten. So he'd have to find out if Matt and Jules Callahan had also remained in town, but that shouldn't be hard to do. Right now, he needed to know more about Deputy Sheriff Glenn Moran.

"Did the deputy sheriff say where he was going?" Daniel asked. "Before he rode out?"

Roberts shrugged. "Not to me. I don't know. You'd have to ask Squire Fuller, I reckon. I'm pretty sure Moran didn't talk to Mark. And we was all pretty much busy. Hell, I don't know if anyone even saw Moran ride out of town." Another pause. "Except Perue."

Daniel's eyebrows lifted. "Perue?"

"Yeah. See, the squire sent me out to find Moran . . . at the inquest, next day. Asked me to fetch Moran, when we realized he wasn't here when it came time for Moran to say what he saw. That's when we all realized we hadn't seen Moran since the morning we found the girl. So I'm about to get up, see if I can fetch him, and Perue says that the deputy rode off that morn. Said he came to the livery, fetched his horse, and headed off."

They looked at each other, Daniel and Roberts, but didn't speak for several seconds. "Did Perue say where?" Daniel asked.

Roberts shook his head.

"No one worried about him?" Daniel asked. "No one tried to find him?"

Roberts again indicated no. "The squire said we didn't need Moran's testimony, anyhow. And, hell, Mark was right about one thing . . . Moran's a good man. He could take care of himself. At least . . ."

"How about you?" Daniel asked. "Any idea as to where Moran was going?"

"To Apache Arroyo," Roberts snapped. "To get his head blowed off."

Daniel knew he had pushed the policeman as far as he could. Nodding his thanks, he turned to walk away, but stopped and said: "He was a good tracker, wasn't he?"

Roberts shrugged. "I don't know about that. Heard he'd scouted for the Army here and there. Before my time. Hunted with him some, though. Yeah, I guess he knew how to read a trail." Roberts had picked up the shell belt, reopened the box of .44-40s, even though all the slots for shells were filled.

Back at the desk, Daniel picked up his notebook and pencil, turned to a new page, but he just stared. Seeing a map form on the paper.

A trail leading from the railroad tracks. North out of town. To a place called Apache Arroyo where the deputy sheriff had met up with the man who had killed the girl who is no more. Where the killer had then ambushed Moran. Killed his horse, and walked casually up to the wounded lawman, put the muzzle right near his forehead, and squeezed the trigger.

In the language of The People, Daniel whispered: "No." Thinking: *It couldn't have happened like that. Not quite. The girl had been killed shortly after midnight. Her body had been found at dawn. Too long. Moran might have found a trail, but he wouldn't have come across the killer. Not after all that time.*

He flipped back the pages of the book till he

found notes from his talk with Squire Fuller. Daniel read: *FULLER. Fraz and Roberts bring Groves to jail, MacLiar gets Dr. & Moran rides off.*

Daniel directed a question at Miguel: "How far away is this Apache Arroyo from here?"

The old Mexican shrugged. *"Ocho* kilometers."

*Five miles*, Daniel thought. *Five hours after the murder of the girl. No, that just doesn't figure.* Sighing, he jotted down in the margins what he had just learned from Hank Roberts, then reread: *Perue said Moran got horse from livery and rode out.*

G.K. Perue. Daniel had hoped he wouldn't have to talk to that foul-mouthed, ugly blacksmith ever again.

He wrote another name down, too. A name that sickened him. The name of someone else who, surprisingly, had remained in town. *Jemez.*

The last words Mark McLyler had issued to Daniel and Manuel before heading out had been a warning: "Listen," McLyler had said. "I told Judge Embry that we need to keep this quiet. At least for now. Word gets out that Glenn Moran's dead, this town will blow up. They'll storm in here, kill y'all, probably not even bother using a rope on Groves."

Daniel had said: "But this means he didn't kill that girl."

"The hell it does," replied McLyler. "Just stay put. We'll be back as soon as we can."

Five minutes after McLyler, Ford, Roberts, Frazer, and two men Daniel had seen around town but didn't know by name had departed, Daniel rose from his chair and said to Manuel: "I'll be back."

Sure, McLyler had told Daniel to stay with Manuel, keep an eye on the jail, protect Francis Groves, but Daniel didn't think there was any real threat to the prisoner. And he hoped that Judge Embry would not throw oil on these flames, that he would not let anyone know that Glenn Moran was dead.

He believed Vince Ford had told the truth, that Deputy Sheriff Glenn Moran was dead in a place called Apache Arroyo. And, for the first time, Daniel felt absolutely certain that Francis Groves wasn't guilty of killing the girl.

"Go on," Manuel said. "I'll be fine."

Daniel left. He moved with a purpose and urgency, making his way through the dark streets toward G.K. Perue's livery stables. What worried him was that she might not be at the stables, not at this time of night, or she might be passed out in one of her stalls. She wasn't, though. Not yet. The loud voice singing told him that much.

I'm glad I fought ag'in' 'er.
I only wish we won.

I ain't askin' any pardon
For anything I done.


The big woman was leaning against the door to an empty stall, both legs splayed out, one boot off, the other on the wrong foot, covered with flakes of hay.

"Hey," he said, looking down at her.

It took a while before her eyes could focus on Daniel. "Where the hell is my Lad?" she sang out. "Where the hell is Ladislaus?"

Daniel kneeled. He pried the jug from her fingers. G.K. didn't resist.

"You seen him?" she asked, and burped.

He sighed bitterly. He might not get any information out of her, not with her in this condition, but he had to try. "I need you to remember something for me," he said. "About when the deputy sheriff rode out of here?"

"Who?"

"Moran!" Daniel snapped, saying the name of the dead man. "The deputy sheriff. During the inquest. He was supposed to testify."

She blinked, and then resumed the out-of-tune wail.

Daniel didn't give a damn. He had a pretty good idea what the *taibos* would say once they looked at the body of Glenn Moran. They would say that, after killing the Rivera girl, Groves had wandered into the desert, only to be found at

Apache Arroyo by a dutiful deputy sheriff named Glenn Moran. Groves had then killed Moran's horse, and wounded, then executed, Glenn Moran himself. Then in a drunken stupor he wandered back to town, back to the place where he had murdered a girl. The Pale Eyes God had exacted His own justice by having Groves stumble along the railroad tracks, hit his head, knock himself out so he would be found that morning by a railroader.

No Pale Eyes jury would ever convict any other *taibo* on such an outlandish theory. But they would definitely believe this is what had happened, because the accused was a renegade white man who had become an Apache. Because this is what they wanted to believe.

He turned to leave, although he remained unsure about his next move. But a massive palm stopped him, shoving him so far back, he almost tripped over one of Perue's outstretched legs.

"What the hell are you . . . ?" Ladislaus Radegunde stopped midsentence. "Hey, you're the damned Comanch' from the train."

Carefully, without answering, Daniel stepped over Perue's leg. The brakeman's breath smelled like he was well in his cups, too, but not as roostered as the woman.

Perue sang out something that made absolutely no sense to Daniel. Or, apparently, to Radegunde, since he ignored her and pointed a finger underneath Daniel's nose, hissing: "Answer me."

Daniel fought down his growing anger, felt his face flush. Then, after letting out a long breath, he said, in what he thought a calm tone: "She saw the deputy sheriff leave here days ago. I just wanted to find out if he told her where he was going."

Radegunde gave Daniel a cold stare, then kneeled down beside Perue. He pulled her toward him, which took some effort, and asked her what Daniel wanted to know. Getting only a blank expression as a response, he cursed her before asking again. He even tried screaming at her. But he got the same result every time. After several moments, Radegunde let out a heavy sigh, looked up, saying: "It's damned hopeless, Killstraight. Come back tomorrow . . . late tomorrow. Hell, maybe the day after tomorrow."

Daniel was already walking outside, heading for the jail. He was angry that Perue had been so drunk, she couldn't add anything that would help Daniel with his theory. No, it wasn't a theory. It was a guess, and probably a wild one. But he was speculating that Jemez had murdered the girl, then, when he saw Moran snooping around, he had followed him to Apache Arroyo, and shot the deputy dead.

Fishing. Again. No bait. No water.

He moved back through the main part of Deming, stopping only briefly as he saw a cadaver of a figure, wearing a tall silk hat, stop in front of the open doors of a boxcar turned into a saloon to light a cigar. Daniel watched as Judge Ichabod Embry drew on the big stogie, and then went inside.

Which made Daniel nervous. He could picture the judge getting drunk, maybe even intentionally, to let the other intoxicated cut-throats of Deming know what had happened to the upstanding deputy named Glenn Moran. They would then storm the jail, kill Miguel, and murder Francis Groves.

Daniel practically ran the rest of the way. He reached the jail, knocked loudly on the door, demanding that Miguel let him in. He felt like a damned fool. He never should have left the old jailer alone. No answer. He called out the old Mexican's name, and hit the door harder. Finally, out of frustration, he grabbed the handle and pushed on the door.

To his surprise, it opened. Miguel hadn't even locked the door, let alone lowered the bar into the slots.

"Miguel!" Daniel cried out.

The door leading to the cells remained open.

Expelling a *taibo* curse, Daniel pulled the door closed, and hurried across the room, through the doorway, stopping when he saw Miguel standing next to the last cell down the hall.

Groves's left arm was around Miguel's throat,

pinning the old man against the iron bars. He had the jailer in a fine choke hold. Daniel grunted, wondering if maybe he was wrong, after all. Maybe Francis Groves was a cold-blooded killer.

"Get me out of here," Groves said, "or I'll bleed out this old Mex like I would a buck deer."

In his right hand, Groves held a fork, the tines directed at old Miguel's throat.

# CHAPTER TWENTY

Daniel said: "You don't have to do this." He watched Miguel as the fork pressed against his throat.

"The hell I don't," Groves said. "Fetch the keys. Get me out of here."

Somewhere, somehow, Daniel heard Rain Shower's voice again, telling him: *Walking Man will help you.*

He said: "I need your help, Groves."

"You need to help this old coot first," Groves replied. "And me." The words might have been desperate, but Daniel detected no panic in Groves's voice. He sounded like an Indian. Not resigned. Not anxious. But somehow steady.

He didn't think Groves would kill the jailer, and from the look on Miguel's face, the Mexican wasn't really afraid, either.

"Will you help the girl who looked like your daughter?" Daniel said.

Groaning, the prisoner closed his eyes tightly. Daniel pressed on. "Two people in this town think you are innocent. Both of us are here tonight." Miguel nodded his agreement, and Daniel noticed the fork pull away from the jailer's throat.

"Get the keys, Killstraight," Groves said. "We don't have much time."

It took Daniel five minutes to find the right ring of keys. He also discovered a pair of manacles, which he fastened to Miguel's wrists, but not too tightly. Likewise, the bandanna used as a gag could easily be pulled down from the jailer's mouth with his fingers—since Daniel had secured the old man's hands in front of him. As Daniel rose, he put a hand on the old man's shoulder.

"When McLyler returns," he said, "make it look good."

"*Yo se*," the jailer said.

"Come on, Killstraight!" Groves said.

"*Gracias*," Daniel told the old man.

"*De nada*," Miguel said.

Groves walked out of the cell. Daniel closed the door, locked it behind him, and tossed the ring of keys onto the hallway floor near the fork that Groves had disposed of.

"You sure we can trust that *hombre* not to cry out an alarm?" Groves asked.

Daniel shrugged. "He was one of the first men here to help me. He knows you didn't kill that girl. Yes, I trust him."

Groves grunted in resignation as they walked down the hall.

"I can walk the five miles to Apache Arroyo without a problem," Groves said. "But you . . ." He snorted after a glance at Daniel, who pulled open the door to the jail office just slightly. "We'll need to steal a horse for you."

Daniel nodded. "I know where we can get one."

He thought about the paint horse he had admired in one of the corrals at G.K. Perue's livery.

They rode northwest in the moonlight, Daniel on the pinto, and Francis Groves mounted on a black Morgan, after having decided that it would be good idea to have a good horse, after all. Neither G.K. Perue nor her husband had been at the livery. Daniel wouldn't call it stealing, exactly, more like borrowing without permission, but he felt good. In the old days, The People had been legendary as the best horse stealers across the Southwest.

As they rode, Daniel ran a theory through his mind again, and kept looking to his right to make sure Francis Groves still rode with him, surprised he had agreed to this idea.

It made sense. Jemez had killed the girl who is no more, then headed out of town, back toward the Four Gates Ranch before deciding he needed to return to Deming. To wait there. To make sure that everyone thought Francis Groves, the stranger in town, had killed the girl. Only, when Moran rode out on the trail Jemez had left, the giant scalp hunter had ridden a wide loop around the deputy. He had reached Apache Arroyo first, waited, then killed the lawman when he reached the spot.

Before leaving Deming, Groves had wanted to study the sign around the trash dump. But Daniel had persuaded him to pick up the trail at Apache Arroyo, saying the trash dump was too risky, that they could be spotted, and that finding a trail a week after the murder would be practically impossible. Besides, he had said, it was dark, and, even though the moon had risen, a man can't find a trail at night.

"I can," Groves had assured him.

Daniel hoped to find the trail Jemez had left when he rode out of Deming. Or find where he had doubled back. Groves figured the arroyo would have blocked out most of the wind, and, since it hadn't rained since the killings, there should be just enough sign, maybe enough evidence, to cast suspicion upon Jemez. If they could tie in Moran's murder with the Rivera girl's, even a turncoat white renegade like Groves himself should be able to drum up enough reasonable doubt.

And if not, if they found nothing at Apache Arroyo, if Miguel let McLyler and the posse know where Groves and Daniel had gone, well, they weren't far from the Mexican border.

Daniel's *puha* would have to be stronger than it had ever been. He knew he was a damned fool, for, as they rode, he realized everything he had not considered. Perhaps even that Groves was a murderer. Furthermore, there might not be any sign left at Apache Arroyo, especially after McLyler's group descended upon the murder site. Not to mention the fact that Vince Ford and his partner, Frank, had been walking around the area.

Nor had Daniel considered the possibility that maybe McLyler would leave one or even two men behind once they had confirmed that there was a dead body at Apache Arroyo and that it was Moran.

Or maybe Moran had been killed by someone who had had nothing to do with the girl's murder.

Or what if McLyler had been right and Ford's claim had been a ruse to pull lawmen out of Deming, so that the cowboys from Rincon could storm the jail and kill Francis Groves?

And there was that statement by Matt Callahan about the scalp hunter: *Jemez would have taken the girl's scalp. Sold it as an Apache's across the border.* Did that rule Jemez out?

Daniel knew there were other things he hadn't even considered. Things that Pale Eyes like Ichabod Embry and Squire Fuller were certain to bring up when Daniel was brought before the *taibo* law to testify. If Hugh Gunter and Harvey P. Noble were around, they would be sure to remind Daniel of everything he had done wrong, every fact he hadn't considered.

He cursed himself in silence for another mistake he had made—the paint horse had a bone-jarring gait.

Groves reined in the Morgan, and stood in the stirrups. Daniel had ridden past, and now let his horse walk back toward Groves, who gestured to the west with his left hand.

"The arroyo bends that way," Groves said. "We'll give the law a wide berth, come in from the north and west." His jaw jutted east. "I figure them boys were riding from Rincon. Means they'd come to the arroyo a mile or so east and slightly south." He looked at the sky filled with stars and a bright moon. "Watch your horse," Groves advised. "A whinny'll carry a long way on a night like this. We'll be upwind of the law, so I'm not worried about them catching our scent, but if one of our horses makes a noise and they hear us . . ."

Daniel said: "I understand."

"You got an idea about what we should do if they leave behind a guard?" Groves asked as if he had read Daniel's mind.

"No," Daniel said, frowning.

Grunting, Groves pulled the carbine from his saddle. Another mistake, Daniel realized. He should have left that saddle at Perue's livery, never should have allowed Groves to take it with him. Or, at least, not the carbine.

"A gunshot," Daniel said, "would be heard a long way, too."

"I know." Clucking his tongue softly, Groves nudged the black forward.

Reluctantly Daniel followed.

When they reached the edge of the arroyo a half hour later, Groves rode around before finding a slope that jigsawed a path to the bottom. Daniel gave the pinto plenty of rein, letting the horse pick its own path. Reaching the bottom, he eased his horse alongside Groves's mount.

Groves still held the carbine, bracing the stock against his thigh, holding it with his right hand, the reins in his left. "Like I said," he whispered, "don't let your horse whinny. This arroyo winds around a lot, so sound won't travel as far, but we don't want to risk anything. Ground's soft, but watch for rocks. A horseshoe on a rock could be heard, too."

Daniel answered with a nod.

"And keep an eye out for rattlesnakes. They like to be out this time of night."

*Something else,* Daniel thought, *that I failed to consider.*

Groves had been right. When they heard McLyler's men, they quickly dismounted, and put a hand over the horses' muzzles. "Keep them quiet," Groves whispered, handing Daniel the reins to his Morgan. "I'll be back." Daniel watched as Groves eased his way out of the arroyo, and took off at a run, crouching, disappearing in the night.

*For a* taibo, Daniel thought, *he moves a lot like an Indian.* Then he waited, watching as the moon arced a path across the sky. Waiting. Waiting. Even for a Comanche, Daniel found his patience being taxed.

He did not know how long he had been alone, but realized that the noise from McLyler and the others had stopped. The two horses slept standing up, and Daniel edged forward, peered around the edge of the arroyo, just saw desert sand in the moonlight. Of course, the posse, the dead body were probably three or four bends into the arroyo away from here.

Daniel didn't hear Groves, but he saw a shadow leap from the top of the arroyo. He sucked in a deep breath, stepped into one of the horses, which snorted and stamped its hoofs. The other horse crow-hopped a bit, but Daniel grabbed the reins, pulled it closer, whispering that everything was all right to calm the animal.

The next thing he knew, Groves came up from behind and took the reins from his hands, saying casually: "It's all right. They're gone. Probably back to town."

"All of them?" Daniel asked.

"Yeah. Must have taken the body along, too . . .

if there was one . . . So, we've got a little time. Unless that Mex guard tells the truth . . ."

How much time was the unanswered question in Daniel's mind. If Miguel did as he promised, McLyler wouldn't know that he and Groves had come to the arroyo. If G.K. Perue sobered up enough to realize two horses had been stolen out of her livery, the law would likely think that he and Groves had headed south to the border.

The posse, both Daniel and Groves believed, would head straight back to Deming.

Still questions raced through Daniel's mind.

*What if Miguel tells them the truth?*

*What if Miguel lies, but McLyler doesn't believe him?*

*What if they look for a fresh trail headed toward Mexico and don't find one?*

*What if we run into someone else from Deming?*

He was beginning to think they should have just fled to Mexico.


Again, Daniel held the horses, watching, waiting.

They had ridden to the spot where the body had been found. The stench of death emanated from Moran's horse. It was an odor Daniel knew well, as did the horses, and they stamped around nervously. But Daniel no longer worried about keeping them quiet.

Daniel realized as he waited that this was no longer Francis Groves at work. This was a

Chiricahua Apache called Walking Man. There was no hurry about this man. He moved slowly, cautiously, and sometimes he didn't move for minutes at a time as his fingers sorted through the information he could glean from the ground, or a clump of creosote. If the moon didn't cast enough light, Groves would strike a match, hold it closer to the thing he was studying, then he would shake out the flame, and step back to think.

Groves moved north to south, then west to east, east to west. The only time Daniel looked away from Walking Man was to check the position of the moon. He worried that the moon would set, or clouds would move in. He also worried that McLyler would come riding in through the darkness.

Finally Walking Man stood and motioned Daniel over to a place that he had been studying for what seemed like a good thirty minutes. Clucking his tongue, Daniel pulled the two horses behind him. Walking Man said nothing, just stared down at the ground.

Daniel waited. He was a Comanche.

When he looked up at Daniel, Walking Man said: "It was not the way you thought it happened."

# CHAPTER TWENTY-ONE

The first to arrive at the arroyo had been a lone man on horseback. At least, that's how Walking Man had read what sign he had found. The second horse to arrive in the arroyo had never left, was lying there, the horse ridden by the deputy sheriff, a patient rider who traveled at a methodical pace. After that, the first horse seemed to disappear, as though it flew away. Well, that's what it looked like, anyway, until Walking Man discovered the impressions in the sand.

"It's an old trick," Walking Man said. "You slip thick hides over your horse's hoofs. To make it difficult to see a trail."

Daniel nodded. Even The People used such methods to fool *taibos*. A cut-throat like Jemez would know of such a trick.

"Maybe that's what Jemez was doing when the deputy came along," Daniel said. "So Jemez killed him."

"No." Walking Man pointed down the arroyo. "The man who tried to hide his trail was likely gone before the deputy arrived." He turned, pointed to the ridge to the east. "There is a third set of tracks."

"McLyler? And his posse?" Daniel suggested.

Walking Man shook his head. "McLyler is not

as big a fool as you seem to think he is. He was smart enough to leave the horses up top."

"The two cowhands? No, not them, either," Daniel said, when he remembered that Frank's and Vince's horses wouldn't go down because of the smell of blood. The cowhands had had to hobble their mounts, leaving them up top before climbing down into the arroyo.

"The third man," Walking Man said, "rode up after the deputy was already here." He moved toward the remains of Moran's dead horse. His head bobbed in admiration. "He was smart, this deputy, but he was also a fool. He was so busy reading the sign, he did not hear the rider coming up.

"The third man shot the horse first. Through the deputy's leg. The deputy cleared the stirrups and saddle as the horse fell." Walking Man pointed. "The man fired again." Walking Man tapped his left shoulder. "Shot him here. Then rode his horse down into the arroyo, dismounted, walked right up to the deputy . . ."

Daniel spit out the taste of gall in his mouth. "And put a bullet through his head."

"Like one who is putting a horse out of its misery."

Daniel thought about this. "The killer's horse wasn't skittish from the blood?"

"His horse," Walking Man said, "is used to such smells."

An image of Jemez came to Daniel, but he said: "Why not hide the body?"

"He couldn't hide the dead horse . . . it was morning. Maybe afternoon. There was light. He would not risk being seen."

Daniel felt a mix of satisfaction and disgust, but the satisfaction quickly evaporated. "If the man who killed the deputy was Jemez," he said, "then Jemez could not have killed the girl in town."

Walking Man shrugged. "You're assuming the man who came into this place first killed the girl. That man could be innocent."

*But why,* Daniel thought, *would an innocent man try to hide his tracks? And why would the deputy sheriff be following this man? No, this rider was not so innocent.*

"Where did Jemez go?" Daniel asked. "After he killed the deputy?"

Walking Man was moving toward their horses. "I didn't say this rider was Jemez. The tracks will tell us later. Maybe."

Daniel followed, took the reins to the pinto, started to mount. "Which way do the tracks lead?" Walking Man pointed up the arroyo, northwest. Daniel nodded, and swung into the saddle. As he looked down, he saw Walking Man turn, and point back toward Deming.

Daniel frowned, then said: "Jemez . . . or whoever it was . . . didn't follow the man hiding his trail?"

"No. At least not at first. He might have doubled back. But it looks like he rode back to Deming." Walking Man mounted the Morgan. "So now we have a decision to make. Which trail do we follow? Which man do you think killed the girl?"

Daniel let out a mirthless laugh. "Well," he said, "I don't think we want to ride back to Deming." He pointed up the arroyo.

"I can't follow this trail at night," Walking Man said. "The one we follow is good . . . hides his trail too well. It was all I could do just to read the sign here. Those damned fools with McLyler almost wiped out what little I did find."

What Walking Man had found did not sound so little to Daniel. He grimaced at what the scout was suggesting. "You want to wait here?"

Already the Morgan was walking north. "We will ride a bit. Then wait for morning."

Daniel cared little for that idea. The plan was to cover as much ground as possible before McLyler figured out where he and Groves had gone. Daniel looked at the stars. It would be three more hours before dawn.

The trail led out of the arroyo three winding miles away from where the deputy had been shot down. Yet it was midmorning before Daniel and Walking Man had reached that spot. In the desert basin, they looked northwest, toward the conical hills and beyond to the rising purple silhouettes of faraway mountains.

Daniel turned, his saddle creaking as he shifted, and looked back toward Deming. He saw no dust.

Walking Man was on his feet again, handing Daniel the reins to the black. The tracker slid the carbine into the scabbard, and moved across the desert floor, slowly, studying everything, sometimes criss-crossing a ten-yard square for countless minutes.

When he had a path charted, Walking Man would mount, and they would ride. Usually his guesses proved correct, but at least three times they had found themselves backtracking to pick up some sign, some clue, that had escaped Walking Man's eyes previously.

At noon, Walking Man picked up a dried horse apple, crumbling it in his fingers. He smiled. "This man is good. Real good. But it is hard to hide horse shit."

Another time, Walking Man saw where the horse had urinated, cutting a line in the dirt near an agave, which had preserved the sign from the wind.

"Could this rider have been Jemez?" Daniel asked Walking Man when he was on his knees, looking at what seemed to Daniel to be just rocks and dirt.

"No. It is not Jemez."

"How can you be sure?"

Walking Man shrugged. "Jemez wears moccasins. When this man dismounted . . ."—he pointed back to a place where he had picked up the trail again—"he was wearing boots." Then he walked to the Morgan, and swung into the saddle. "He is getting confident," Walking Man said. "He is not so concerned about hiding his trail. But he is still good. Just not as good."

That pleased Daniel. Maybe the trail would become easier to follow. "So if it isn't Jemez, who is it?"

"I don't know. But he's left-handed."

Daniel remembered his father had once taken him and a young friend on a hunting trip. Maybe they were nine or ten, for it was after Daniel's father had given his son his name and taken Marsh Hawk as his own. His father was following a small herd of antelope. Daniel and his friend were merely following his father, in total awe.

"You do not follow a trail," Marsh Hawk had told them. "You become the one you follow, whether it is an antelope, a buffalo, a wild pony, a *taibo*, a Pawnee. You know what it is doing, what it will do. You do not guess. You do not even anticipate. You already know."

Walking Man reminded Daniel of Marsh Hawk. He wasn't guessing. He wasn't even reading the sign any more. He knew what the man on the horse with the hides over the hoofs was doing,

271

thinking. He knew everything about this man. That he was a Pale Eyes who wore high-heeled boots and rode a good horse, a gelding, and that he was left-handed.

He knew everything, except who this *taibo* was.

Yet even now, with the man no longer so careful about hiding his trail, it seemed to be taking an eternity for Walking Man to follow his trail. They had come to another arroyo, a path between two hills with deep, thick sand. Walking Man was studying the ground ahead of Daniel, who held the reins to the black Morgan.

Daniel had given up trying to determine how Walking Man detected the trail, figuring it would always remain a mystery to him—just as he and his friend could never figure out how Marsh Hawk knew which way the antelope herd was running.

Neither Daniel nor Groves saw the man ease his horse out of the trees along the old creekbed until Police Chief Mark McLyler cocked the Winchester rifle and said: "I knew you two bastards wouldn't go to Mexico."

Daniel looked up, cursing himself. He was supposed to keep an eye out for dust, and he had, but always behind him. McLyler must have ridden ahead and around. Just as the killer of the deputy sheriff had done about a week earlier.

Quickly the lawman raised the rifle barrel

and pulled the trigger. His horse side-stepped a bit, but McLyler managed to keep his blood bay steady as he levered another round. He fired two more shots into the air, then, after jacking a fresh round into the chamber, trained the barrel at Daniel.

"Slowly pull that carbine out of the scabbard, Killstraight," McLyler ordered. "And pitch it behind that yucca."

Daniel looked at the saddle on the black, then back at McLyler. Walking Man remained kneeling in the sand, seeming to be unconcerned about the policeman.

"Now," McLyler ordered.

"He is following the trail of the killer," Daniel said.

McLyler repeated. "Now. Or I bring you in face down over that saddle."

Walking Man continued to read the sign on the ground.

Daniel slid from his saddle, and stepped to the Morgan, putting his right hand on the black's neck, rubbing it in a circular motion, as he moved to the saddle. He reached up, put his right hand on the stock.

"Careful," McLyler said.

Daniel drew the powerful Springfield from the leather.

"Now pitch it," McLyler said.

Instead, Daniel thumbed back the heavy

273

hammer. He didn't bring up the rifle, didn't do anything threatening, other than cocking the weapon. He read anxiety in McLyler's face.

"How did you know," Daniel said, "that we would come this way?"

That got Walking Man's attention. He looked over at McLyler. The lawman wore boots. He rode a good horse. True, he seemed to be right-handed, but Daniel had known some men who were good with either hand.

"What the hell are you talking about?" McLyler said as he steadied the rifle still trained on Daniel's chest. "Damn it, throw that gun away. I don't want to kill you."

"Did you want to kill the girl who is no more?"

McLyler shifted in the saddle. He almost lowered the Winchester. "What . . . ?"

"I am not throwing down this gun," Daniel said. "So that you might kill us."

"If you don't throw it down, and I don't shoot you, Frazer or any of the ten men riding in my posse will gun you both down, you dumb red bastard." The rifle was tight again in McLyler's arms. He was sweating, but it was a hot day.

Daniel still refused to lower the carbine. "How did you know we would be here?" Daniel asked again.

"I guessed, damn it. Roberts took ten men south. But I didn't believe than Miguel was so damned stupid he'd let that killer escape. And I

274

know that both of you want to believe that Jemez killed Melody, but, damn it, you're wrong. Put the rifle down, Killstraight. Frazer will be here soon. He's sure to have heard my shots. That was the signal."

Instead, Daniel said: "Why would Jemez be riding this way?"

"Christ Almighty!" McLyler roared. "The Four Gates Ranch headquarters is four miles up this trail."

It was Walking Man who broke the stalemate. "That way," he said, and began walking again.

Confusion and indecision froze McLyler. He swung the barrel toward Walking Man, who didn't even glance at the lawman, just walked casually past him, moving north and west, following the sandy path. Realizing he had taken his eyes off a man with a cocked carbine, McLyler jerked the Winchester back toward Daniel, but Daniel had not moved. The police chief didn't know which man to watch. His horse, sensing his confusion, jerked this way and that.

It was then that Daniel knew that Mark McLyler had killed no one. He lowered the hammer on the Springfield. The heavy metallic clicks brought McLyler's Winchester barrel toward Daniel, who held the Springfield loosely before putting it into the scabbard. Then he moved to the pinto and climbed into the saddle.

"Don't make me kill you," McLyler said, but they were just empty words. Nothing more.

Daniel took his reins in one hand, and with the other the reins to the Morgan. He kneed the pinto into a walk, and signaled toward Walking Man.

"We follow him," he said. "He will find the killer of the girl who is no more, and the deputy sheriff who is also dead."

The paint horse carried Daniel right past McLyler, and he half expected a bullet to slam into his back. To his surprise, he heard the sound of creaking leather and knew Police Chief Mark McLyler had put away his Winchester. Moments later, McLyler had eased his blood bay mare alongside Daniel.

"You better be right," McLyler said. "You damned well better be right."

# CHAPTER TWENTY-TWO

He saw the scattered cattle, rangy, stringy, half-starved longhorns that were even worse than the cattle the *Tejanos* brought to the reservation in Indian Territory, right before they crossed a shallow creek, where they let their horses drink before continuing along a clearly marked trail. On the far bank, Walking Man pointed to odd depressions, long dried in the mud, that led out of the creek, disappearing as the sand ended and the trail became hard.

"What's that?" McLyler asked.

"The horse of the killer," Walking Man said. He kept walking.

"Horse?" McLyler asked.

"He used hides to cover his mount's hoofs," Daniel said, and explained what Walking Man had learned from the sign. Daniel reasserted his theory that if the deputy sheriff had been following the killer's trail out of Deming, that meant Groves could not have killed the young girl. On the other hand, Daniel didn't bother bringing up the idea that there had to be two killers. That might just confuse the lawman.

"What's he going to do?" McLyler asked. "Follow the tracks to one of Mister Callahan's corrals? You don't think the killer would have left the hide on his horse's hoofs?"

Daniel wasn't listening. He was looking behind them, watching the dust cloud that had to be coming from Frazer and the posse. It worried Daniel. The young deputy wasn't as patient as Mark McLyler. He might shoot down Walking Man and Daniel on sight.

"Trail might not lead to the ranch," Walking Man said. "He could be going to Silver City. Or all the way into Arizona Territory."

Daniel knew better. Maybe he couldn't read sign like his father or Walking Man, but he knew enough about the man they were following. He knew his trail would lead right to the Callahan Ranch.

It wasn't what he had expected, this *taibo* ranch. No grand sign announcing the owner's name or brand, like those he had seen in Texas. The buildings were small, merely dug-outs rather than adobe or stone houses. The horse barn was the best structure on the premises, stoutly built.

A small group of cowhands were gathered around one of the nearby corrals. Daniel could hear them joking and laughing, could see dust rising from inside the corral. There was a burst of cheering as the head and torso of a cowboy rose above the hats of the men sitting on the top rails of the corral, hung in the air for a moment, then dropped out of sight below the row of watchers.

"Ha!" came a boisterous voice. "Ain't that a fart-knocker."

Daniel had never understood the cowboy method of breaking their mounts.

One of the cowboys on the fence turned, must have seen Daniel, Walking Man, and McLyler. He punched the arm of the man sitting to his right, and within moments the cowboys were climbing off the corral railing. Inside the fenced area, the horse twisted, snorted, and bucked even though it had been abandoned by its rider who was exiting the corral between the rails. A tall man in a Mexican sombrero waited for the rider.

One of cowboys yelled out: "Hey, boss!"

At the shout, the door of one of the dug-outs opened, and a tall man stepped out, and, across the grounds, two men emerged from another, larger building, which Daniel assumed to be the bunkhouse or the chuck house.

From among the group of cowhands, the sound of a gun being cocked could be heard.

"You let me do the talking," Mark McLyler said as he dismounted. He stepped out and pushed back his duster so that everyone could see the sun reflecting off his badge. He glanced back, and added: "At least to start off."

Twisting in the saddle, Daniel looked back at the dust cloud being raised by Jasper Frazer and his posse of ten. It was nearer. But not near enough. And Daniel surprised himself, by wishing they would hurry.

"What the hell are you doing here?" Matt Callahan demanded as he approached the trio. Today he was without his duster, looking more like one of his ranch hands in a work jacket, gloves, and striped britches. He also had a Colt revolver stuck in his waistband. Callahan pointed with disgust. "And with them two birds?"

"Mister Callahan," McLyler said as he took a few steps forward. "Glenn Moran's dead."

"The hell you say?"

"Murdered at Apache Arroyo."

Callahan shot a quick glance at Jemez, who stood to the left. The scalp hunter had come out of one of the dug-outs with another man who was even bigger than the Mexican, with a flat-face and ham-sized arms. As Daniel studied the fellow, who upon closer inspection looked more like a boy than a man, except for his size, he decided this had to be the simpleton son of Matt Callahan, Jules.

Callahan's glance at Jemez had been lightning quick, so quick that Daniel had been lucky to even catch it. But in doing so, he also saw that although Jemez did not carry his machete, he had a gun stowed in his pants pocket. Jules Callahan did not appear to be armed, but just about all of Callahan's ranch men were.

"You didn't answer my question," Callahan said.

"We followed the trail," McLyler said, and pointed uncertainly at Walking Man. "Well, actually, Groves did."

The rancher spit tobacco juice into the dust. "Him? You let that murdering black-heart out of jail so he could follow a trail almost a week old?"

Daniel slipped out of the saddle. Callahan's right hand moved toward his gun as did Jemez's. Yet Daniel moved casually, and stepped ahead of McLyler. At the same time the cowboys moved slowly around, forming a half circle, flanking the newcomers.

"We did not follow the trail of the man who killed the deputy," Daniel said. He could feel McLyler's stare bore through his back. "It was the trail of the man who killed the girl who . . ."

McLyler cut Daniel off, knowing what he was going to say. "Melody Rivera."

Callahan blinked. "I thought you said Moran was dead."

"He is." McLyler cleared his throat.

"Hell, I don't believe that."

"Boss!" shouted one of the cowhands, and pointed up the trail. Daniel watched the *taibos* look, but he did not turn around. He knew they were seeing Frazer's men riding into view.

"Yes," Daniel said, "you believe it."

Callahan moved his hand closer toward the Colt. "Believe what?"

"That the deputy is dead."

The rancher stared.

"How else would you have known the trail was a week old?" Daniel asked.

"Leave him alone!" roared Jules Callahan.

Daniel caught just a glimpse of Callahan's son as the boy came flying at him. He was fleet for a person of his size.

"Jules!" the rancher cried out. "No!"

But a heavy shoulder slammed low into Daniel's side, and he felt himself being lifted off his feet, carried almost, past Walking Man and McLyler, past Matt Callahan. He seemed to feel, rather than see, or even hear, the cowboys scattering as Jules plowed Daniel the fifteen yards straight into the round corral where the unbroken horse pawed the earth, and then began snorting at the commotion.

The juniper rails crushed against Daniel's side. His breath exploded out of his lungs. He might have grunted. He might have even screamed. He heard the sounds of the rails of the corral give, but not break. Then he was slammed to the ground, certain that a few of his ribs had been broken.

He tried to breathe, but his chest felt paralyzed. No air could reach his lungs. His mouth would not work. Sounds seemed distant. He spit, not sure whether it was saliva, or vomit, or blood. Hundreds of tiny orange bolts of lightning darted past his eyes. He waited. Then, slowly he opened them.

He saw that flat face of young Callahan, the brute the brakeman had told him about. Then a massive hand grabbed at his hair, ripped, pulled his head off the ground. Then slammed it against the hard-packed earth. Daniel cursed, or at least wanted to. He felt his head being jerked up again and slammed down. He sucked in air, and this time he knew he screamed, because his hearing had returned.

"You . . . won't . . . hurt . . . ," Jules was saying. Then his hands moved to Daniel's throat and clamped down. Daniel couldn't breathe as the boy's thumbs, as strong, as powerful as hammers, pushed down.

Groves leaped on the young Callahan. And the giant's left arm released its hold on Daniel's neck only long enough to fling aside the former scout like a horse's tail flicking away a fly. Someone else tried to pull the over-grown kid off Daniel, but was also hurled away.

"Stop him! Callahan! Stop him!"

Daniel wasn't sure who was shouting. He didn't even know if he had actually heard it, or just dreamed it.

Daniel's eyes able to focus clearly now, looked into Jules Callahan's enraged face, and behind and standing above him the face of Jemez . . . who was laughing.

Then slowly as blackness began to envelope Daniel, he heard a loud explosion, and felt the hands release his throat and blood splatter across his face.

# CHAPTER TWENTY-THREE

As Daniel opened his eyes, he prayed that Rain Shower would be there to guide him across the trail to The Land Beyond The Sun.

"Well, boy," Dr. Walter Commager said, "you ain't dead."

Daniel closed his eyes. He knew he was breathing, because every time his lungs moved, his chest burned. He also knew that he wasn't dead, because his throat felt raw, his arms were sore, and he ached all over. Even his teeth hurt. But his ribs hurt the most.

Rough, dry hands began lifting his head, trying not to hurt him, but failing miserably. Above his own moans, Daniel heard Commager say: "Drink this."

"What is it?" Daniel asked even though speaking hurt his throat. Even his teeth ached.

He wasn't sure the doctor had even heard him until Commager answered gruffly: "Laudanum. Open . . ."

"No," Daniel said, and sealed his lips, and Commager cursed, but lowered Daniel's head back onto a rock-hard pillow.

"You're stubborn, Daniel."

When he opened his eyes again, Commager was sipping from the bottle of laudanum. The doctor licked his lips, and slipped the bottle into his pocket, then looked down at Daniel.

"What happened?" Daniel asked, and slowly lifted one of his hands to his throat, ignoring the burning in his side, touching the cloth that rested over his throat.

"Well, you got five busted ribs. But you're lucky, kid. None of them punctured a lung. Or your heart . . . if you have a heart. Throat's badly bruised, but not crushed. You had a dislocated shoulder, but I fixed that." Doc Commager snorted. "Should have heard yourself scream, Daniel. Worse than a woman giving birth. Well, no, maybe not that bad."

Daniel swallowed. Even that took an effort. "Walking Man?" he asked.

"Who . . . oh, Groves?" He pointed a finger across the room.

Daniel feared he meant the section of the boxcar where the doctor did his undertaking work, but when he turned his head, he saw another bed nearby.

"The kid tossed him so hard," the doctor explained, "he busted one of Groves's ankles pretty damned bad, but he's all right. That kid snapped the wrist of one of Callahan's waddies, too." Doc's face turned soft, almost sad, as he shook his head. "Damned shame." Then he reached into his pocket, and pulled out a thin slip of paper and not the laudanum bottle that Daniel thought he was retrieving. "Matt just come in here . . . wrote me this check."

"For . . . ?" Daniel whispered.

The doctor's face turned into a bitter grimace. "For Jules, his son. For his . . . funeral . . ."

As Doc's words trailed off, Daniel began to remember. He could see and feel Jules Callahan straddling him, pounding his head, choking the life out of him. He recalled the gunshot, and reaching up, touching his face, but it wasn't his blood.

Doc Commager crumpled the check, and faced Daniel with the saddest expression he'd ever seen on a Pale Eyes face. "God forgive Matt Callahan . . . but God bless him, too. He killed his own son, Daniel. To save your life."

That man with the mind of a child, Jules Callahan, had killed Melody Rivera, Doc Commager explained. "He followed the couple. He wasn't hiding. Probably just came after them, mad as hell, and he picked up a crowbar, knocked out Francis Groves, and strangled the poor girl to death. Slammed the crowbar on the girl's neck. And dumped her body in the garbage. Then he had fled. Must have gotten lost in the night. A boy like that couldn't think clearly on the best of days, and so addled by what he had done, well . . . you couldn't blame the boy. His mind had never been right. He didn't know any better. But when

Glenn Moran wandered into Apache Arroyo the next morning, Jules killed the deputy, probably thinking Moran was on to him. That's when Jemez had arrived. Sent the boy back toward the ranch. Rigged up the boy's horse's feet to make it harder for anyone to follow the trail. To protect him."

The doctor fished for the small bottle, took another, larger, sip of laudanum. "Felt it was his duty to protect his boss's simple-minded kid. Matt Callahan didn't know until . . . until . . ." There was a stirring from the other bed.

"Hey, Comanche!" Walking Man called out. "Glad you didn't die."

Daniel smiled. "I'm not." He really didn't know how he felt. Oh, he understood the physical pain, and he was glad he had saved Francis Groves from the gallows. Yet, he had wanted Jemez to have been guilty of something, something other than trying to protect his boss's son. Yet, it made sense. Jules Callahan had loved the girl, had been jealous, and the violence he had displayed toward Daniel proved that he was capable of murder. As for Matt Callahan? Daniel had wanted him to be guilty of something, too. But Callahan would pay for the rest of his life. He would have to live with two horrible facts. That his son was a murderer. And that he had killed his own flesh and blood.

Doc Commager reached into his pocket. "When they brought in the boy's body," he said softly, "I found these in his pocket." He passed the tintype of the dead girl to Daniel, along with a broken leather thong that held a crucifix.

They hadn't been stolen for their value, Daniel knew. *Then for what?* Daniel wondered. *Trophies? Souvenirs? Reminders of a girl who the Callahan idiot had loved, and brutally murdered?*

In the back of his mind, came a whisper from Rain Shower: *No.*

That's when Daniel knew.

"Doctor," he said tightly, "help me up."

"What?"

"Now," Daniel barked, and immediately regretted it as pain shot through his body. He gasped as he tried to push himself into a seated position on the uncomfortable bunk, so Commager helped to ease him up. Daniel grabbed his side gently, felt tears of pain welling his eyes, had to bite his bottom lip to fight the pain. A wave of dizziness came and slowly passed. As did nausea. He spotted Groves's Springfield carbine leaning in the corner, beckoning him, telling him what he had to do.

"What the hell are you up to?" Walking Man called out.

"Is Callahan still in town?" Daniel asked Commager.

"He was having breakfast at the Harvey House," the doctor answered.

"Killstraight?" Walking Man demanded. "What is it?"

Gingerly Daniel's feet touched the floor. Damn it, he thought, staring at his bare feet. He needed his moccasins. Then he realized that he was wearing one of Doc Commager's over-size nightshirts, about as large as a teepee.

"Where's . . . McLyler?" Daniel got out the two words, and immediately wanted to lie back down.

"I don't know," Commager stammered. "Office? Jail? Court's in session. He might be there."

"Find him." Daniel mumbled, as he pushed himself up. Then he was moving, not fast, and with every step he thought he might pass out.

The doc told him he was an idiot, then, realizing the pointlessness of arguing with a Comanche, he left through the boxcar door to find Deming's police chief.

Walking Man was sitting up, warning Daniel to think about what he was doing. He knew the former tracker couldn't get up when he glimpsed his ankle, swollen and bandaged. Without a cane or crutch he couldn't walk, couldn't interfere.

Daniel was on his own, unless Commager found McLyler fast. Standing still to catch his breath, Daniel tried to calm himself and adjust to the pain as he stared at the door which looked to be miles from where he stood. Attempting to continue to move sent pain rifling through his entire body. He almost wet himself. He knew he wouldn't make it without some help, so he reached for the carbine propped nearby, to use as a crutch. He gripped the barrel with both hands, planted the stock on the floor. Then one small step. Another . . .

Outside, it wasn't so hot, but sweat poured out of his body like a sieve. A woman gasped at the sight of him, and quickly crossed to the other side of the street. An old Mexican crossed himself, and stepped aside. Daniel progressed slowly, painfully. He could see the Harvey House through the sweat that poured down from his forehead. But he had to keep moving.

He had to be right. This time. He had been wrong too many times about this case. And if he didn't hurry, he would be too late.

Jemez and Callahan had come out of the Harvey House. They were mounting their horses, as Daniel stepped into the street, shuffling his feet now, unable to lift his legs, hardly able to walk.

It was Jemez who saw him while backing his horse away from the hitching rail. The Mexican turned the big gelding, said something softly to the rancher, who turned in the saddle, staring at Daniel with a look of contempt. Callahan's big horse turned in the street.

Both men faced Daniel. Out of the corner of

his eye, he saw several people standing under an awning, watching.

The rancher leaned forward in the saddle, and spat out his bitterness. "I got nothing to say to you, boy."

Raising his voice loud enough for the rancher to hear him sent spasms through his chest, but he managed to say: "You owe me my spondulicks."

The word must have confused Callahan, because he leaned back in the saddle, and said: "Your what?"

"Five hundred dollars," Daniel said. "For finding the killer of that girl. Remember?"

Callahan's face reddened in anger. "You damned dirty son-of-a-bitch."

More people were gathering in front of the Harvey House, and across the street as well. Black porters and Mexican freighters now stood at the depot. Daniel heard a few snickers, saw one or two people point at this ridiculous-looking Indian, wearing a striped teepee and standing in the middle of the street to confront the most powerful rancher in the area.

Jemez reached for his machete, but Callahan stopped him. "No. I'll pay the greedy red bastard." He reached inside his jacket, brought out a leather-covered checkbook. "It's payable to bearer," he said, as he dug for a pen. "The bank won't give you any trouble. Cash it . . . and then don't ever let me see you around

Deming, or even in this territory, again." The pen disappeared back inside his pocket as soon as he was done scribbling. Callahan ripped the check out of the register, blew on the ink, then wadded up the check and tossed it at Daniel's feet. The wind blew it across the street, but Daniel wasn't concerned with the check. He just stared at the rancher and the scalp hunter.

"You're left-handed," he announced to Matt Callahan.

"So what?"

"You killed that girl," he said. "Then you killed your own son to cover up your crime."

Callahan's face darkened with rage. "I ought to kill you for that," he snapped. "It's bad enough what I had to do to save your sorry hide."

Daniel merely shook his head.

"Hell, boy, I offered you five hundred dollars to find the real killer."

"So McLyler would not suspect you."

Jemez snorted. Callahan spit. "You're full of shit."

Daniel shook his head. "The tintype," Daniel said. "The cross. That's what will hang you."

Jemez's face, Daniel noticed, suddenly paled. The black-hearted bastard understood now, even though Matt Callahan had yet to figure it out.

"They were found in my boy's pocket!" Callahan roared.

"Because you put them there," Daniel stated.

Oddly enough he didn't hurt quite so much at the moment. And he felt calm. "Your son couldn't have taken the tintype. It was on the girl's coffin at her funeral. He wasn't there. But you were. You loved her, but you still killed . . ."

He saw Callahan's hand grasp for a revolver, but Daniel was already moving, surprised that he could move. He dropped the carbine in the dust, lunged at the horse, felt an intense pain shoot through his chest. The wind caught the over-size nightshirt, billowing it like a giant cloud.

It wasn't how he planned it, for he really had no plan, just an idea, a suspicion. No, it was more than that. He was like a tracker, like Walking Man on the trail. He knew. The horse reared as Daniel stumbled. Callahan screamed as the big blood bay fell, and that was all Daniel saw. Pain blinded him temporarily, his lungs burned, and he suspected that he had landed on the steps to the Harvey House. He heard the horse's squeal, a man's ear-piercing shriek, and a gathering of women and men gasping, yelling, cursing.

He sucked in as much air as he could manage, bit back the pain, looked up, vomited. Callahan's horse had rolled over, regained its feet, was galloping away from the Harvey House. He didn't see Callahan. Just Jemez. The man wasn't holding the machete, though. He held the Springfield that Daniel had dropped, was bringing the stock to his shoulder, thumbing back the hammer, squeezing the trigger.

*Click.*

"Jemez!" a voice roared.

The scalp hunter bellowed something, raised the big gun over his head, started to bring it down. Then something popped behind Daniel, and through the tears from the pain, he saw the scalp hunter falling backward, away, away, away. . . .

# CHAPTER TWENTY-FOUR

Daniel stood at the depot, leaning on his crutches, shaking hands with G.K. Perue, Judge Embry, Squire Fuller, Ladislaus Radegunde, practically everybody in Deming. It hurt like hell, but, somehow, it also felt pretty good.

It had been another story during that inquest. The solicitor, Dave Barber, wanted blood, but he wouldn't get any from Francis Walking Man Groves or from Daniel Killstraight.

Doc Commager had testified that Jules Callahan had not been at the funeral, and that the tintype of the dead Rivera girl had positively been present on the girl's coffin. Jules Callahan could not have stolen it. He hadn't been in town. Three cowboys for the Four Gates Ranch had testified they had brought Jules home after the 4th of July celebration. The boy hadn't acted like a murderer. On the other hand, they hadn't seen their boss, nor had they seen Jemez, that night after the dance. The boss had told them to make sure the boy got home, but those orders had been issued before the dance was over, before Francis Groves had left with Melody Rivera. Matt Callahan had left the dance early, and the hired hands said he looked madder than the devil himself.

G.K. Perue, on the other hand, who was sober enough to testify, said she had seen Jemez. Saw him ride out of town after Deputy Sheriff Glenn Moran had gotten his horse out of the stable late on the morning of July 5th. She hadn't really thought much about it, she testified, but it sure looked like that black-heart was following the deputy.

Maybe they didn't dot every i and cross every t, the way they always liked things at the Carlisle Industrial School, but it proved to be enough. There would be no bill of indictment. The coroner's inquest ruled that Matt Callahan had clubbed Francis Groves with intent to kill, and then had murdered Melody Rivera in a jealous rage. Later, Matt Callahan had murdered his own son and tried to pin the murder on the simpleton. Jemez had killed Glenn Moran to keep him from following Matt Callahan's trail to the ranch headquarters.

Callahan's neck and back had been broken when his horse fell while in the act of trying to shoot down Daniel Killstraight. An accidental death, which, by the stroke of good fortune, saved the county the expense of a murder trial and an execution. Jemez had been shot dead before he could kill Daniel Killstraight. It was what the *taibos* called a justifiable homicide.

So at the depot, Daniel shook hands with the Harvey House owner, L.J. Vanderhider.

"Thank you," Daniel said.

The merchant shrugged. "I never liked that fat Mexican, anyhow."

Beside him, Doc Commager laughed. "I told you L.J. once ran restaurants in Houston and New York. You got to be tough to handle towns like that."

Vanderhider had been fined $10 and court costs for firing a gun inside the city limits. Daniel would never understand the laws of the Pale Eyes.

The doctor moved out of the crowd, and put his hand on Daniel's shoulder. He leaned closer, whispering: "I cashed that check Callahan wrote you. Bank didn't give me any trouble. Gave the money, just like you wanted, to Missus Rivera. She broke down in tears. Wanted me to thank you, and let you know how much she appreciated it. She couldn't bring herself to come here, though. Poor woman's still heartbroken." Commager turned around. "Thought that boy of hers would be here to thank you, see you off, but, criminy, you know. Pride and all."

The conductor yelled that the AT&SF had a schedule to keep, and if Daniel Killstraight didn't get on now, he'd have to wait until the next train came through.

"We don't want that, Killstraight," Mark McLyler said, grinning as he shook Daniel's hand. He picked up Daniel's grip for him, and motioned toward the frowning railroader who kept waving his watch. "Thanks for everything."

"Thank you," Daniel said, and he turned to another man on crutches. "And thank you, too," he told Walking Man. He pointed at the crutches. "I don't think you'll be walking too far, though. Not with those."

"Maybe not," he said. "But I've got somewhere to go. I think."

"Florida?" Daniel asked.

Walking Man's head shook. "No." He gazed far off to the south. "Might see if I can find Jlin-Litzoque and his people."

Daniel understood. Some Chiricahuas had escaped the government roundup, were living in the Sierra Madres south of the border. "Good luck," Daniel said.

"I'll need it," Walking Man said.

They did not shake hands. They did not have to.

"Come on!" the conductor roared.

Daniel turned. McLyler had climbed aboard the train with Daniel's grip. A black porter and Radegunde, the train's brakeman, helped Daniel up the steps, giving him, Daniel thought, the respect due any white peace officer, or whatever it was that Joshua Biggers had written in that letter of introduction. At least, Daniel wouldn't have to ride all the way to Dodge City with the livestock. People across the territory had heard about Daniel Killstraight. He was something of a celebrity, but he knew he'd have a lot of explaining to do once Agent Joshua Biggers had him in that dark office on Cache Creek.

"Killstraight!"

As he turned back, Daniel saw Walking Man pointing one of his crutches in the air.

Daniel looked into that pale desert sky.

"Thank you," Walking Man called out, "for helping me find my way! Maybe that hawk will help you."

Overhead, the great raptor circled, cried out, then flapped its large wings, and soared away.

Smiling, Daniel straightened, and slid aside to let Police Chief Mark McLyler step off the train.

"This way, sir," the porter said, holding the door open for Daniel. Radegunde had already gone toward the caboose.

Daniel gave a final wave at the Pale Eyes who had gathered at the depot to see him off, nodded gratefully at Walking Man, and then stepped inside the coach.

The hawk was flying northeast. Going home. Just like Daniel Killstraight.

# ABOUT THE AUTHOR

Johnny D. Boggs has worked cattle, shot rapids in a canoe, hiked across mountains and deserts, traipsed around ghost towns, and spent hours poring over microfilm in library archives—all in the name of finding a good story. He's also one of the few Western writers to have won six Spur Awards from Western Writers of America (for his novels, *Camp Ford*, in 2006, *Doubtful Cañon*, in 2008, and *Hard Winter* in 2010, *Legacy of a Lawman*, *West Texas Kill*, both in 2012, and his short story, "A Piano at Dead Man's Crossing," in 2002) as well as the Western Heritage Wrangler Award from the National Cowboy and Western Heritage Museum (for his novel, *Spark on the Prairie: The Trial of the Kiowa Chiefs*, in 2004). A native of South Carolina, Boggs spent almost fifteen years in Texas as a journalist at the *Dallas Times Herald* and *Fort Worth Star-Telegram* before moving to New Mexico in 1998 to concentrate full time on his novels. Author of dozens of published short stories, he has also written for more than fifty newspapers and magazines, and is a frequent contributor to *Boys' Life* and *True West*. His Western novels cover a wide range. *The Lonesome Chisholm Trail* (Five Star Westerns, 2000) is an authentic cattle-drive story, while *Lonely Trumpet* (Five Star Westerns, 2002) is an historical novel about the first black graduate of West Point. *The Despoilers* (Five Star Westerns, 2002) and *Ghost Legion* (Five Star Westerns, 2005) are set in the Carolina backcountry during the Revolutionary War. *The Big Fifty* (Five Star Westerns, 2003) chronicles the slaughter of buffalo on the southern plains in the 1870s, while *East of the Border* (Five Star Westerns, 2004) is a comedy about the theatrical offerings of Buffalo Bill Cody, Wild Bill Hickok, and Texas Jack Omohundro, and *Camp Ford* (Five Star Westerns, 2005) tells about a Civil War baseball game between Union prisoners of war and Confederate guards. "Boggs's narrative voice captures the old-fashioned style of the past," *Publishers Weekly* said, and *Booklist* called him "among the best Western writers at work today." Boggs lives with his wife Lisa and son Jack in Santa Fe. His website is www.johnnydboggs.com.